David leaned over to look down into Honor's sleeping face.

Even in her sleep she was smiling. What was she dreaming of—him? He grimaced a little at his own vanity and then wondered if she would still be smiling if she knew the truth about him.

In reality they hardly knew one another, but there had been an honesty, a purity, about their coming together that had elevated it way, way above anything cheap or carnal.

Honor had talked to him openly about her life, her past, but he had not been able to be similarly honest with her.

There was no real point, he reminded himself. Their time together could only be brief, the relationship transitory, and once she knew the truth she was bound to reject him. Who could blame her? But he knew he would have to tell her, even though he couldn't really understand the compulsion that was drivng him to do so. Just as he didn't understand why he had felt that he must come home.

"Honor..."

Reluctantly, she opened her eyes.

"There's something I have to tell you," David began.

Dear Reader,

When I first started to write, my favorite reading was
sagas, stories spanning not just generations but centuries,
with young brides who grew to become loved matriarchs,
aggravating younger sons who matured into fine strong
men and daughters who, like their mothers, kept a watchful
maternal eye on their children—and their children's children.

As an author, I have concentrated on the modern-day
romances I enjoy writing so much. But the desire to write a
series of novels based around one family has never left me—
partly because my own personal ideal is to live in a small
country town surrounded by a network of family connections.
And I am fortunate to live in a part of the English countryside,
Cheshire, which is steeped in history, the perfect setting for
my family series.

I very much wanted to write about the emotion, joy and often
sadness that bond a family together, and with this series I feel
that I have in some sense fulfilled a part of myself—the name
Crighton originally belonged to my husband's mother's family.
I hope you will take my fictional family to your heart and love
them as much as I do.

Penny Jordan

The Crighton family novels

Penny Jordan

COMING HOME

HARLEQUIN®

TORONTO • NEW YORK • LONDON
AMSTERDAM • PARIS • SYDNEY • HAMBURG
STOCKHOLM • ATHENS • TOKYO • MILAN • MADRID
PRAGUE • WARSAW • BUDAPEST • AUCKLAND

ISBN 0-373-83452-7

COMING HOME

First North American Publication 2000.

Copyright © 2000 by Penny Jordan.

Penny Jordan has been writing for more than fifteen years and has an outstanding record of over one hundred novels published. Among these are the phenomenally successful **To Love, Honor and Betray, A Perfect Family, Power Games, Cruel Legacy** and **Power Play,** which hit both the *New York Times* and London *Sunday Times* bestseller lists.

An internationally acclaimed author, Penny Jordan has over sixty million copies of her books in print. She was born in Preston, Lancashire, and now lives with her husband in a beautiful fourteenth-century house in rural Cheshire.

The Crighton Family

Haslewich branch of the family

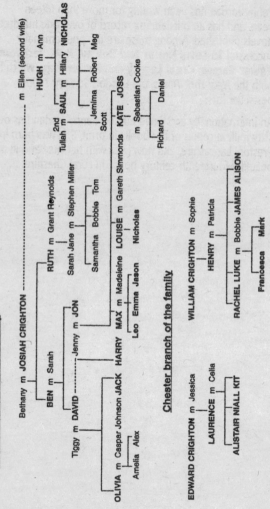

Chester branch of the family

CHAPTER ONE

'How's Gramps?'

'Not too good, I'm afraid, Joss,' Jenny Crighton admitted in response to her youngest child's question, looking past the tall, gangly shape of the seventeen-year-old to where her husband Jon was standing, frowning a little.

'Maddy managed to have a word with me in private after I'd been to see him,' Jenny told her husband. 'She's very concerned about the way he seems to be deteriorating. Despite the fact that medically both his hip operations have been a success, he still complains that he's in pain and that his joints ache. He's quite definitely losing weight and Maddy's worried that he isn't eating as well as he was. He's looking positively gaunt.'

'He is in his eighties, Jen,' Jon reminded her, but Jenny could see that he was still frowning and she knew he was troubled. Ben was his father after all and even though they all knew that Ben could not possibly receive better care than that given to him by Maddy, their daughter-in-law, the wife of their eldest son Max, Jenny also knew that Jon still felt that he should be the one to carry the main responsibility for Ben, just as he still felt guilty because...

'Aunt Ruth says that Ben is turning into a curmudgeonly old man,' Joss informed them both. 'She says he actually enjoys being grumpy.'

'Grumpy perhaps,' Jenny allowed, 'but no one enjoys being in constant physical pain, Joss,' she reminded him gently.

Joss had always preferred the company of Great-Aunt Ruth to that of his grandfather, and Jenny knew that she could hardy blame him. Ruth had been far more of a grandparent and a mentor to Joss than Ben had ever been.

Out of all his grandchildren, there was only one for whom Ben Crighton had ever shown any real liking and that was for Max. Not that such favouritism had had either her or Jon's backing. Once there had been an acute degree of antagonism between Max and his parents, but thankfully that rift was now healed. Jenny only had to watch Max with his wife Maddy and their three children to feel overwhelmed not just with love and pride but with a humbling gratitude to whomever or whatever had drawn the master plan for her son's life.

To say that Max had completely changed virtually overnight from a human being even she as his mother had sometimes come close to loathing to one whom everyone who now knew him spoke of with respect, admiration and love sounded overly dramatic and theatrical, but it was no less than the truth. But in order to undergo such a transformation, Max had had to sail terrifyingly close to the fine, dark edge that separated life from death. Not willingly or voluntarily but through the trauma of a vicious physical attack that could have ended his life or left him permanently injured.

Mercifully, it had not, and Max had returned to them to begin a new life here in the small Cheshire town of Haslewich.

Families! Jenny gave a small sigh, but she wouldn't be without hers, not a single member of it, including her irascible father-in-law, Ben.

The Crighton family was a large one with several branches. But one thing that linked all of them together, one inheritance they all shared, was their fascination with the legal world, the world of lawyers, solicitors, barristers and judges. It was an in-joke in the family that every Crighton child, just as soon as he or she was old enough to know what the words meant, when asked what they wanted for Christmas or birthdays, would respond eagerly, 'I want to be a QC.'

Queen's Counsel. It had been a goal to which Ben had strived unsuccessfully, the goal to which he had relentlessly tried to push his own son and then more recently his grandson Max.

There had been a time when Jenny knew that had Max attained that goal, she would have felt it was somehow tainted and wrong, but when, the previous year, Max had come over to tell them that he had heard on the grapevine that he was going to receive this accolade, Jenny had been filled with love and pride for him. So, too, had Jon, who had embraced Max with emotion as he congratulated him.

But, typically, when Ben Crighton had praised his favourite grandchild on his achievement at a family gathering, he hadn't been able to resist adding brusquely, 'It should have been my son David. It would have been David,' he had told them all fiercely, giving his granddaughter Olivia an angry glower, 'if it hadn't been for *your* mother.'

Olivia hadn't responded, but Jenny had seen the

look of pain in her eyes and the anger in her husband Caspar's and she had felt for her.

There had been no point in trying to console or comfort Olivia by reminding her that Ben Crighton gave as little value and love to her own daughters as he did to Olivia. Ben might have been born into the twentieth century, but he had never embraced its ethos to the extent of accepting that women were as professionally capable as men. The achievements of the female members of his own family were something Ben either ignored or criticised as women taking jobs that should more rightfully belong to men.

'Is Gramps going to die?' Joss asked his mother now, the anxiety in his eyes reminding Jenny that despite her youngest son's growing maturity, the sensitive side of his nature, which had so marked him out as a child, could still hold him emotionally hostage to his fears.

'I don't know, Joss,' Jenny answered him honestly. 'According to the doctor, there is no physical reason why he should.' She paused, choosing her words carefully. 'But your grandfather has never been a man who has enjoyed life. He—'

'He still misses Uncle David, doesn't he?' Joss cut in.

Jenny and Jon exchanged speaking looks. Joss

had accurately and swiftly highlighted the true cause of Ben's deep-seated malaise.

David Crighton, Jon's twin brother, had disappeared just a few weeks after their joint fiftieth birthday party, only a short time ahead of Jon's discovery that David had fraudulently plundered the bank account of an elderly widow whose business affairs he had been responsible for.

Had it not been for the fact that Jon's aunt Ruth had stepped in and offered to repay every penny of the money David had 'borrowed', the resultant scandal would have damaged not just the guilty but the innocent, as well. David could have put into disrepute the family's legal firm in which he was the senior partner although, in truth, it had been run by his quieter and less flamboyant brother, Jon.

Even so, Jon had argued passionately against Ruth's decision, insisting that the interests of truth and honesty must be put before those of the family and himself.

In the end, though, Ruth had prevailed upon him to listen to what she was saying because, as she had insisted at the time, since David had disappeared, none of them had any means of knowing if David himself had intended to repay the money or indeed if the now deceased widow had actually loaned or given it to him.

Initially, only Jon, Olivia and Ruth knew the truth, but after an emotional discussion it had been decided that they would tell their 'nearest and dearest' because, as Ruth had put it, secrecy between couples and close family members could be very hurtful and damaging. But the truth had been kept hidden from Ben for the most altruistic of reasons.

Since his disappearance, nothing had been heard of David despite Jon's attempts to discover his whereabouts.

The last contact they had had from David had been from Jamaica, but when Max had flown out there to look for him, no trace could be found. All Max had got for his pains was a vicious knife attack on one of the local Jamaican beaches.

After David's disappearance, his wife Tania had returned to her parents' home on the south coast. The marriage was well and truly over and Jon and Jenny had brought up Jack, David and Tania's son, alongside their own.

There were only a couple of years between Jack and Joss. They had always got on well together and were as close as brothers.

Right now, though, Jenny's concern was not for

the younger contingent of the Crighton family, but for its oldest member, Ben, who was visibly getting frailer with each month that passed.

'He called me David last week,' Joss told his mother sadly.

Jenny frowned. There was no way Joss looked anything like his uncle.

'Do you think Uncle David will ever come back?' the boy asked.

Jenny looked helplessly at her husband.

'I doubt it, Joss,' Jon told him gently. 'David was…is…' He stopped and shook his head, not wanting to tell his son that David had not just been a braggart and as careless with other people's feelings as he had been with their money, but that he had been a coward, as well. Thanks to their father, David had grown up believing he could do no wrong. Ben had shielded David from the harsh consequences of his behaviour all through his life, often at Jon's own expense. David was the favoured child, the blue-eyed boy, and Ben had set him upon a pedestal, which, it seemed now to Jon, was so high, it was inevitable that sooner or later he would have had to fall.

Despite the cruel comparisons his father had made over the years, Jon had always loved David—did still love him—but no longer with the blind love that his father had compelled him to give his sibling, no longer in a way that meant he had to subjugate his own needs and feelings to those of his brother.

Without David's presence casting its dark shadow over his life, Jon's personality had flourished and blossomed, but that did not mean that he had stopped loving his twin—not for a moment.

'I don't think he would ever *want* to come back,' Jon offered quietly.

'Not even if he knew how much Gramps wants to see him?' Joss asked.

Helplessly, Jon looked at Jenny.

'It isn't quite as easy as that, Joss,' Jenny told him. 'There are problems…and—'

'Because of the money,' Joss interrupted her. 'But he could *still* come back. He could *still* see Gramps. Surely if he knew how much Gramps wants him…'

'Maybe *if* he did,' Jenny agreed. Privately, she didn't think it would make the least difference. David had always been self-absorbed and selfish; a vain, weak man who had never put another person's feelings or needs before his own in the whole of his life. 'But since we have no idea where he is nor any way of contacting him—'

'But he and Dad are twins,' Joss interrupted, startling them both by adding not entirely jokingly, 'There's supposed to be a bond between twins that means they are telepathically linked.' When neither of his parents responded, he reminded them urgently, 'Katie and Louise have it.'

Jenny sighed. It was true their twin daughters *did* have that special bond that twins *do* sometimes experience, that ability to know when the other was in need or in pain despite the miles separating them.

'Joss, I don't think...' she started to respond, then stopped, turning to look at Jon.

'David and I were never close in that kind of way,' Jon told Joss gruffly.

'But you could *try*,' the boy persisted. 'For Gramps's sake.'

Uneasily, Jenny studied his set face. Something *was* bothering him, something that he wasn't saying.

'Joss—' she began gently, but as though he had read her mind, Joss continued quickly.

'When Gramps mistook me for David, he...' He hesitated and then told her chokily, 'He started to cry...he said that he had missed me...and that life hadn't been worth living without me. I never really had much to do with Uncle David and I know what you all think about him. Even Jack says he wishes that *you* were his father, Dad, but Gramps…'

Wordlessly, Jon reached out and put his arm around his son. Tall as he was, just that little bit taller than Jon himself now, his body, his bones, still had that terrifyingly vulnerable feeling of youth.

As he hugged him fiercely and ruffled his hair, Jon knew that the tears he could see gleaming in his son's eyes were mirrored in his own.

'We've tried to find him, son,' he told him huskily. 'But sometimes people just don't *want* to be found. He could be anywhere,' he added gently.

'But what about Gramps? Doesn't he care that Gramps is missing him and that he's getting older?'

Not knowing what to say, Jon sighed as he heard the emotion breaking up his son's voice.

His twin and their father had always been close, far closer than he had ever been to either of them, but it had been a closeness founded on their mutual promotion of David into a person he had never actually been. Keeping up that kind of fiction, that kind of falsity, year after year, decade after decade, had ultimately resulted in the relationship self-destructing or being destroyed, which, in effect, was what David had done with his disappearance.

Of course, Jon knew how much his father missed David, but the David Ben missed was someone he himself had created.

Jon suspected that the realisation that he was not the superhuman that his father had always lauded him as being had been as traumatic to David as its discovery would have been to their father. But that was in the past now. David's dramatic exit from their lives had heralded a series of transformations that had seen his own marriage develop into the deeply fulfilling emotional and physical bond he had always longed for.

If David were to return now, Jon suspected that he would be thoroughly bemused by the changes that had taken place. David's daughter, Olivia, was now married and a mother. Jack, his son, had grown from a boy into a young man, just nineteen and about to start his first year at university. Max, Jon's son, was married and the father of three.

Yes, there had been plenty of changes and a whole new generation of babies born, including David's own granddaughters.

Olivia, he knew, had never forgiven her father for what he had done nor for the fact that his actions had almost resulted in the destruction of her relationship with her husband, Caspar.

Her mother, Tania, a victim of the eating disorder, bulimia, had been more the child in the relationship between herself and Olivia than Olivia herself had ever been, and although she had never said so, Jon knew that Olivia placed a large part of the blame for her mother's disorder on David's shoulders.

Olivia. Jon frowned as he released his son. He had become increasingly concerned about his niece over the past few months. When he had tried to suggest to her that she was working too hard and that for her to be at the office before him in the morning and still there when he left at night was an excessive devotion to duty, she had snapped crossly at him.

Later, she had apologised, explaining tiredly that it was impossible for her to take work home. 'Caspar feels that when we're at home we should spend as much time as we can with the children. Of course I agree with him, but sometimes when I've got statements or counsel's opinions to read through...'

Jon had given her a sympathetic smile, but he couldn't help thinking a sense of responsibility to one's work was one thing, but using it as a means of putting a barrier between oneself and one's family was another entirely. Perhaps he ought to ask Jenny if she could have a word with Olivia. They had always got on well together.

A LITTLE LATER that evening as they were preparing for bed, Jenny told Jon musingly, 'I was just thinking about that time when Louise gashed her leg so badly and Katie, who was miles away at the time playing with a school friend, insisted on coming home because Lou had hurt her leg and needed her to be with her. Do you remember?'

'Mmm...' Jon acknowledged, guessing what his wife was leading up to.

'When you were boys, did you and David ever...?' Jenny persisted, then stopped as she saw the look in his eyes.

'David and I never shared the kind of relationship that Lou and Katie have. You know that,' Jon told her quietly and then added almost brusquely, 'Do you think if there was any way, any way at all I could bring him home for Dad that I wouldn't use it?'

As she heard the pain in her husband's voice that couldn't be masked by his anger, Jenny went up and put her arms around him.

Even though he was in his fifties and had a relatively sedentary lifestyle, Jon still had a very sexy body—well, she certainly thought so, and after all the sterile, weary years of having to hide her feelings for him, to be able to caress it...*him*...freely and openly was something that never failed to give her joy, but the caress she gave him now was one of tender emotion rather than teasing sensuality.

Like all the Crighton men, Jon was good-looking, tall, broad shouldered with a very masculine profile. His hair was thick and closer to caramel colour than blond. Women's eyes still followed him when they went out and hers followed them. Not that Jon ever noticed their glances of discreet female appreciation. He was a wonderfully loyal and loving husband and she was a very lucky woman to have such a fulfilling marriage, such a truly loving and lovable man, but Jon was no saint. He could be stubborn and even a little blinkered at times, but for him to be angry was a very rare occurrence indeed and she knew that the fact he was now was an indication of how deep his feelings went over the issue of his twin.

A man with a weaker personality than Jon's, a man lacking in his emotional strength and compassion, might have been badly warped by the obvious and relentless favouritism of their father for David. But Jon was too kind, too caring a person to fall into that trap, and Jenny loved him all the more for what his father had once so contemptuously dismissed as Jon's softness.

'Come on,' she said now, kissing his chin. 'Let's go to bed.'

JON GLANCED at the bedside clock. Jenny was asleep at his side, curled up next to him like a little girl. He smiled as he looked down into her sleeping face. They had made love earlier and she had fallen asleep almost immediately afterwards, *his* prerogative as a male, surely? And to be fair to Jenny, he was the one who normally fell asleep first, but tonight for some reason he just hadn't been able to do so.

For some reason... There was only one reason why he couldn't sleep—David. Not even to Jenny had he confided...admitted...how often he thought about his twin, or how much he missed him. It was ironic, really, because he knew damn well that David wouldn't be thinking about or missing *him* and he knew, too, that without David's presence in it, his own life had improved immeasurably.

Where was David now? Did he ever think of

them…of him? Deliberately, Jon closed his eyes, letting his mind drift back through the years to their shared childhood. Those childhood years had been so painful for him, pushed as he was by their father into the shadows, ignored and unwanted, unloved, he had always felt, constantly reminded by their father of just how lucky he was to be David's brother.

'David is the first-born,' their father used to say, and Jon had known almost before he could analyse what that knowledge meant how important it was that David should *be* the first, the sun, the star, and that he should never attempt to pre-empt David's role.

As they grew up, it had become second nature to him to remain in the shadows, to withdraw into himself so that his twin could be first.

David… Stored away in his memory, Jon had a thousand, a million different images of him. David…

'YOU SEEM…PREOCCUPIED. Is there something on your mind?'

David smiled warmly at his companion and teased him gently. 'Once a Jesuit priest, always a Jesuit priest.'

The older man laughed. 'I confess that there are

times when the habit of encouraging another's confession is too strong to resist, but purely for the most altruistic of reasons, I hasten to add.'

Looking away from him, David said passionately, 'On a night like this, I can't help wondering what it is about us human beings that compels us to behave so imperfectly when we have been given the gift of such a perfect universe, the potential to enhance our lives, to be the best we can be....'

'It is a perfect evening,' Father Ignatius agreed gravely as he sat down slowly next to David on the rocky outcrop of land from which it was possible not just to look up into the star-studded Jamaican sky above them but also out to sea. 'But there have been other equally perfect evenings and they have not resulted in such a philosophical outburst.'

'Philosophical.' David shook his head. 'No. To be philosophical is to be detached, to talk about the human condition in general terms, whereas I was thinking...wishing...regretting...'

He stopped whilst the priest looked at him and said knowledgeably, 'You want to go home.'

'Home!' David gave a mirthless laugh. 'This is my home and a far better one than I deserve.'

'No, David,' the priest corrected him gently.

'This is where you *live*. Your *home* is where your heart is. Your *home* is in England…in Cheshire…'

'…in Haslewich,' David supplied wryly for him. 'I dreamed about my father last night,' he said to the priest abruptly. 'I wonder what they have told him…about me…about my disappearance. I wonder if…'

'From what you have told me of your family, your brother, your *twin*,' the priest emphasised, 'I doubt they will have told him anything that might hurt him. But if you really wish to know, then you should go back,' he said gently.

'Go back,' David repeated brusquely. 'No, I can't do that.'

'There is no such word as "can't",' the priest replied sturdily.

'I'm a thief, a criminal. I stole money,' David reminded him sharply.

'You sinned against one of God's laws,' the priest agreed. 'But you have repented your sin, acknowledging it with humility and genuine contrition. In God's eyes, you are making atonement.'

'In God's eyes, maybe,' David agreed grimly. 'But in the eyes of the law, I am still guilty.'

'Which is more important to you, David?' the priest questioned him softly. 'The burden of guilt you carry for the debt you owe your family or that which you carry in the eyes of the law?'

'My father might no longer be alive.'

'You have other family,' the priest pointed out. 'A brother…a daughter…a son…'

'They are better off without me,' David told him curtly, turning his head away so that the priest couldn't see his expression.

'Maybe…maybe not.'

'I *can't* go back,' David repeated, but the priest could hear the uncertainty and yearning in his voice.

Ever since he had read the report of David's nephew, Max's knife attack, in the island's paper, he had been preparing himself for this moment. David had become as close to him as a son and the love he felt for him was that of a father, but he was *not* David's father, and had he been he knew perfectly well that it was the duty of a loving father to set even his most beloved child free to live his own life.

Since David had been working here helping him in his self-appointed task of nursing the island's terminally sick, those too poor…too shunned by society to merit any other kind of help, Father Ignatius had come to realise just how solitary and lonely his life had been.

He had found David lying drunk in one of Kingston's stinking gutters and even now had no real idea just why he had stopped to help him, a man who had cursed him and who, when he was sober enough, had blamed him for not allowing him to die.

It had been months before David had finally brought himself to start talking to him about his life, his past, but once he had done so, the priest had not passed any judgement. Why should he? Judging others was not what *he* was here for. Helping them, healing them, loving them; *those* were his duties.

Originally, when he had entered the priesthood, he had been filled with such ideas, such visions, but then had come the faith-shaking discovery that the man he most admired, his inspiration and guiding light, had been guilty of one of the most unforgivable of sins. Father John had broken his vow of chastity and had not just had a secret relationship with a woman but had also given her his child. Torn between conflicting loyalties, tortured by what he should do, in the end the younger man had simply felt obliged to speak up.

The result of his action had been catastrophic. Father John had taken his own life and he, Francis O'Leary, known by the church as Father Ignatius, had been to blame. Totally and absolutely. Even the bishop had seemed to think so.

He had been sent away out of the area, hopefully to get a fresh start, but the news of his role in the tragedy had followed him and he had become untouchable, defiled, someone to be avoided, a priest whose faith not just in others but in himself had been destroyed. He had volunteered for missionary work and had been granted it.

'Even if I wanted to go home, I couldn't,' David said, bringing the priest back to the present. 'There's no way I could raise the cost of the airfare.'

It was true they lived very simply and meagrely, growing as much of their own food as they could and relying on the generosity and gratitude of the patients and their families for the rest of it.

'There are other means of travel,' Father Ignatius pointed out and then added, 'There's a yacht in the harbour now waiting to be sailed back to Europe. The captain was in the Coconut Bar yesterday saying that he was looking for a crew willing to work their passage.'

'A yacht bound for Europe? What's her cargo? Drugs?' David asked him drily.

'No, but her owner is dying and he wants to go home.' The two men exchanged looks.

'AIDS?' David asked him forthrightly.

'I imagine so,' the older man agreed.

A very large proportion of the priest's patients were in the final stages of that ravaging disease, abandoned by their frightened families and friends. Working alongside him, David had learned to respect the disease and those who suffered from it. To respect it and not to fear it.

'I can't go...not now....' David resisted, but there was no denying the longing in his voice.

'Do you often dream of your brother?' Father Ignatius asked him obliquely.

'Not like I did last night,' David admitted. 'I dreamed about when we were children. It was so vivid. It was when we got our first bikes, but the odd thing was...' He paused and frowned. 'In my dream, though I could see myself riding my bike, my *feelings* were Jon's.'

The older man said nothing. He knew David had seen Jon Crighton from a safe distance when he had come to the island to visit Max in hospital and eventually take his son home. Life was so precious, and because he was becoming increasingly aware of just how frail his own physical strength was getting, the priest prayed that Jon

Crighton would find it in his heart to welcome home his twin.

'I can't go,' David was saying, but the older man knew not just that he could but that he would.

CHAPTER TWO

'Yes, Mrs Crighton...very well, Maddy,' Honor corrected herself into the telephone receiver with a warm smile as she responded to her caller's request that she use her Christian name. 'I'd be very happy to come and see your father-in-law, although I can't promise...'

She paused. Over the years she had grown used to the fact that her patients and their families, having failed to find a cure for their illnesses through conventional medicine, tended to expect that she could somehow produce something magical to restore them to full health.

'Herbal medicine is not some kind of black art. It's an exact science,' she sometimes had to tell them severely.

Many modern drugs were, after all, originally derived from plants even if more latterly scientists had discovered ways to manufacture them synthetically in their laboratories. In her view, synthetic drugs, like synthetic foods, were not always

sympathetic to the human system, and to judge
from the increasing number of patients consulting
her, other people were beginning to share her
views.

Honor had not always been a herbalist. Far
from it. She had been at medical school studying
to become a doctor way back in the seventies, a
sloe-eyed brunette burning the candle at both
ends, studying and partying and desperately trying
to deny her aristocratic background and connections to become part of the London 'scene'. Ironically, it had not been on the London scene that
she had met her late husband but through one of
her mother's friends.

Lady Caroline Agnew had been giving a com-
ing-out party for her daughter, and Honor's
mother had insisted that Honor had to attend.
Rourke had been there photographing the event.
Lady Caroline had contacts at *Vogue* and he was
the 'in' photographer of the moment, more used
to photographing long-legged models than chubby
adolescent debs.

Honor had been fascinated by him. Everything
about him had proclaimed that he belonged to the
world she so longed to join. His clothes, his hair,
his laid-back manner and, most of all, his sharp
cockney speech. Somehow or other she had man-

aged to catch his eye and they had left the party together.

Three months later they became lovers and three months after that they married and she dropped out of medical school.

For two years she had been so passionately and completely in love with him that she had blinded herself to reality, his unfaithfulness, his drinking, the drugs he was taking with increasing regularity, the bills that mounted up because he refused to pay them, the unsavoury characters who hung like dark shadows on the edges of his life, *their* lives, and then she had become pregnant.

Their first daughter Abigail had been less than six months old the first time he left her.

Her parents, who had never really forgiven her for her marriage, had refused to have her home, but her father had given her a tiny allowance just enough to cover the rent on a small flat, and she had found herself a job working in a small family-owned chemist's shop. It had been whilst working there that her interest in medicine had been reactivated. The shop was old-fashioned, its upper room stuffed with all manner of things amongst which Honor, who had been sent upstairs to tidy it, had found the herbal book that once opened she had been unable to put down.

Rourke, his affair over, had turned up on her doorstep one dark, wet night and foolishly she had taken him in. Nine months later Ellen was born. Rourke had already embarked on another affair with a rich older woman this time.

On her own again, Honor had become fascinated by herbal medicine and cures, so much so that when she learned of a local herbalist in a magazine she was reading in the dentist's waiting room, she made a note of her address so that she could get in touch with her.

Now a fully trained herbalist herself, Honor always made a point of advising her patients to make sure they went to similarly trained and accredited practitioners whenever they chose alternative forms of healing.

Her own training had been long and thorough and one of her main reasons for coming to live here in the rather dilapidated house she had just moved into on her second cousin Lord Astlegh's Cheshire estate was because of the land that went with it—land on which she would be able to grow some of her own herbs in a way that was completely natural and free from pesticides and any kind of chemicals. The house, which was miles away from any other habitation, might have drawn cries of despair from both her daughters, who had protested at its lack of modern amenities and creeping damp, but Honor had assured them that once she had time to get someone in to repair and improve the place, it would make a very snug home indeed.

'It's a hovel,' Abigail had said forthrightly.

'A wretched hovel,' Ellen had agreed.

'The locals will probably think you're some kind of witch,' Abigail had joked.

'Thank you very much,' Honor had told her daughter drily. 'When I want my ego boosted, I shall know where to come.'

'Oh, no, Mum, I didn't mean you *look* like a witch,' Abigail had immediately reassured her. 'Actually, you look pretty good for your age.'

'Mmm... Nowhere near forty-five,' Ellen had agreed.

'Forty-four, actually,' Honor had corrected her with dignity.

'Honestly, Mum,' Abigail had told her. 'With all the money you inherited from Dad, you could have bought yourself somewhere *really* comfortable. I know you had to scrimp and scrape whilst we were growing up, but now...'

'Now I have *chosen* to come and live here,' Honor had told them firmly.

She was still not totally over her shock at the

amount of money she had inherited from Rourke. She hadn't expected him to die so relatively young and certainly not from something so ridiculous as a cold turned to pneumonia. She was even more surprised to discover that since they had never divorced, she was his next of kin. The young leggy model he had been living with had been quite happy to accept the fact, simply shrugging her sparrow-like shoulder-blades and gazing at Honor with drug-glazed eyes as she shook her head over Honor's concern and explained in a small, emotionless voice that she was really quite rich herself.

Rourke's unexpected wealth had come not from his current work as a photographer but from his earlier and highly original work as a young man, which had now become extremely valuable collector's pieces, selling for thousands upon thousands of pounds.

She had insisted on sharing the money with the girls, her daughters...Rourke's daughters. Both of them were adults now and they often tended to treat her as though *she* were the one in need of parenting. Whilst both of them loved their mother's elderly second cousin and thought that his Palladian home, Fitzburgh Place, and the philanthropic way in which he was developing the estate's resources were both worthy of their highest approval, they were united in disapproval of the ramshackle place their mother had chosen to make her home.

'I can't bear to think about your living like this,' Ellen had said, grimacing in distaste as she wiped a fastidious finger along one grimy window-sill the weekend her mother had moved into Foxdean.

'Then *don't* think about it,' Honor had advised her gently.

Much as she loved them, her daughters, both wonderful girls, clever, independent, good fun to be with and undeniably beautiful, could, at times, in their attitudes and conversations, remind her disconcertingly of her own mother.

'Honoraria has always been…wayward,' her mother had been fond of saying exasperatedly, and Honor knew how pained and bemused her mother in particular had been at what she had seen as her daughter's determination to turn her back on the kind of life they had expected her to lead.

If her decision not to go to Switzerland following in her mother's footsteps and attending an exclusive finishing school but instead to study medicine had shocked and confused her parents, then the way she had ultimately lived her life, the man she had married, the friends she had made had earned her their wholehearted disapproval. But as she sometimes pithily had to remind the more conventional members of her large family, their aristocratic forebears, of whom they were so proud, had received their lands and titles for acts that had been little short of outright theft and barbarism.

Her parents had tried their best, poor darlings. No one could have been more true to stereotype than her father. His family, although not quite as noble as her mother's, was nonetheless extremely respectably provenanced. No doubt the Victorian son of the Jessop family, who had so providentially married the only daughter of an extremely wealthy mill owner, had been more than happy to exchange his upper-class connections for her wealth. Honor's mother's family had always managed to marry well, which was, of course, the main reason why her second cousin, unlike so many of his peers, could afford to be paternally benevolent towards his tenants and keep his large estate in tiptop condition.

Apart, of course, from her house.

What she had not told her daughters, and moreover had no intention of telling them, was that the main reason the house was so dilapidated was because of the history appertaining to it.

Local legend had it that originally it had been built on the instructions of the younger brother of the then Lord Astlegh to accommodate his mistress. He would visit her there, often spending several days with her much to the disapproval of his elder brother and the rest of his family who had arranged a profitable marriage for him with the daughter of another landowner.

The young man refused to do their bidding. The only woman he wanted, the only one he could love, was his mistress, the wild gypsy girl for whom he had built the house but whom he would often find wandering barefoot through the woods scorning the comforts of the home he had given her.

'Come with me,' she was supposed to have begged him when he told her of his family's plans for his future. 'We can go away together…be together….'

He had shaken his head. He loved fine food, fine wines, fine books.

'I can't stay here,' the gypsy girl had told him. 'It hems me in. I need to travel, to be free. Come with me.'

'I cannot,' he had told her sorrowfully.

'You are a coward,' she had returned contemptuously. 'You have no fire, no passion. You are weak. You are not a true man, not like a Romany man. A Romany man would kill for the woman he loved.'

Her voice had been scornful, her eyes flashing, and in the darkness of the small copse where they had argued, he had mistaken her tears for a gleam of taunting mockery.

It had been said later when the bodies were found that she had bewitched him and that only by killing her and then killing himself had he been able to break free of her spell.

He came from a powerful family, *the* most powerful family in the area. James, his elder brother, the then Lord Astlegh, used his position to have the affair hushed up, but news of what had happened quickly spread amongst the local population and with it claims that the copse and the house itself were haunted. Tenants who pooh-poohed the warnings and moved sturdily into it very quickly decided to move out again!

It was a reasonably sized house, a well-built, pretty Georgian red brick building with its own small porticoes and elegant sash windows, the kind of house that the upper-class women Honor had grown up with would drool over as the ideal country retreat, but her cousin was unable to successfully find a tenant. It was he who told Honor of the legend surrounding it.

'Have you ever seen a ghost there?' she had asked him, intrigued.

Immediately, he had shaken his head. 'Dashed nonsense if you ask me,' he told her gruffly. 'But wouldn't want you not to know about it. Give it to you rent-free. Can't sell it—part of the estate. Have to do your own restoration work on it…local workforce shun the place.'

Honor who had fallen in love with the house the moment she saw it had been delighted.

Her chance visit to her second cousin had really been a duty visit since she had heard on the family grapevine that he was suffering badly from a colicky stomach disorder that the doctors seemed unable to relieve. She had guessed that she was being subtly asked if she could do anything to help, but the visit had had the most advantageous outcome. She had been looking for a new home for some time.

Rourke's inheritance meant that she could actually afford to completely renovate the place and fulfil the ambition she had been harbouring, not just to prepare her herbal remedies but to grow the herbs themselves, as well. Foxdean, with its surrounding land, was perfect for her purposes. Why, she might even be able to persuade her cousin to allow her to erect a glass house where she could grow some of the more tender, vulnerable herbs.

A visit to Haslewich's excellent health-food shop and a long chat over lunch with its owner had resulted in her being contacted by so many potential patients that her diary was becoming quite full. This was why, as she listened to Maddy Crighton outlining her grandfather-in-law's problems, she had to tell her, 'I can't do anything for Mr Crighton until I have seen him, of course, and unfortunately, my first free appointment is not for a few weeks.'

There was a small pause at the other end of the telephone line, then she heard Maddy saying, 'Oh dear. Well, in that case we shall just have to wait until then.'

As she pencilled the appointment into her diary, Honor asked Maddy several questions about her grandfather-in-law.

'He's had two hip operations in the past few years, but he's still complaining about the pain he's suffering,' Maddy informed her. 'But it isn't just his pain that's concerning us. Just lately he seems to have lost interest in life. He's always been rather dour and a little bit tetchy, but these past few months...'

'If he's in constant pain, it will be having a debilitating effect on him,' Honor responded, 'if his GP hasn't prescribed some painkillers.'

'Oh, he has, but Gramps threw them away. He isn't very good about taking medicine...he doesn't have a very high opinion of the medical profession.'

'Oh dear,' Honor sympathised, guessing that Ben Crighton was the kind of patient who made most doctors' hearts sink.

'I'm afraid I must be painting a rather gloomy picture,' Maddy apologised. 'Gramps can be a little bit difficult at times, but I hate to see him in so much discomfort. He isn't so old after all, only in his early eighties. I know it must be frustrating for him not being able to get about as much as he used to. He doesn't drive any more and he can't walk very far.'

'Try to persuade him to take the painkillers his doctor has prescribed,' Honor advised her.

'Do you think you'll be able to do something to help him?' Maddy asked tentatively.

'Hopefully, yes. You'd be amazed at the difference even the smallest fine-tuning of someone's diet can make where joint pain is concerned. Then there are poultices that can be applied to the damaged joints and a variety of herbal medicines that can help. I'll be better placed to discuss these with you, though, once I've seen Mr Crighton.'

After she had finished speaking, Honor went through to the old-fashioned back kitchen that she was in the process of turning into her still-room. In the passage that led from the kitchen proper to this room, she had put up bookshelves and she looked quickly along them, extracting a volume that she carried back with her to the kitchen proper. She sat down in a chair whilst she looked for what she wanted.

The book was one she had found tucked away amongst a pile of fusty documents at the back of a little bookshop in the cathedral town of Wells. As it was entitled *A Medieval Herbal*, she had pounced on it straight away. Now as she turned the pages, she paused at the one headed 'Bramble' and read it with a small smile. 'For sore of joints take some part of this same wort, seethe in wine to a third part and with the wine then let the joints be bathed.'

As she closed the book, Honor sat back in her chair. Herbalism had come a long way since its early days, but its principles were still the same as they had always been—to heal the sick.

In the high-pressure world of modern drugs the race was on to comb the most remote tracts of land searching for the plant that would give the world a panacea that would cure mankind of all his ills and give him eternal youth.

Personally, Honor felt that their efforts would be better employed in preserving the rain forests instead of letting them be destroyed. Surely the increasing incidence of childhood asthma and eczemas was proof enough of what polluting the earth's atmosphere was doing. Trees cleaned the air. Without them...

Already she had plans to plant a new grove of trees on her rented land. She knew that her views, her beliefs, often exasperated Ellen who, as a biologist, took a somewhat different view of things, whereas Abigail, an accountant, tended to view everything in terms of profit and loss.

It often amazed her that she had produced two such practical daughters—or was it that the hand-to-mouth peripatetic existence they had all had to live when the girls were young had made them overly cautious?

As she got up to fill the kettle and make herself a cup of coffee, the black cat, who had appeared from out of nowhere the first week she moved in and adopted her, strolled through the door.

None of Honor's enquiries had brought forward an owner for the cat, who had now fine-tuned her timetable to such a precise degree that Honor knew without having to look at the kitchen clock that it must be three o'clock.

The cat, she assumed, must have found its way to the house along the old bridle-way that passed in front of it, leading from Haslewich to Chester across her cousin's land.

She frowned as she glanced towards the kitchen door. Like the rest of the house, it was very much in need of repair if not replacement. She was going to have to renew her efforts in finding someone to work on the place soon.

The two large building firms she contacted had given her what she considered to be extortionate quotes and the three small 'one-man' businesses she tried had all turned her down with a variety of excuses.

Thoroughly exasperated when the third man who had been recommended to her claimed to be 'too busy', she challenged him, 'Don't tell me that people around here *still* actually believe those idiotic stories about the place being haunted?'

The man had flushed but stood his ground.

'They ain't just stories,' he had told her grimly. 'Uncle of mine broke his leg working here. Aye, and had to have it cut off—infection set in.'

'An accident,' Honor had responded. 'They do happen.'

'Aye, they do, and this house has had more than its fair share of them,' he had answered bluntly.

'I can't believe that people are actually refusing to work on the house because of some silly story of its being haunted,' Honor had complained to her cousin a few days later when he invited her up to Fitzburgh Place to have dinner. 'I mean... it's just so...so...ridiculous.'

'Not as far as the Cooke family are concerned,' he had retorted. 'They're closely related to the gypsy tribe the girl was supposed to have come from, and in a small town such things aren't easily forgotten.'

'Oh, I'm not saying that there wasn't an affair nor that it didn't end tragically. It's just this silly idea of the house being haunted.'

'Mmm...well, the Cookes are a stubborn lot, a law unto themselves in many ways. You could try bringing someone in from Chester.'

'I *could* try paying nearly double what I should be paying to a high-priced fancy builder, as well,'

Honor retorted drily, adding with a twinkle in her eye, 'I'm beginning to think my "bargain" home with its peppercorn rent wasn't quite the bargain I first supposed.'

'Ah well, my dear, you know what they say,' Lord Astlegh told her jovially. '*Caveat emptor.*'

'Let the buyer beware,' she translated.

REMEMBERING the pleasant evening she had spent with her cousin, Honor smiled. He was a kind man, well-read and interesting to talk with. A widower now without any children to inherit from him, he was determined to do everything he could to safeguard the estate from being broken up when it eventually passed into the hands of the next in line. It was to that end that he was trying to make the estate as self-supporting as possible, using a variety of innovative means.

The outbuildings that he had converted into small, self-contained working units for a variety of local craftspeople were now in such demand that he had a waiting list of eager tenants. The antiques fairs and other events that the estate hosted brought in not just extra income but visitors to the working units and to the house and gardens and its tea and gift shops.

He was now talking about renovating the or-

angery and getting it licenced for weddings, and
Honor had to admit it would make a perfect setting for them. Large enough to hold even the most
lavish of receptions, the orangery ran along one
wall of the enclosed kitchen garden. Enthusiastically, he had described to her how he planned to
have the garden subtly altered with the addition
of bowers of white climbing roses and a fountain.

As she listened to him, Honor had discovered
that most of his ideas came originally from the
man who was responsible for organising the antiques fairs—Guy Cooke.

'Nice chap,' he had told Honor. 'Must introduce you to him and his wife. Pretty girl. One of
the Crightons but on the wrong side of the blan-
ket. Still, can't say too much about that with our
colourful family history, can we?'

THE CAT MIAOWED demandingly and to oblige it
Honor went to get some food. Tomorrow she
would make a concerted effort to find herself a
builder—unless fate was kind enough to send her
one.

'A HERBALIST! I can't see Gramps... Do you
think that's a good idea?' Max Crighton asked his

wife dubiously. 'He's bad enough about conventional medicine and I don't think—'

'We don't have to tell him that she's a herbalist,' Maddy said gently. 'I don't want to deceive him, but I'm so worried about him, Max. He looks so weak and frail even the children are beginning to notice.'

'Mmm. I know what you mean,' Max agreed absently, picking up one of the fresh scones Maddy had just placed on a wire rack to cool and then shaking his fingers as it burned them.

'Wait until they're cool,' Maddy scolded him. 'You know they'll give you indigestion if you don't.'

'Indigestion.' Max's eyes danced with laughter. 'That's what marriage does for you. The woman you love stops seeing you as someone who is sexually exciting and thinks of you instead as someone with indigestion.'

'I wouldn't say *that*,' Maddy responded with a small smile.

'No?' Max questioned, his voice muffled as he took her in his arms and buried his mouth in the warm, soft, creamy, cooking-scented curve of her throat.

'Nooooo...' Maddy sighed.

The truth was that it would be hard to find a

man who was *more* sexually attractive than her husband. Max wore his sexuality with very much the same panache and air of self-mockery with which he wore his barrister's robes, a kind of dangerously sexy tongue-in-cheek, wry amusement at the reaction he was causing, coupled with a subtle but oh so sexy unspoken invitation to share in his amusement at it.

'Why is that lady looking at my daddy?' Emma had once asked Maddy as Max had met them both on their way home from school. He had stopped his car and got out, causing all the other mothers to gawp at him with varying degrees of bemused appreciation.

'The lady' in question had been almost as stunningly attractive as Max was himself, but for all the notice he had taken of her she might as well have been the same age as his aunt Ruth.

To the envy of Maddy's friends, Max was a totally devoted husband and father.

It hadn't always been that way. The Max who had married her had been a dangerous predatory man who had treated the emotions of those closest to him with a callousness it was hard to imagine now.

If, by some horrible blow of fate, the changes within him brought about by his frighteningly close brush with death in Jamaica should ever be reversed and he should revert to the man she had first met, Maddy knew that she could not and would not go back to being the girl she had been, the girl who had such low self-esteem that she had quietly and humbly allowed Max to emotionally abuse her.

Those days were gone and so was that Maddy. Now she and Max were equal partners in their marriage. Max didn't just love her; he respected her, as well.

'Where are one, two and three?' he murmured against her throat as he nibbled hungrily, referring to their three children.

'At your mother's,' Maddy told him huskily.

'Mmm…let's go upstairs.'

'What's wrong with down here?' Maddy teased him daringly, giving him a flirtatious look. 'Ben never comes in here and there's no one else in the house.'

'Here?'

Max raised his eyebrows, but Maddy could tell that her suggestion had excited him.

'You look so wonderfully sexy in your court clothes,' she whispered in a small breathy voice.

Max started to laugh but immediately joined in her game, reaching out towards the tray of scones and saying sternly, 'So what is this? I see that one scone is missing and you, wench, are the only one who could have taken it. Such a theft demands a very heavy sentence.'

'No...no...' Maddy cried, trying to tug her hand out of Max's grasp, but he refused to let her go, skilfully backing her against the table.

'A very heavy punishment,' he repeated huskily. 'Unless, mayhap, you have not eaten the stolen sweetmeat but secreted it about your person, in your pocket, perchance,' he demanded. 'Or...'

As his hands lifted towards her breasts, Maddy exploded into laughter. 'Oh, Max.' But as she saw the look in her husband's eye, her laughter died.

'Oh, Max, what?' he challenged as he moved his body over hers and slid his free hand inside the blouse he had just unfastened. His palm felt heavy and warm against her breast, her nipple hardening immediately.

'We can't,' Maddy breathed. 'Not here...'

'No?' Max challenged her, letting go of her wrist to push her blouse off her shoulder and unclip the front fastening of her bra before lifting her onto the table.

An hour later, a flushed and floury Maddy just managed to finish fastening her blouse before her three children and her mother-in-law came into the kitchen.

'Jenny.' Maddy beamed as she responded to the older woman's affectionate hug. 'Thanks for having them. Have you been good for Grandma?' she asked her two elder children whilst Max expertly scooped their youngest out of Jenny's arms.

'Your skirt is all floury,' Leo pointed out to his mother.

'Yes, and so is your blouse,' Emma chirped.

Blushing, Maddy turned away.

'Mummy's been very busy,' Max told them tongue-in-cheek.

As Maddy turned towards him to give him a wifely look, Jenny remarked in amusement, 'There's flour all over the back of your skirt, as well, Maddy...and Max's suit—'

'Caught in the act,' Max admitted cheerfully. 'Well, almost...'

'Max!'

Both Jenny and Maddy protested at the same time.

'What does Daddy mean?' Emma demanded, tugging insistently at Maddy's skirt.

'Uh-huh, bath time for you, baby,' Max announced quickly, walking towards the kitchen door.

'Men!' Maddy expostulated to her mother-in-law after he had escaped.

'Hmm. Talking of which, how's Ben?' Jenny asked her.

'Not really any better,' Maddy admitted. 'He just doesn't seem to... I've arranged for this herbalist I've heard about to come and see him. The problem is that she's so busy it's going to be a few weeks before she can come.'

'A *herbalist*...?'

'Herbal medicines *are* proven to work,' Maddy began defensively, but Jenny shook her head.

'I wasn't criticising, my dear. *I* think it's an excellent idea.'

'Do you? Good. In fact, I've been wondering if we mightn't use it somehow at The Houses.'

'The Houses' were the units of accommodation originally sponsored and started by Ben Crighton's sister Ruth to provide secure homes for single mothers and their babies. They had since been extended to provide not just accommodation and rooms where young fathers could visit their children, but also to give access to educational opportunities to help equip the young mothers to earn their own living.

'What are you planning to do?' Jenny asked

Maddy in some amusement. 'Train all our teenage mums as potential herbalists?'

Maddy laughed. 'No, of course not. No, what I was thinking was that we could perhaps utilise the kitchen garden here and combine a programme on gardening with nutritional awareness and simple, basic home remedies of the type our grandmothers would have used. It would be another step towards making our mums independent and add to their sense of self-worth.'

'Well, it's certainly worth thinking about,' Jenny agreed.

After her late marriage to the man she had loved and believed lost to her, the father of her illegitimate daughter, Ruth had handed over day-to-day control of the charity she had founded to Jenny and Maddy, thus allowing her to split her time between her home in Haslewich and her family in America.

'Mmm…and you know that land that was used for allotments—the land the council owns down by the river—it's all overgrown and untidy now. Well, I was thinking, if we could persuade them to allow us to use it, the boys could perhaps be encouraged to clear it. It could be a community project.'

As she listened to the enthusiasm in her daughter-in-law's voice, Jenny reflected that Ruth couldn't have chosen anyone better to be her successor. Maddy had transformed herself from the shy, downtrodden bride Max had married into a woman of such enormous capability and compassion, of such energy and love, that Jenny felt blessed to have her as a member of the family.

'Joss is most concerned about Ben,' she confessed quietly to her daughter-in-law. 'He asked Jon if he thought David would ever come home.'

Maddy gave the older woman an understanding look. 'Gramps has become increasingly withdrawn and morose, as you know, but when he does speak, increasingly the sole topic of his conversation is David, and just recently he's no longer talking about *if* David comes back but *when* he comes back.'

'Oh dear,' Jenny sighed. 'Do you think…?'

Maddy shook her head. 'Oh, no, he's perfectly sensible. No sign of any dementia, according to Dr Forbes. No. I think that Ben is just so desperate to have David home, so determined that he *will* come home, that he's convinced himself that it *is* going to happen. Do you think he will come back?' Maddy asked.

'I don't know,' Jenny replied thoughtfully. 'He wasn't…isn't…like Jon. He…'

'He's like Max was before,' Maddy agreed. 'Yes, I know.'

'Well, yes, but David never really had that…that hard-edged aggression of Max's,' Jenny told her. 'He was selfish, yes, breathtakingly so, but weak. He must have known for years about Tiggy's eating disorder,' Jenny used the nickname for Tania the whole family knew her by, 'but he never once attempted to do anything about it so far as we can tell. He never made any attempt to defend Olivia from Ben's unkindness when she was growing up or to encourage her in her ambition to become a solicitor. And as for poor little Jack…'

'Olivia has always said that he wasn't a good father.'

'No, he wasn't,' Jenny concurred soberly and then felt obliged to add in her brother-in-law's defence much as she knew Jon would have done, 'But against that you have to set his upbringing and the appalling indulgence with which Ben treated him. He put David on a pedestal so high that it not only gave him a warped idea of his own importance, but it must have been frightening for him at times.'

'Frightening?' Maddy queried.

'Mmm… He must have worried about falling

off it,' Jenny told her simply. 'And Ben never stopped insisting to Jon that he must virtually devote his life to his first-born twin brother. He also paradoxically and probably without thinking deliberately did everything he could to drive a wedge between them. Their loyalty to one another was never left to develop naturally. Jon was practically ordered to put David first.

'It all stemmed, of course, from the fact that Ben lost his own twin brother at birth. His mother, who I am sure never realised what she was doing and was perhaps following the way of the times, seems to have brought Ben up in the belief that his dead brother would have been a saint and that Ben's life and hers were blighted because he was not there to share it with them.

'Having a twin is such a special relationship,' Jenny added soberly. 'To have another person made in one's exact physical image and to have shared the intimacy of the womb with him and yet to know oneself to be completely separate from him.'

'Olivia would hate it if David were to return,' Maddy said with insight.

'She does have scant reason to want him back. As we've agreed, he wasn't a good father. Add to that the fact that she had to deal with not just her mother's bulimia but David's fraud, as well, at a time when her own relationship with Caspar was going through a bad patch, and I can understand why she feels so negatively towards him.'

'Yes, so can I.' Very carefully, Maddy drew an abstract outline on the kitchen table with her fingernail before saying slowly to Jenny, 'I don't think Olivia is feeling too happy at the moment.'

As she lifted her head and looked into Jenny's eyes, the older woman's heart sank. Olivia was as close and as dear to her as one of her own daughters—more so in some ways—and although Olivia had said nothing to her, Jenny, too, had noticed how strained and unhappy she was looking.

'Jon has told her that she is working far too hard,' Jenny responded.

There was a small pause and then Maddy said uncertainly, 'You don't think there's anything wrong between her and Caspar, do you?'

Jenny looked searchingly at her. 'What makes you ask that?'

'Nothing. Well, nothing I can explain logically,' Maddy admitted. 'It's just…well, I've noticed whenever I go round that there's a sort of atmosphere.'

'Olivia has mentioned that she feels that Caspar ought to refuse an invitation they've received to attend a wedding in the family,' Jenny told her carefully. 'Perhaps...'

'No, Olivia told me about that. I think it's more than that. They just don't...they just don't seem happy together any more,' Maddy told her hesitantly. 'And the children...' She stopped and shook her head. 'Olivia isn't the type to discuss her most personal thoughts and feelings freely, but I know how much you and Jon think of her and would hate—'

'Olivia has always been a very private person,' Jenny quickly agreed. 'Her home life made her very independent from an early age. That was one of the things that helped her to bond so closely with Caspar, I think, the fact that they both experienced difficult childhoods, Caspar with his parents' constant remarriages and Olivia with David and Tiggy's problems. We were very close when Olivia was younger, but she seems to have changed since Alex's birth.' Jenny gave a small sigh. 'I suppose it's only to be expected—she has Caspar now and the children, and Caspar adores Amelia and Alex. He's a wonderful father.'

'Yes, I know,' Maddy agreed, turning away from Jenny as she asked a little awkwardly, 'I was wondering if *that* could be part of the problem. Oh, I know that Olivia loves them, too, but—'

'You think that she might be a little resentful of the fact that because of their different careers, Caspar has taken over the main parenting role?' Jenny guessed. 'Olivia loves her children,' she added protectively.

'Her children—yes,' Maddy replied before saying uncomfortably, 'I probably shouldn't mention this, but the other week when we were over there for dinner, Olivia really snapped at Caspar over something trifling and it wasn't just an ordinary husband-and-wife grizzle. She's told me, too, that she thinks Caspar has become far too protective of the children. Whilst we were there, she said to him, quite vehemently, that Haslewich wasn't New York.'

'Max is a very caring father, too,' Jenny said.

'Mmm…but not to the extent of correcting me about what size socks the children wear and whether or not they need new underwear,' Maddy told her simply. 'To be quite honest, I can imagine that in Olivia's shoes *I* might easily feel just a little shut out and I—'

'You didn't have Olivia's upbringing when she learned in the most painful way that as a girl, as *herself*, she wasn't properly valued. I understand what you're saying and I *can* see the problem, but *seeing* it and knowing what to *do* about it are two different things.'

'Yes, I know. I did offer to have the children for a weekend so the two of them could go away together, but Olivia said that they simply didn't have the time. ''I'm far too busy at work'' and ''Caspar would never leave the children'' were her exact words.'

'Mmm…' Jenny was thoughtful.

'Oh, and speaking of children, I almost forgot. Did Leo say anything to you about seeing a strange man?'

'No!' Jenny denied immediately, looking alarmed. 'Where? What…?'

'Well, you know what a vivid imagination my son's got.' Maddy gave Jenny a rueful look. 'But he keeps talking about a ''nice man'' who he wants to be his friend. He says he's seen him in the garden. ''Grampy Man'' he calls him, whatever that means! But whenever we've gone out to look, we haven't seen a sign of anyone.'

'Oh, Maddy, have you told the police? These days…'

'Not yet. Leo knows, of course, about not talking to strangers or going near them, but the odd thing is that he keeps referring to this man as a nice man, but when I asked him what he meant he couldn't explain. He's normally very cautious, too, but—'

'*Where* exactly has he seen him?' Jenny asked worriedly.

'In the garden. But when I wanted to know what the man was doing, Leo said, "Nothing. He was just standing looking." Not at him, apparently, but at the house.'

'I think you really ought to mention it to the police,' Jenny cautioned.

'Yes, but if it's just some poor itinerant looking for an empty shed to spend the night in—'

'Maddy, you've got a heart of gold,' Jenny told her, shaking her head.

'Maybe, but I'm still making sure that the children don't go out of my sight when they're in the garden,' Maddy assured her.

As the grandfather clock on the stairs struck the hour, Maddy gave a small groan.

'Is that the time? I haven't given Ben his medicine yet this afternoon.'

Jenny laughed not unsympathetically as she told her, 'Perhaps if your herbalist's remedies work, you won't have to any more.'

Maddy laughed with her. 'Wouldn't *that* be something? You wouldn't believe the lengths he goes to not to have to take his pills and yet, after refusing them, he goes on to complain about the pain he's in. He says they make him feel sleepy and he's even accused us of trying to sedate him into senility. He apologises afterwards, of course, but when he's having a bad day...' She shook her head.

'You're a saint. Do you know that?' Jenny told her fondly as she got up and gave her a loving hug.

CHAPTER THREE

'...MADDY WAS SAYING that when she and Max went to dinner with Olivia and Caspar, Olivia was... Jon, you aren't listening to a word I'm saying,' Jenny protested.

'Sorry, Jen. What was that?' Jon apologised, giving his wife a penitent look.

'I was just trying to talk to you about how concerned both Maddy and I are about Olivia and Caspar,' Jenny told him mock sternly and then sighed and asked him more gently, 'What is it, Jon? What's wrong?'

'Nothing,' he denied swiftly, too swiftly in Jenny's wifely opinion.

'Yes, there is,' she insisted. 'Tell me.'

'It's David,' Jon admitted with reluctance. 'I just can't stop *thinking* about him. I don't want to. Heaven knows I've got a hundred other things I *ought* to be thinking about—at least—but no matter how hard I try to keep him out, he keeps coming into my mind.'

Because she understood and loved him, instead of allowing him to see her curiosity by demanding further details, she simply smiled and said nonchalantly, 'Oh, I expect it's just because we've been talking about him recently.'

'Mmm…that's what I thought,' Jon agreed in relief. 'Where are you going?' he asked as Jenny suddenly got up out of her armchair and hurried towards the sitting-room door.

'Oh, I just remembered that I need to give Katie a ring. She was saying the other day that she had no idea what to get her mother-in-law for her birthday and I saw the very thing for her in the shop, the prettiest Dresden inkstand.'

The antiques shop in Haslewich, which had originally been owned and run by Jenny and her partner, Guy Cooke, but which was now owned solely by Guy and run by one of his cousins, Didi, was a favourite stopping-off point for Jenny whenever she went into town. Still, Jon couldn't help giving a faint, pained male sigh of incomprehension and bewilderment at his wife's sudden and to him inexplicable need to speak with their daughter right in the middle of a discussion about something else.

'I thought you wanted to talk to *me* about Olivia and Caspar,' Jon complained.

'Yes. I did…I do,' Jenny agreed. 'But you know what I'm like. If I don't ring Katie now and tell her about the inkstand, I'll probably forget.'

Jon blinked a little in surprise at this disarming statement since, as he had good cause to know, Jenny never forgot *anything*. She could, he often privately thought, have masterminded the provisioning and deployment of an army were she called upon to do so, so excellent was her grasp on all the many different threads of her life. Still, who was he as a mere male, a mere *husband*, to question the intricate thought patterns of a master tactician?

'Katie?' Jenny answered her daughter's hello as she picked up the telephone receiver. 'Do you ever find that Louise sometimes pops into your thoughts, sometimes when you don't really expect her to be there?'

'As though she's trying to get in touch with me, you mean?' Katie responded to her mother's question with immediate insight. 'It did happen, especially when we were younger and she wanted to borrow money off me.' She laughed before saying more seriously, 'Yes, I do get her in my thoughts. Why do you ask?'

'Oh, it's nothing, not really. Oh, and by the

way, I saw the ideal present for Seb's mother in
the shop the other day. It—'

'—the antique inkstand. I've already bought it
for her,' Katie told her mother triumphantly. 'I
was in town myself this afternoon and the moment I saw it I knew she'd love it. I bumped into
Maddy, as well. She said something about consulting a herbalist to see if she could do anything
to help Gramps.'

'Mmm…she was telling me all about it earlier,'
Jenny said.

'It isn't a herbalist he really needs,' Katie told
her sadly. 'It's a magician, someone who can
wave a wand and bring Uncle David back for him.
Speaking of which, this herbalist of Maddy's
wouldn't be the woman who's moved into Foxdean, would it? She was in the health-food shop
when I went in the other day. *Very* attractive. Tall,
dark-haired, with the most amazingly piercing
blue eyes, and despite her casual clothes she had
that unmistakable look of elegance about her—if
you know what I mean. After she had gone, Didi
told me that she's related to Lord Astlegh, a second cousin or something.'

'Well, Guy will know. He's very close to Lord
Astlegh and he goes over to Fitzburgh Place

pretty regularly. Foxdean. It's very brave of her to have moved in there.'

'Because of the ghost? Oh, come on, Ma, *you* don't believe in that, do you?'

'No, of course not. What I meant was that she was brave to move in there because of the state of the house. Look, I must go. Your father will be waiting for his supper. We'll be seeing you on Sunday, though, won't we?'

'You certainly will. Seb says that nothing would stop him from eating one of your Sunday lunches.'

After replacing the receiver, Jenny went over to the fridge, opened it and removed some of her home-made pâté. Jon loved cheese and pickles with fresh, crusty bread for his supper, but it gave him the most dreadful indigestion. He would complain about being given the pâté instead, of course, but he would still enjoy it.

Was it a sign that they were becoming old that the very predictability of her husband's reactions was something she found reassuring and comforting as well as amusing rather than boring or irritating? If so, then as far as she was concerned, it was a definite plus point. The heady excitement that accompanied the early stages of being in love might have been denied to her and Jon for a variety of complex reasons that were now past history, but Jenny felt she had been more than compensated for its absence by the deep and richly joyous loving contentment and companionship they now shared. And for her, sex, too, was something that had improved and become infinitely more pleasurable in these past few years.

It now seemed odd to think that she had once envied David and Tania their outwardly so perfect marriage, feeling that everyone who knew them must pity Jon because his plain, dull wife in no way matched up to the exciting glamour attached to being married to an ex-model.

Quietly, she picked up the supper tray and headed for the sitting room, the new fitted carpets they had splashed out on the previous autumn muffling the sound of her footsteps as she pushed open the door.

Jon was standing with his back towards her, studying one of the photographs she kept on the small antique bureau. Silently, Jenny watched him.

The photograph was one that had been taken on the night of David and Jon's shared fiftieth birthday party. Jenny forgot who had taken it, but it had caught David and Jon in mid-conversation with one another and conveyed a closeness that in reality had not existed, a rapport that for some reason made them look even more physically alike than they actually were.

Although he rarely spoke about it to her now, Jenny knew just how much David's disloyalty and dishonesty had distressed Jon.

'If my father knew what Ruth and I were doing by covering up for David, he would be shocked senseless,' Jon had sadly said to Jenny at the time his brother's fraud came to light.

Jenny had said nothing. If David had committed a murder, Ben would have expected and even demanded that Jon claim the crime was his to spare David any punishment.

'If you didn't let Ruth pay back the money, could you ever forgive yourself?' Jenny had asked him.

The bleak smile he had given her had supplied the answer. Jon was the most honest and upright man there could be and Jenny knew how torn he was by his own conflicting desires to protect their clients from the results of David's weakness and to save David from the consequences of his actions.

Nor could she forget, either, that David had suffered a heart attack at that very birthday party, one brought on by the stress he was under. Jon might live a far healthier lifestyle than his twin brother, but it wasn't unknown for twins to share the same health problems, which was one of the reasons she was so insistent on Jon's not working too hard at the practice.

But her concern for Jon's health did not mean that she wanted to see Olivia putting a strain on her own marriage by trying to do too much. Perhaps she ought to suggest to Jon that he consider taking on another full-time qualified solicitor.

The arrival of Aarlston-Becker, the huge multinational drug company, in the area some years ago had brought a dramatic increase in the firm's workload. Aarlston had their own legal department, of course, part of which was headed by Saul Crighton, another in the family caught up in the field of law.

As the tea tray gave a faint rattle, Jon quickly replaced the photograph and turned round to face her. Giving no indication that she had noticed anything out of the ordinary, Jenny smiled her thanks at him as he pulled out the small table they used for their suppers.

'You won't believe it, but Katie actually saw the inkstand and bought it. She sends her love,' Jenny added chattily, but she could see that Jon still wasn't really giving her his full attention.

Now wasn't the time to probe and pry. Ben's distress over David's absence was obviously affecting Jon, but what if David were to come back? Such an event would give rise to all manner of problems and conflicts and *she* certainly had no wish to see her beloved Jon pushed into second place again or made to feel that he had to shoulder the burden of protecting his brother.

Would it be very wrong of her if she were to offer up a tiny prayer that things could continue as they were and that the warm contentment of their lives should not be disrupted? Maybe not wrong, she acknowledged, but perhaps a little selfish.

As DIDI FINISHED cataloguing the weeks' sales from the antiques shop for its owner, Guy Cooke noticed that his normally chatty cousin seemed rather preoccupied.

'Is something wrong?' he asked her quietly when they had finished their business discussion and had moved on to talk about family matters and the forthcoming eighteenth birthday of Didi's son, Todd.

'I'm a bit concerned about Annalise,' she admitted worriedly. Annalise was her niece, the eldest child of her brother, whose acrimonious divorce had caused a good deal of discussion within the family four years earlier when it had taken place.

'Paul's eldest?' Guy asked, surprised. 'But Paul was saying only at Christmas how well she was doing at school.'

'Yes, but in the past few weeks she's apparently changed completely, neglecting her schoolwork, going out and refusing to tell him where she's been or whom she's been with. Paul says that she's either lost in some kind of day-dream or snapping at the boys, so much so that she actually made little Teddy cry the other day when she told him off for forgetting to bring his sports kit home from school. And Paul said he has to speak to her at least half a dozen times on some occasions before he gets any kind of response from her.'

'Sounds like she could be in love,' Guy suggested.

'Yes. That's what Paul's afraid of,' Didi admitted.

Guy gave her a rather wry look. 'Girls of seventeen do fall in love,' he pointed out with a small smile, 'or at least they think they do.'

'Well, yes, but because of her parents' divorce and her own rather serious nature, Annalise isn't perhaps quite as *aware* as most other girls of her age. In some ways as a little mother to the others, she's very mature, but in other ways—so far as boys go—she's quite naïve.

'Paul has tended to be a bit overprotective of them all since the divorce from their mother was a particularly unpleasant one. There had been… relationships with more than one other man before she eventually left with a lover. As you know, his wife's a Cooke, too, another member of our large family and you also know how old gossip and exaggerated histories tend to be exhumed at times like this. Paul has been determined that his children, and especially Annalise, should remain free of any taint of ''carrying the wild Cooke genes''. I have tried to hint gently to him since Annalise started to grow up that there is such a thing as being too protective where boys, sex and relationships are concerned, but you know how prickly Paul can be at times.'

'Yes, a difficult situation, whichever way you look at it. Do we know who it is that Annalise has fallen so deeply in love with or—'

'We do, and it poses a problem. It's a boy called Pete Hunter. Paul is not disposed to think kindly of him because he's the lead singer with a local group that's all the rage at the moment.'

'You mean Salt?' Guy asked, naming the group of five young local boys who all the teenagers raved over.

'Mmm…that's them.' She gave Guy a curious look. 'I'm surprised you know the band's name. I wouldn't have thought their kind of music was to your taste, Guy.'

'It isn't,' he agreed, 'but Mike, my sister Frances's boy, is a member of the group.'

'Oh, yes, of course he is. So you'll know Pete, then?'

'Sort of. A tall, dark-haired lad with what I personally feel is just a little too much "attitude",' Guy returned wryly.

'That's the one,' Didi sighed. 'I mean in one way I doubt that Paul needs to be too worried. Pete is very self-aware and very sure of himself and what he wants from life. I doubt that normally he'd look very hard in Annalise's direction. Not that she isn't attractive, she is, and she's going to be even more so, but right now she's still very much a seventeen-year-old and a young seventeen-year-old at that.

'From what I've heard, the girls Pete normally squires around are rather more streetwise and, dare I say it, bimboish, and if Paul hadn't been silly enough to go storming round to Pete's parents' house and demand that Pete stay away from his daughter, I'm sure her crush would have died a natural and early death. Of course, Pete being the type of young man he is, Paul's interference has had exactly the opposite effect from the one he wanted and now, apparently, Annalise has been seen in several clubs around the area where the band has been playing, very much a member of the band's entourage.'

'And does Paul know about this?'

'I'm not sure, but once he does find out, as he's bound to do... Annalise is at a very vulnerable age and if Paul starts trying to come the heavy father—'

'Or if in his anxiety he panics and starts telling her she's going to end up like her mother...'

'Exactly,' Didi agreed. 'I've tried to talk to Paul, but he just doesn't want to know. He can be so stubborn at times. I suspect whilst Annalise believes herself to be deeply in love with Pete, as only a young, idealistic girl can be, Pete is anything but in love with her. I hate to use such an ugly word, but my feeling is that he's just using her and that once he's bored he's just going to push her to one side.

'Normally, I'd say that that kind of experience is just a part of growing up. We all go through the pain of teenage heartache, but the disparity between Annalise and Pete makes me very anxious for her. Of course, I'm anxious for Paul, as well, especially since the whole thing is inevitably going to be conducted in public...'

'Mmm...and of course it couldn't come at a worse time for Annalise's education, what with her A levels ahead of her,' Guy added.

'Exactly.'

'Oh dear, the perils of a father of teenage daughters,' Guy sighed. 'Well, if there's anything I can do to help...'

Since his marriage to Chrissie, who was seen to have tamed this wild Cooke, not quite knowing how or why it happened, Guy discovered that he had been elected to the role of paterfamilias within the Cooke clan and that inevitably, at some stage or another, various members of the family would bring their problems to him.

This was one problem where he suspected that Chrissie's gentle touch would be much more beneficial than his own.

'We've got a family gathering looming soon, haven't we?' he asked Didi. 'I'll see if Chrissie will have a tactful word with Paul, if you like.'

'Would you?' Didi smiled in relief. 'I haven't dared say anything to Paul, but I have heard a whisper that Annalise has been bunking off school to be with Pete. The band practises in an old barn out at—'

'Laura and Rick's farm, yes, I know,' Guy said, nodding. 'They used to use Frances's garage, but she gave Mike an ultimatum and told him that there was no way she would continue to allow them to use it unless they agreed to keep the noise level down. Laura stepped into the breach and offered them the use of one of their barns.'

'Well, as I said, it seems that Annalise has been sneaking off school to spend time with them there.'

'Leave it with me. I'll do what I can,' Guy promised.

DAVID TENSED as he watched Maddy's car come up the drive towards Queensmead. He had been watching the house ever since his arrival in England some days earlier, sleeping at night in unlocked garden sheds and open hay barns. After several weeks at sea sharing cramped quarters with the rest of the crew, the solitariness of his present existence was a relief. He missed Father Ignatius, of course; the two of them had become very close in the time they had worked together. As well as missing him, though, David was also concerned about him. Despite the priest's vigour and positive attitude towards life, David had sensed recently that the older man was not quite as stalwart as he had once been.

Had he done the wrong thing in leaving him to come home? Had he made the selfish decision—again?

In the car with Maddy were her three children, the second youngest, Emma, with her solemn eyes and determined expression reminding him so much of his own daughter Olivia's at the same age. It was odd the things that memory retained without one's being aware of it. If asked, he would have been forced to admit that he had paid scandalously little attention to either of his children as they grew up. Olivia had spent more time with Jon and Jenny than she had done at home, getting from Jenny the loving mothering she had never received from Tiggy, his frighteningly fragile and vulnerable ex-wife. Given the number of years he had been away, David had assumed Tiggy would have divorced him by now and this had indeed been confirmed when he overheard a comment about her having moved away and established a new life for herself with another man. David was shamed to realise that he felt more relief than grief at this discovery. His ex-wife's

loss was one thing; seeing Emma in the garden
with her brothers Leo and Jason and being reminded of Olivia was quite another.

But was it his nephew's children David had really come to see, familiar to him now by name
and expression as he watched them play and call
out to one another? They tugged at his heartstrings in a way that reinforced how much he had
changed.

The eldest child, Leo, who was physically so
very much a Crighton, seemed fascinated by him.
David had ached to talk to the children and to
hold them, but he had restrained himself. Seeing
them, though, reinforced just how much he had
lost. Man and child had not spoken with one another, but David sensed that both he and Leo felt
the tug of the blood bond that existed between
them. 'Grampy Man,' Leo had wailed in protest
as David made a hasty exit from the garden when
Maddy had come to the garden door.

Was it, then, his own adult daughter and almost
adult son who had brought him back home like a
lodestar? Or had it been his need to see his father?
He was an old man now, who spent most of his
day in a chair apart from his twice daily walk
around the garden with Maddy or Jenny, Jon's
wife, or sometimes with Max.

Max!

Max had surprised David. What had happened to the selfish, hedonistic young man who had looked up to him and on whose adulation David had often preened himself, whose envy of him had fed David's own always vulnerable sense of self-esteem?

Only two days ago he had watched as Max walked in the garden with his younger brother Joss, the two heads close together as they talked earnestly. At one point they had stopped walking and Max had put his arm around the younger man's shoulders in a gesture of comfort and very real affection. There had been no mistaking the closeness between them and no mistaking, either, the love and pride in Max's eyes as he played with his own children.

Seeing Max with his wife and children and witnessing the total transformation of his character had left David with a sharp sense of pain and regret.

The day he walked out of the nursing home where he had been recuperating from his heart attack and out of his old life, he had done so because he could no longer tolerate the unbearable weight not just of his own guilt but of his father's expectations.

The onus of being the favourite son, the first-born twin, the good-looking husband and charming brother-in-law, the isolation of being the one all the others looked up to, had become so burdensome to him, so resented by him, that he had felt swamped by it.

He had needed to break free; to step away from the image others had created for him and be himself. At least that was what he had told himself at the time; that and the fact that he had every right to put himself first, that his brush with death had released him from any and every obligation he owed to anyone else; that his heart attack was a warning to him to live his own life.

A faint smile touched his mouth, creasing the lean planes of his face.

He weighed a good deal less now than he had done when he had left home and his body possessed the taut, muscle-honed strength of a man used to hard physical work. His skin was tanned by the Jamaican sun and the sea air, and his streaked blond hair was only just beginning to show some grey. But it wasn't just his body that looked different; the long hours spent in often painful reflection and the even longer hours in discussion and debate with his friend the priest had also left their visible mark on him. His eyes now looked out on the world with reflection, compassion and wisdom, and he was able to smile warmly, generously and even sometimes tenderly at the frailties of his fellow man.

A stranger looking properly at him now would have found him something of an enigma. His physical appearance was that of a tough manual worker, but married to it was a depth of awareness and intelligence in his eyes that suggested a man of letters and deep reflection. But David no longer courted the approval of other people; he no longer needed either their admiration or their company. Solitude, physical, mental and emotional, had become his chosen friend rather than his feared foe.

It had taken some months of working beside Father Ignatius before David had been able to start confiding in him.

'I have no family, no friends,' David had told him. 'If I were to go back home, they would disown me and rightly so. I have committed an unforgivable crime.'

'No crime is unforgivable in God's eyes,' the priest had replied firmly. 'Not if one truly repents it.'

'What *is* true repentance?' David had asked him, adding sardonically, 'I've never been the sackcloth-and-ashes type. Too much of a sybarite, I suppose, and too selfish.'

'You say that and yet you are prepared to acknowledge that you have sinned. It takes a brave man to submit himself to the judgement of his peers and an even braver one to submit to his own judgement and God's. If to admit the existence of one's sins is the first step on the road to self-forgiveness, then to make true atonement for them is the second.'

'True atonement! And how am I supposed to do that?' David had asked savagely. 'There is no way I could ever repay the money I stole or undo the damage I have done.'

'There is always a way,' Father Ignatius had insisted, 'but sometimes we can make it hard for ourselves to find it.'

Always a way! David shook his head as he remembered those words now. If he had imagined that his leaving, his absence, had created an emptiness in the lives of those he had left behind, he was discovering how vain that assumption had been. The jagged edges of the destruction he had caused had been repaired, and in the days he had spent silently witnessing the lives of his family, he had also discovered just *who* was responsible for the new closeness and harmony that now permeated their lives.

Jon, the brother he had always secretly pitied and sometimes openly mocked.

Jonathon. Only the previous evening his twin had walked so close to David's place of concealment in the dusk-shrouded garden of Queensmead that by moving a few yards David could have been at his side.

His brother had changed, grown taller, or was it simply that his bearing had become more upright? As he watched him, David had been aware of how much more confident Jonathon seemed, of how much more content. Was it because *he* was no longer a part of Jon's life?

David hadn't always been kind to Jon or valued him as he ought to have done. It shamed him now to remember how often he had allowed their father to insist that Jonathon step back into the shadows to allow him to become more prominent, how easily and vainly he had allowed himself to be put up on a pedestal and fêted as the favourite son—to his twin's detriment. How conceitedly and selfishly he had laid claim to all the virtues of their shared heritage, pinning on Jonathon the label of the one to inherit all the weaknesses. The truth was that, of the two of them, it was Jonathon who was the stronger, the purer of heart and deed.

He was beginning to feel hungry. He had very little money and no wish to be recognised by anyone. Last night he had raided Maddy's vegetable garden. Tonight...

A car was coming down the drive. Not Maddy's this time. This one had a different engine sound. Swiftly, he withdrew into the protection of the shrubbery surrounding the lawn, watching as the car came to an abrupt halt and a young woman got out, her cap of hair shining in the sunlight.

Olivia...

David's heart skipped a beat as he watched his daughter head for the house. She looked preoccupied and much more on edge than either Maddy or Jenny appeared to be. A sharp surge of paternal anxiety plucked fiercely at his heartstrings.

Olivia was worrying about something. Why? What?

OLIVIA FROWNED as she hurried into Queensmead's kitchen. She had come hoping to see Maddy who had obviously gone out.

'She said she'd be back, that she wouldn't be very long,' Edna Longridge, the retired nurse who came to Queensmead a couple of times a week to keep an eye on Ben, explained to Olivia.

'I can't wait,' Olivia told her. 'I've got a meeting in half an hour.'

'Oh dear, can I give her a message for you?' Edna asked.

'No, it doesn't matter.'

Her decision to pay Maddy a call had been an impromptu one, an impulse of the moment, a need to talk over her present disenchantment with her life and her marriage with someone she knew would understand.

Maddy and Max might be happy together now, but their marriage had not always been a happy one. No one knew better than Maddy what it was like to be married to a man who didn't love you...a man who was unfaithful to you....

Olivia tensed.

But Caspar did love her and so far as she was aware he had certainly never been unfaithful to her.

Not yet! That small, sharp inner voice that had become increasingly vociferous recently berated her smartly.

Not yet...not ever. Not Caspar...

No? Then why was he so irritable with her? He might claim that it was because he felt shut out of her life, because he felt that her work had become more important to her than either he or the children were. He must know that that simply wasn't true. He must know how haunted she was by her fear that if she didn't do everything she could to prove that she was not like her father—unreliable, selfish, incompetent, dishonest—she would be letting not just herself down but their children, as well. She would be condemning them to be tainted with their grandfather's sins. It was all very well for Jon to claim that *she* bore no responsibility for her father's crimes; that no one would ever think that just because her father had been dishonest she was going to be the same. Somewhere, deep down inside herself, Olivia could not bring herself to believe him. She was scared beyond measure that Jon was lying to her, that he really didn't trust her, and that was why she drove herself so hard, why she felt compelled to prove herself over and over.

Only the previous week she had come back from an appointment out of the office to find Jon standing beside her desk. Her stomach had clenched with sick fear as she had a flashback to the day she discovered what her father had done. Was Jon simply in her office because he needed a file, as he had said, or had he been checking up on her?

She had tried to discuss her fears with Caspar, but her pride, that same stubborn pride that had always been her major sin had got in the way.

What if Caspar shared Jon's suspicion of her? He certainly didn't trust her to be a good mother. Look at the way he criticised her for going back to work full time after the birth of their second child, Alex.

'I have to work,' she had told him, unable to find the words to explain the fear that had so inexplicably taken over her life. It had grown from a tiny seed of doubt, which had somehow come into being after Alex's birth, into the terrifying dark force it now was.

Only the other week, Max had remarked on the new car they had recently bought, and immediately Olivia had become agitated and anxious. Did Max think she had stolen money from their clients to pay for the car?

'You shouldn't have bought such an expensive car,' she had told Caspar critically. 'There was nothing wrong with the old one.'

'No. Except for the fact that it really wasn't big enough for all of us,' Caspar had pointed out quietly, adding, 'What is it you're really trying to say, Livvy? I know that you're the major bread-winner of the family at the moment and that the bulk of the money for the car came from you, but if you're trying to suggest that I put pressure on you to buy a new car as some kind of macho ego trip, then—'

'No, of course I'm not,' Olivia had hastily de-nied, but as so often seemed to be happening these days, within seconds they were both stiff with hostility as they each took up a defensive stance. It was impossible for her to explain just what it was that was causing her so much anxiety when all Caspar seemed to be concerned about were his own feelings and needs.

They had gone to bed that night in a mutually antagonistic silence, lying with their backs to one another, and, as had become an increasingly fre-quent event in recent months, neither of them had reached out to the other to make things up before they had fallen asleep. But why should *she* be the one to give in all the time, to make amends? Surely if Caspar *really* loved her, he would see…understand…know…if he really cared…*if* he really cared….

Olivia couldn't remember the last time Caspar had looked at her as though he loved her, touched her as though he loved her. They hadn't even had *sex* in weeks, never mind made love. Not that she wanted to have sex; she was so exhausted by the time she went to bed that it was the last thing on her mind. It seemed to be the last thing on Caspar's, as well—at least with her!

The previous weekend, just as she was on her way out of the house, she realised that she had forgotten her jacket. Hurrying back upstairs for it, she had rushed into the bedroom to find Caspar on the telephone, his voice soft with a laughter he had stilled the moment he saw her. He had quickly ended the call and hadn't offered her any explanation of whom he had been talking to. She, of course, had been too proud to ask him.

Last night's row was the worst they had had so far. She had come home from work after a particularly gruelling client meeting to be met with a furious accusation from Caspar of being a neglectful mother because she had forgotten to pick Amelia up from her after-school dancing class.

'But I rang the school and explained that I was going to be late and I left a message with Maddy asking if *she* could collect her for me,' Olivia had defended herself.

'You left a *message*?' Caspar had cut across her explanations sharply. 'My God, Livvy, what's happening to you? Being a mother isn't something you can simply delegate to someone else. Do you realise that Amelia had to ask the teacher to ring me because no one turned up to collect her? You do understand that *anything* could have happened to her if she hadn't had the sense to speak to her teacher…if she had for instance tried to walk home on her own.'

'I did my best,' Olivia had argued defensively. Through the sick storm of guilt and fear for her daughter that was flooding her, she recognised the truth of what Caspar was saying.

'Did you? Well, you certainly may have done your best for yourself, but you didn't do your best for Amelia,' Caspar told her savagely.

His accusation that she had neglected her daughter's needs in favour of her own had hurt her badly—just as she knew that Caspar must have intended it to. After all, he knew better than anyone else how much the parental disinterest and neglect *she* had suffered as a child had hurt her and how determined she had always been that her children would grow up knowing they were loved.

'You don't *have* to work full time,' Caspar had pointed out to her when she returned to the family practice after Alex's birth. 'We could manage on less.'

'But not here in this house living the way that

we do,' Olivia had replied sharply, unable to stop herself from defending her own decision. She was equally unable to explain to Caspar the dark pit of anxiety she knew was waiting to claim her if she broke faith with the pact she had made with herself to prove that she was not her father's daughter.

No one else knew how she felt, of course. She was a woman, an adult, not a child, and whilst the family might discuss anxiously the effect of her father's behaviour on her younger brother Jack and enfold itself protectively around him, no one seemed to feel that *she* might need...

What?

What it was exactly that she *did* need, Olivia wasn't sure. Not any more. Once she would have said that the thing she wanted and needed most was Caspar's love, but that had been a long time ago, and now...

She was glad in a way that Maddy had been out. What good would discussing her problems with her do anyway? She had to face them alone just as she had always done.

The icy cold explosion of fear that rocked through her body stopped her in mid-step as she hurried back to her car.

From the protection of the shrubbery, David

watched. Her down-bent head, her frown, the quick, impatient way she moved—all were indicative of a young woman who was not happy either with herself or with her life.

As she passed right by him and got into her car, David had an overwhelming urge to reach out to her, to go and hold her in his arms, to tell her how much he loved her. She was a woman and yet, as he watched her walk unseeingly past him, the expression in her eyes was that of a lost child.

'My going back now can serve no purpose other than to salve my own conscience,' he had told Father Ignatius in frustration when the older man had urged…insisted…that it was time for him to leave the protection of their enclosed world.

'In *your* view,' the priest had agreed. 'But we must never forget that there is another higher authority and His overview overrides the narrowness of ours, just as His will supersedes ours.'

'I am not a religious man,' David had protested.

The priest had chuckled as though enjoying a private joke. He said, 'You don't have to be.'

Not a religious man now, but he had seen enough, learned enough, in the time he had worked alongside Father Ignatius to understand

and accept the complexity of the needs and emotions that gave mankind its humanity.

His daughter wasn't happy and David could feel the sharp, aching tug of her distress.

He had felt a similar emotion in Jamaica over his son Jack, who had been caught up in that same vicious attack as Max. Were his children the reason, after all, that he had been compelled in some way to come back?

Olivia had driven away. As he looked towards the house, David could see his father seated in his chair in the library. Outwardly, the two of them had shared a very close bond. He had always been Ben's favourite, but inwardly, their relationship had been based upon Ben's need to re-create the twinship he believed he had lost when his own twin brother died at birth. Ben was as much a victim of his own upbringing and loss as David and Jon had been of theirs.

David wondered where Olivia had gone—back to the solicitor's practice where he'd once been senior partner? The senior partner so far as the world at large was concerned, but in reality it had been Jon who had had the better qualifications and who had handled all the more complicated cases. Jon on whose overburdened shoulders the full weight of the responsibility for maintaining the family's professional reputation had actually rested, although no one within the family had ever given him credit for it. David himself least of all.

So many debts that he had walked away from and left unpaid…debts that perhaps could never be repaid.

This train of thought reminded him his small store of cash was dwindling away very rapidly. He needed to earn some money and find himself some proper accommodation. Not in the town itself, of course, where he would be recognised. No, not there. An outlying farm, perhaps, or better still, Lord Astlegh's estate. Surely he could pick up several days' work there.

It was a good few miles away, but walking that kind of distance meant nothing to David now. He smiled rather wryly to himself, remembering the other David who would have grimaced in disdain at the thought of walking any farther than a few yards unless it was on the golf course!

CHAPTER FOUR

HONOR WAS WORKING in her garden when she saw David walking along the bridle path in the direction of Fitzburgh Place. He was, she noticed, moving with the carefully controlled step of someone who was used to walking long distances, yet he did not look like a hiker or a rambler. Although Honor couldn't have said exactly why she thought that something seemed different about him, she sensed acutely that there was something that set him apart from others.

He was dressed ordinarily enough in faded jeans and a worn checked shirt, his feet encased in sturdy boots, and he had a small canvas haversack strapped to his back. Tall, lean-featured and tanned, he quite definitely merited a second look Honor's female instincts informed her approvingly.

Straightening her back, she smiled warmly at him and said hello. David paused to smile back.

Honor wasn't the first person to speak to him on his walk, but she was certainly the most alluring.

His ex-wife throughout their marriage had used every artifice she could find to at first enhance, and then frantically maintain, the beauty she felt she needed to hide behind, to offer as a sacrificial gift to others in exchange for their acceptance and approval.

David couldn't remember ever seeing Tiggy in public, or indeed anywhere other than in bed, without any make-up on, but this woman who was watching him with her head tilted slightly to one side, her luminous enchantress's eyes liquid with laughter, wore no cosmetics at all, nor indeed did she need them.

She wasn't young; he could see the tiny fan of lines around her eyes and the wisdom and maturity that etched her smile. All the same, David suspected that in a room full of much younger and more conventionally pretty girls, *she* would still be the woman everyone would look at.

'Are you thirsty?' Honor asked him. 'I was just about to stop for a drink.'

Thirsty! David's expression showed his surprise.

As she watched him, Honor wondered if he knew how much his expression gave him away.

In it she could see not just surprise but also a faint touch of male disapproval, even protectiveness.

'That's very kind of you,' David began, 'but—'

'But a woman of my age should have more sense than to invite a strange man into her garden.' Honor chuckled. 'Ah, but you see,' she teased him, 'I have special magical powers that enable me to tell what a person is really like. I'm a witch, you see,' she added mock solemnly, her eyes dancing with laughter as she put down her spade and walked over to the gate, opening it invitingly. 'So...dare you come in?'

'A witch?'

The smile David gave her, a flash of white teeth in his sun-browned face, made Honor's heart flip over in a double somersault of heady excitement. Careful, she warned herself chidingly as David walked towards her. He really was a quite devastatingly attractive man with an air of unconventionality and uniqueness about him that made her pulse race. She felt secure in her judgement that it was safe to let this stranger enter her home.

'Well, no, not really,' Honor admitted with a smile as she led the way towards the kitchen. 'I'm actually a herbalist.'

'A herbalist...?'

As she heard the interest in David's voice, Honor paused to turn and look at him.

'Is herbalism something that interests you?' Honor asked as she pushed open the kitchen door.

The room inside was low-ceilinged and dark, too much so for practicality, Honor knew, but she was loath to attempt by herself to cut back the large overgrown hedge that shadowed the kitchen windows. Perhaps when she found her builder, he might be able to recommend a tree surgeon to her.

'It isn't a subject I know very much about,' David admitted honestly, 'but I have a friend who believes very strongly that the answer to all our modern diseases can be just as effectively found within nature as it can within a laboratory.'

'I completely agree,' Honor responded warmly, then asked, 'Does your friend live locally? I'm Honor Jessop, by the way. I'm new to the area and as yet I haven't had much time to meet any kindred spirits.'

David hesitated and shook his head. 'No, he lives in Jamaica.' He paused and then said quickly, 'I'm David—Lawrence.'

Yes, she liked his name even though he had obviously been reluctant to give it to her.

'Jamaica... I wondered where you'd got your enviable tan. Do you go out to visit him often?'

'No,' David told her shortly, then realising how rude and almost aggressive he must have sounded, he softened his denial a little by explaining, 'I lived out there for…for some time. That was how he and I met. But now…' He frowned as he turned his head in the direction of Honor's dripping kitchen tap.

'Aggravating, isn't it?' Honor agreed. 'I've tried to unfasten it to replace the washer, but the wretched thing just won't budge.'

'It probably needs greasing first,' David suggested, glad of the opportunity to change the subject. 'I'll have a look at it for you if you like.'

Half an hour later as David unrolled his shirtsleeves, having not only fixed the dripping tap but also emptied the waste trap, he pointed out a little severely to Honor that the lead piping leading into her kitchen ought to be replaced and the outside pipes lagged if she wanted to avoid the risk of their freezing during the winter.

As she watched David moving about her kitchen, Honor had recognised how complete he made the place look and how right it seemed to have him there. She felt comfortable around him, and his presence made her sweetly aware of herself as a woman. A small smile touched her mouth at this last thought. Her daughters would be shocked if they knew what she was thinking right now.

She had always been a faithful wife, but she knew that there was a strong sexual side to her nature that her current circumstances and lifestyle had caused her to contain and repress. Good sex was one of life's pleasures, a life-enhancing experience that everyone had the right to enjoy. Bad sex, on the other hand, was like bad food—poisonous to the human system, destructive, sometimes even fatally so.

Honor was both a realist and a fatalist. Life offered many opportunities, but one had to know how to recognise them and take advantage of them.

Without saying a word, whilst David washed his hands, she went to the fridge and opened it, removing the chilli she had made the previous day.

'This won't take long to reheat,' she told him conversationally. 'I ought to warn you, though, that you may find it a little on the hot side. My daughters complain that—'

'You have children?'

'Mmm…two girls. Well, they're adult women now. And you, do you have any family?'

'I have two children as well.'

'But no wife?' Honor asked quietly.

'No wife,' David agreed. 'And you?'

'I'm partnerless, too,' Honor acknowledged.

'I take it you live here alone?' David questioned a little later when they were seated opposite one another at the kitchen table eating Honor's chilli.

From the hunger with which he had tucked into the meal, eating it with absorbed concentration, Honor guessed that it had been a while since he had last eaten. He was an educated man, well-spoken and well-mannered, and he certainly wasn't someone she felt uneasy about being with on her own—quite the opposite—but she was beginning to recognise that he was no mere walker out for an afternoon's hike. Although he had answered all her questions, she sensed how carefully he was editing his responses and patrolling his privacy.

'You sound disapproving.' Honor smiled.

'Well, the house is very isolated—'

'And very dilapidated. Yes, I know,' Honor agreed. 'I've been trying to find a builder to take on the work that needs doing, but I can't get anyone local because of its reputation.'

'Its reputation? Oh, you mean that old story about it being haunted,' David guessed.

Honor had insisted on pouring him a glass of her home-made wine. The effect of it combined with the warmth of her kitchen and a full stomach was making him relax his guard a little.

He knew about the house's reputation. That meant he must be local, Honor thought, but she didn't say anything, simply commenting instead, 'Not many walkers use this bridle-way. I think you're the first I've seen all week. I expect you were heading for Fitzburgh Place.'

'Yes. I'm looking for some casual labouring work—and somewhere to stay,' David admitted. 'I thought it might be worthwhile asking Lord Astlegh's estate manager if he needs anyone.'

'Mmm... Well, you're in between seasons for casual work now,' Honor warned him. 'Most of the harvesting is done by machinery, and although they do take on beaters for the shooting season, I don't think they're looking for anyone right now.'

As she watched David's face, an idea was beginning to take shape in her mind.

'You did a very professional job on that sink. I'm looking for someone who can take on the task of making this house weatherproof for the winter. The pay wouldn't be very much, but I could certainly offer bed and board.'

David gave her an astonished look. 'You're offering *me* a job? Are you serious?'

'Are *you* serious about needing work?' Honor countered.

'But you don't know the first thing about me,' David protested.

'I know you have clean nails and good manners,' Honor half joked. 'And I know that you can fix a leaking washer and you like my chilli.'

'I don't *believe* this,' David maintained, shaking his head. 'Have you any idea of—'

'If you're going to read me a lecture about the dangers I could be inviting, the risks I could be taking, then please don't,' Honor advised him firmly. 'I'm an adult woman and perfectly capable of making my own judgements and decisions. The offer stands. Whether or not you accept it is up to you. Apple pie?' she asked, standing up to collect their empty chilli bowls.

'Er...please...yes. Look, let me get those,' David insisted. He stood up quickly and reached out for the bowls at the same time as Honor did.

As they touched, Honor was conscious of the lean strength of his hands and their warmth. He had long fingers and his movements were economical and deft. When he touched a woman, his touch would be firm and carefully judged. But would it also be sensual? Would the cool hesitancy, the watchfulness she could sense in him, be burned away by the heat of passion? Or was he the kind of man who remained impervious to real desire and was perhaps even a little afraid of it? If so, then he was not a man who would hold her interest for very long.

But perhaps she would not *want* to hold him for very long…perhaps—

'What exactly would it involve, this work you're offering me?' David broke into her thoughts.

'Er…well, as I said, I'd like to get the house as weatherproof as possible before winter sets in. You said yourself just now that those pipes need lagging. There's a leak in the roof and some of the windows are desperately in need of repainting—one or two of them have panes of glass missing. There's an awful lot of heavy work to be done in the garden and there's a greenhouse up at Fitzburgh Place that my cousin says I can have. I just have to find someone to put it up for me.'

'Cousin?' he questioned sharply.

'Yes,' Honor responded openly. 'Lord Astlegh is my cousin. That's how I've come to be here. He's letting me live here for a peppercorn rent.'

'You mean you're actually paying someone to live in this wreck?' David grimaced.

Honor gave him an arch look. 'Now you sound *exactly* like my daughters,' she told him drily.

David thought quickly. He needed somewhere to live and he had to eat. Honor wasn't local, so there was no danger of her recognising him. Nor from what she had told him did she socialise, apparently preferring her own company. He was surprised that she was allowed to keep so much to herself, given the extraordinary sensuality she possessed. Or perhaps that was why. Very few women, no matter how happily or securely married, would want to risk their husbands for too long in the company of a woman like Honor. David knew how dangerously aware of her, how dangerously aroused by her, *he* already was, which was a very good reason for turning down her suggestion.

But if he wanted to stay in the area, could he afford to turn it down? *If* he wanted to... He had a momentary mental image of Olivia as she had looked earlier. Bowed down...unhappy...in need...

'I'll take the job,' he told Honor quickly.

'Good,' she responded and then asked him

wryly, 'Aren't you going to ask me how much I intend to pay you?'

'Bed and board, I thought you said,' David reminded her.

Bed and board! He was prepared to work for *that*. Why? Honor wondered curiously. But she sensed that any attempt on her part to question him would only result in his withdrawal from her and even perhaps his rejection of the offer she had made.

'I thought to begin with, for a trial period of, say, a month, I would pay you fifty pounds a week,' Honor suggested, naming a sum that she knew to be risible, but she was interested to find out what David's response would be.

When he accepted calmly and without question, Honor knew then that she had every reason to feel curious about him, curious and suspicious, perhaps? Her daughters most certainly would have been. But she was not her daughters, Honor reminded herself firmly. She preferred to trust her own inner judgement rather than to doubt it.

Fifty pounds a week. Riches indeed when compared with the tiny income he and Father Ignatius had eked out in Jamaica. But this was not Jamaica, David warned himself.

What was he hoping to achieve? Why had he

really come back? To ease his own conscience? To see his family? His unanticipated witnessing of Olivia's unhappiness earlier in the day had given him far more to think about than his own feelings. Why did he sense so strongly that Olivia needed him? She had Jon to turn to after all. Jon, whose company she had always preferred to his, just as Max, Jon's son, had turned more to his uncle. But Max and Jon were now very obviously close.

Honor was refilling their glasses with her home-made wine. Lifting hers towards him in a toast, she proclaimed, 'To a very successful and enjoyable relationship between us.'

The slow smile she gave him, even more than the ambiguous way she had phrased her words, made David look sharply at her. Honor was a stunningly attractive woman but not, he guessed, a sexually predatory one. She wouldn't need to be. In Jamaica he had met women who had spoken quite openly of their desire to have him satisfy their sexual hunger and their willingness to pay him for doing so.

There was a glint of curiosity in Honor's eyes when she looked at him, but David knew instinctively that it was a curiosity she would curtail and control unless he made a move—and even then...

There was something about her that fascinated
him. She was so open, so seemingly careless of
her physical and emotional safety and yet at the
same time he had the distinct impression that she
was very well protected, that she had a wisdom
and a strength that came from experiencing life's
pains as well as its joys.

As he drank his wine, David wondered what
Father Ignatius would make of his present situation. Would he approve of what he was doing?
David smiled inwardly to himself, imagining the
older man's response to such a question.

'Do *you* approve?' was what he would be more
than likely to say. 'Your own approval of your
actions and your thoughts should be more important to you than mine. It is far harder to deceive
ourselves than it is to deceive others and thus we
are our own sternest critics.'

'Yes, o master,' David would sometimes tease
him at the end of one of his homilies.

'There is no master here,' the priest would correct him gently. 'Only two pupils.'

David had no qualms about his ability to do the
work Honor wanted doing. After he left England,
he had spent some time in Spain, and whilst he
was there had earned his living working illegally
building villas for foreign buyers.

'Tell me a bit about yourself,' Honor invited.

It was potent wine, especially for a man who had virtually not touched a drink since the night Father Ignatius had picked him up out of one of Kingston's gutters. His drinking binges had been a pathetic and solitary attempt to destroy what was left of his life. It hadn't worked—thankfully—but his own disgust at his behaviour, coupled with the abstemious way the priest lived, had meant that alcohol was something David's system was no longer used to. Careful, he warned himself as he felt it warming his blood and loosening his tongue.

'There isn't very much to tell,' David responded cautiously.

Honor's eyebrows lifted, but she didn't argue with him, commenting instead, 'You mentioned that you had children.'

'A son and a daughter,' David agreed heavily. 'But I'm not in contact with them any more.'

Cursing himself under his breath, David wondered what on earth had made him tell her that, but to his relief, instead of pouncing on his admission, Honor merely remarked calmly, 'It does happen. People divorce, and despite everyone's good intentions, sometimes it just isn't possible to maintain contact. My husband had very little to do with our daughters. He was a photographer. My family never really approved of him and I've always suspected that at least a part of the reason he walked out on us was for the perverse pleasure it gave him to prove them right. He was like that.'

'It must have been hard for you, bringing up your daughters on your own,' David told her politely.

Honor gave him a wry look. 'Not really. What was hard was trying to bring them up to live with him. We were young,' she added by way of explanation. 'He took to the excesses of the time like a duck to water. Drink, drugs, sex, money—he wanted them all and had them all, as well. He's dead now.' She saw David's look of surprise. 'And by one of those quirks of fate, I inherited his estate. I can't pretend that the money hasn't been very welcome. My family washed their hands of me when I married, and even though I later left him, so far as they were concerned I had made my bed and I should, therefore, continue to lie in it with or without my husband.

'Are you divorced?' Honor asked him in her straightforward way.

'Yes. At least I understand a divorce went through,' David answered tersely. 'I haven't had any contact with my wife or my family for some

time, but the marriage was effectively over before…before I left. What made you become interested in herbalism?' he asked, to change the
subject.

'What makes anyone become interested in anything?' Honor countered. 'I liked the idea of using
nature's own healing powers. Perhaps I'm more a
child of my time than I like to admit.' She gave
a small shrug.

'If you ever manage to find a plant-based
method for weight loss, you'll become a million-
airess overnight,' David told her drily.

'Nature *has* already provided one,' Honor re-
joindered tartly, and then explained as he looked
queryingly at her, 'It's called famine.'

David had the grace to look a little shamefaced.

'I'm sorry. I didn't mean to belittle your work.'

'Or me?' Honor asked him with a direct look.

There was a brief pause before David responded. 'I have no right to belittle anyone or to
sit in judgement on them. By rights I should be…'
He stopped.

'You should be where?' Honor encouraged
him.

'Somewhere else,' David told her abruptly.
What would she have said if he had finished his
original sentence and told her that by rights he

should be in prison, serving a fully deserved sentence for the crime he had committed.

'Somewhere else. You mean with your family?' Honor guessed, sensing that something was disturbing him and that the potency of her home-made wine had pushed down barriers he would much rather have kept erected against her questions.

'No, I do *not* mean with my family,' David told her angrily. 'My family...my family would probably turn away if they saw me in the street, and who could blame them? No doubt they'd like to pretend that I no longer existed...that I never existed—and with good reason. They have every right to feel shame at being related to me. Me—their father...brother...son...uncle—a thief and a coward.'

'A thief?'

Honor breathed a small, inward sigh of relief. Thank goodness for *that*. Just for a moment she had wondered what on earth it was he might have done. Theft, whilst a deplorable crime to any right-thinking, conventional, law-abiding person, hardly merited too much concern to someone whose ancestors had for many generations indulged in that same crime on a grand scale.

'Really, Honor, you do yourself no favours

with such radical thinking,' her aunt once chided her icily when Honor had questioned this relative's sanitised, not to say sanctified, version of their family history. 'Your great-grandfather was one of the most respected men of his generation and your great-uncle was Lord Lieutenant of the county.'

'Yes, I'm sure that they were as upright and honest as anyone could possibly be, but what about our real ancestors, the ones who raped and murdered and stole?'

'That was centuries ago when everyone did that kind of thing,' her aunt had insisted, adding critically, 'You really are the oddest girl. I don't know why you must bring up such things. It really isn't done.'

Done or not, there was no escaping the facts and she doubted that whatever crime David might have committed came anywhere near equalling the atrocities of her ancestors.

The wine was finished and Honor could tell that David was regretting what he had revealed to her. Another few minutes and he would be saying that he had changed his mind and that he had to leave. She didn't want that. Oh, no, she didn't want that at all.

Standing up, she gave him a small smile and

told him calmly, 'If you'll come up with me, I'll show you your room and then tomorrow we can discuss which repairs should have priority.'

A little muzzily, David got to his feet. He had been on the point of telling Honor that he ought to go. Her questions about his family had brought home to him the danger and stupidity of what he was doing. He was the last person they would want back in their lives. In their place, he knew that was how he would feel.

'It's this way,' Honor was saying, and somehow or other David found he was following her into the hallway and up the stairs.

The bedroom she showed him was down a small half-landing at the back of the house.

'It isn't as large as the rooms at the front, but I'm sleeping in one of them and the girls have bagged the others for when they visit,' she said apologetically as she snapped on the light and stepped to one side so that he could walk past her.

The room wasn't large, it was true, but compared with the places David had been sleeping in since he came home, what did size matter? It had a bed—luxury indeed so far as David was concerned. It had furniture, too, a wardrobe and two chests, not that he would need those. He travelled light; all his possessions were in the haversack on his back and they wouldn't even fill one of the two chests.

There were curtains at the window and a carpet square on the floor. That they were rather threadbare scarcely mattered to him. The room still had its own fireplace and the air smelled faintly damp and cold.

'The house does have central heating—of a sort,' Honor told him as though she had guessed what he was thinking. 'But as yet I haven't found a way of making it work.'

'Mmm...what priority on the list is that to have?' David asked her drily.

'Well, it will come somewhere before trimming the hedge but after fixing the leak in the roof,' Honor answered with that little glinting smile of hers that did such interesting things to his hormone levels.

As a young man, David had taken his sexuality and his body's response to a pretty woman for granted. He had met and wanted Tania—Tiggy— in the heady days of the sixties when sex was a free-for-all of snatched goodies grabbed and consumed greedily without thought.

They had married and had two children. Then had come the fallow years of their marriage, years when sex had become a ritual, a duty, a chore, and then later still, a resented payment at the shrine of Tiggy's insecurities and his own guilt.

In Spain and Jamaica there had been women who had approached him, middle-aged, eager, avaricious, their demands falling little short of aggression, wanting not just his body but his spirit, as well. He had resisted them all. The celibacy of recent years had served as a welcome oasis of peace. He had assumed he had no regret that he had become both physically and emotionally impotent so far as sex was concerned. Yet here he was becoming aware of Honor, reacting to her with bemusingly unexpected potency.

'The bathroom's the third on the left,' Honor informed him. 'You'll find plenty of towels in the airing cupboard. Luckily, the immersion heater is one of the few things that does work, so there is always plenty of hot water. Oh, and I always leave the landing lights on, but with your bedroom door closed they shouldn't disturb you,' she told him casually as she turned back to the door.

'You *always* leave them on?' David questioned. 'What for, the ghost?'

He could see the tension in her departing back as she suddenly went very still.

'Perhaps,' she agreed, but he could hear the faint tremor in her voice and guessed, with a small shock of surprise and compassion, that she must be afraid of the dark.

It seemed such an unexpected and almost childish fear in so strong a woman that for a moment he was almost tempted to laugh, but just in time he managed not to do so.

'Well, they won't disturb me,' he assured her gravely instead.

His reward was the look of relief in her eyes as she turned round to face him. She said in a slightly wobbly voice, 'We still have overhead power cables here and every time there's a storm the power tends to go off. I keep a supply of candles—just in case.'

'Candles can be a fire hazard,' David cautioned her gently. 'It might be worth your while to think about investing in a generator.'

'Yes, I had wondered about that,' Honor agreed.

Whatever it was that made her afraid of the dark, it was obviously a very big fear, David recognised. He turned round again and walked across his bedroom. It took him a while to fully analyse the feeling it gave him knowing that she had allowed him to see her vulnerability. It was pride, male pride and machismo...coupled with a desire to protect, to *be* her protector.

'No, no,' David warned himself as he put down his haversack and started to unpack. 'Oh, no, you don't. *That* isn't what you are here for, David Crighton. That isn't what you're here for at all.'

CHAPTER FIVE

DAVID WAS AWAKE at first light, momentarily disorientated by the unfamiliarity of his room and the comfort of the old-fashioned, soft-mattressed double bed.

He had neglected to close the curtains the previous night, and through his window he could see the trees forming the woodland that belonged to Fitzburgh Place cloaked softly in dawn mist, the sun only just on the rise.

In Jamaica, this had always been his favourite part of the day, when the air was still and relatively cool up in the mountains where Father Ignatius had his refuge.

There was nothing like an English autumn. Others might rave over the wonderful colours of a New England fall, but here in the Cheshire countryside one could feel totally in tune with the changing season and the fading year. There was a haunting melancholia heightened by the lingering warmth of the sun, reminiscent of summer days. At the same time, the air was sharpened by the cool tang of early-morning mists and the enveloping darkness of evenings that brought the coming winter sharply to mind.

Stretching his body, he got up and padded naked across the floor as quietly and softly as a jungle cat. Living in the tropics had taught him how to be economical with his body's store of energy. Living alongside Father Ignatius had shown him how to value the wisdom of the older man's experience.

At first he had laughed a little unkindly at the priest's insistence on his morning shower beneath the cold waterfall close to the refuge, followed by a brisk exercise routine.

'The body is like a piece of equipment. With a little care it can serve us well, but like any other piece of machinery, if we neglect or abuse it, our laziness and lack of respect will show up in our later years.'

'Providing one *makes* it to one's later years,' David had reminded him a little grimly. The priest had inclined his head in acceptance of David's caveat.

'To take pride in one's faculties—physical, mental, emotional and spiritual—is the mark of a truly wise man,' the priest had responded. 'And perhaps it is vain of me, but I should not wish to be judged by myself or others as lacking the wisdom to respect the gifts that nature has given to me. Besides,' he had added with his lightning-quick, almost boyish smile, 'I like feeling clean and energised both in body and spirit.'

'A typical Jesuit teaching,' David had pronounced a little contemptuously.

'Cleanliness being next to Godliness,' the priest had quoted drily to him. 'I cannot speak for that, but I can say that cleanliness is quite definitely the first step towards controlling and eradicating disease, and since that is our task here...'

David had shrugged his shoulders, but he knew that the older man had a point. He was, as David had already observed, meticulous about boiling all the water they used in the hospice and keeping everything as spotless and sanitised as possible.

And, after a while, David discovered that he not only no longer felt any defensive need to taunt Father Ignatius for his habit of showering and changing from one shabby set of clothes into another clean set at the end of their day's work, but he himself was actually beginning to enjoy following the same morning and evening ritual.

One pair of threadbare shorts and an unmatched shirt might look the same as another, but there was no doubt that the clean ones felt a whole lot better.

In Spain he had earned enough to buy himself the kind of basic clothes he needed and to pay a woman in the village to wash them for him. But he had had to leave Spain in a hurry, only one step ahead of a deportation order for working there illegally. The offer of work crewing on a yacht bound for Jamaica had been too opportune for him to refuse. At the end of the trip, though, the skipper had announced that the only wage David was going to receive was his free passage.

In Jamaica the only paying work that was available to him involved working as a 'mule' for one of the drug-smuggling gangs, bringing drugs into the UK. Whatever sort of man he might be, David had too much sense to get involved in drug running and so he had found himself in a situation where he had to live day-to-day, from hand to mouth, and count himself lucky if he earned enough to feed himself.

Pulling his jeans on, he headed for the bathroom. He doubted that Honor would be up yet, which meant that…

Honor. What a fascinating woman she was. It amazed him that she was actually living alone. Her choice, no doubt about that. The effect that thinking about her had on his body both amused and amazed him. He couldn't remember the last time he had been so immediately and so firmly aroused. Tiggy would definitely have trouble believing this and be astonished if she could see him now.

Even before Jack's conception there had been times when he had had to fake orgasm, when he had had to pretend that the excitement and arousal he was feeling were real, that his need to interrupt their 'lovemaking' to go to the bathroom was because of a weak bladder, when in reality...

David gave a small grimace of distaste as he stepped out of the shower. Tiggy's sexual appetite had mirrored her disordered appetite for food. Wild binges of excess had been followed by self-revulsion and self-punishment. Whilst at the time he might not have recognised her symptoms for what they were, and most certainly had not possessed either the expertise or the compassion to help her, he had been as eager as her to maintain the outward façade of their 'perfect' marriage. He, too, had made a show of their highly charged and very sexual relationship, entered willingly into those little playlets of fake sexual intimacy and loving adoration that they enacted together in public. And like so much else in his life, eventually the burden of maintaining such a fiction had destroyed whatever genuineness might have existed, leaving in its place a ghastly, destructive, numbing fear that somehow he might slip up and that others would see him as he really was.

Just about the time he had started using his client's bank account as though the money was his own, he had started having terrifying dreams that he was walking through Haslewich's main town square, but no one he saw seemed to recognise him. When he paused and looked at his reflection in a shop window, he realised why. He looked nothing like he should have done.

He had turned round to face the street, calling out to those watching him, his brother Jon, his wife, his father, his cronies at the golf club, but all of them had refused to listen, shrugging him off as though he were a stranger importuning them.

Easy enough to understand the message of his dream now, when ironically he could walk through the square and be recognised physically as himself, the same David Crighton who had walked away from his family and his home, but inwardly...inwardly the man he was now was as much a stranger to them as though they had never met. A stranger sometimes to himself, as well, given the extent of his own bemusement over his physical reaction to Honor.

Once dressed, he went downstairs into the kitchen where he filled the kettle with water. Whilst he waited for it to boil, he studied his surroundings. One of the window sashes had rotted, leaving the window unable to close properly. There was a gap beneath the ill-fitting outer kitchen door. As he already knew, the stairs creaked badly and beneath the carpet on the landing a couple of floor planks were out of alignment.

Honor had obviously attempted to brighten up the kitchen, which was painted in a strikingly warm shade of ochre, while the dresser against one wall was adorned with vibrant, Mediterranean-coloured pieces of china.

In the alcove over the large, old-fashioned range, a variety of what he imagined must be herbs were tied to a wooden drying rack. But despite these touches, the room felt cold and slightly damp, and when David went over to the range and touched it, he realised that it had gone out. After a moment's hesitation, he got down on his knees in front of it. He then opened the doors and proceeded to clean it out.

He had just managed to light it when the

kitchen door opened and Honor came in with a large wicker basket over one arm.

'You're up early!' she exclaimed as she smiled at him.

'I could say the same to you,' David returned as he closed the doors of the range and went to the sink to wash his hands.

'Oh well, a lot of the plants and herbs I use are best gathered when they are at their freshest. They are more effective then.'

'That sounds suspiciously like medieval mythology to me,' David teased.

Sharing his laughter, Honor added, 'But it wasn't just plants and herbs I went out for.' She opened the draw-string top of her basket and removed a handful of mushrooms. Her eyes lit with pleasure as she showed them to him. 'Look, breakfast!'

'Are you sure they're edible?' David asked.

'Trust me, I'm a herbalist,' Honor responded tongue in cheek.

As he walked over to the range to open the door and added more logs to the glowing flames, her mischievous expression changed to one of amazement as she saw.

'Oh, good, you've managed to light the range. It's been threatening to go out on me for the past week and I've only just managed to keep it going with a lot of elbow grease and prayer.'

'No spells? You disappoint me.' David shook his head.

'It's a dreadfully temperamental old thing,' Honor continued, ignoring his teasing comment. 'I intend to replace it. Fortunately, I don't have to rely on it to cook with. I've got a small portable stove and a microwave.'

'You mean I've gone through all this for nothing?' David complained.

Honor laughed. 'Well, no, not for nothing. You see,' she told him, wide-eyed, 'the range is the only thing big enough to take my cauldron and I can carry on now that you've lit it!'

'OK, so you're a ''Rent-a-Witch'',' David said gravely, his eyes warm with laughter as he looked at her. She was wearing jeans and wellington boots, and where the top of her boots met her jeans, the fabric was dark with the heavy dew from off the fields. The cream cotton sweater she was wearing looked as though it had originally belonged to someone else—a male someone else—her husband? A lover? He frowned as he felt the unmistakable sharpness of a very male and ludicrously inappropriate shaft of jealous possessiveness.

Oversize though her sweater was, it still didn't disguise the full, soft thrust of her breasts as they jiggled enticingly with her movements, hinting at a deliciously promising unfettered naturalness.

Tiggy, despite her periodic desperate craving for sex, had been almost aggressively uptight about her body. She claimed that the underwear she wore would have been considered irresistibly provocative and arousing by any other man, but to David it had given her body all the appeal of a plastic doll, stiff and unyielding, cold and sanitized.

Honor, he suspected, would not smell of expensive perfume or set out to be deliberately alluring by wearing bras designed to give her extra cleavage or stockings worn self-consciously and anxiously in a 'refuse to be turned on by me if you dare' kind of pose.

No, Honor would be lusciously and deliciously female rather than artificially feminine. She would be warm and womanly, abandoning herself to her sexuality with a natural hedonism that couldn't fail to arouse her mate.

Her mate! But he wasn't that...wasn't and never could be. He—

'I don't know about you, but I like to start my

day with a proper breakfast,' Honor was saying to him warmly.

A proper breakfast. In Jamaica breakfast, like every other meal, had consisted of fresh fruit from the trees, some fish they had caught and whatever other food they had either bartered for or been given by their patients and their families.

'A proper breakfast,' David repeated her words back to her.

Where had he gone? Where had his thoughts been just then, Honor wondered, musing curiously over the inwardly concentrated look she had seen in his eyes.

'Well, you know what they say,' Honor told him cheerfully. 'One should eat breakfast like a king, lunch like a lord and dinner like a pauper.'

'You're the boss,' David reminded her with a brief shrug of his shoulders. Tiggy had never eaten breakfast—at least not in his presence—and he had hated the chaos of the family kitchen. Early in the morning he had snatched a cup of coffee and waited until he reached the office to satisfy his hunger on the sandwiches and croissants his secretary would send out for.

He could remember how irritated he had felt when Olivia had looked accusingly at him as he gulped his coffee, shouting from the bottom of the stairs to Tiggy, still in bed, that he was leaving.

In the kitchen, Olivia, dressed in her school uniform and wearing the shirt she would have had to iron herself, would be carefully pouring a bowlful of cereal for Jack.

How those memories hurt him now, but at the time if he had felt any guilt, it had been well buried beneath his own self-centredness and his belief that as his father's favourite son he was greater than the sum of all the other members of his family.

Like Tiggy, although no doubt for different reasons, he had found as many excuses as he could to spend as little time as possible with his children, at best bored and at worst irritated by their claims on his attention.

How easy it had been to slip into the habit of arranging evening 'business meetings', to go straight from work to the country club, arriving home when Olivia and Jack were doing their homework or in bed.

'Come back.'

Honor's soft command brought him out of his introspection. Smiling ruefully at her, he admitted, 'I was just remembering family breakfasts when the children were young.'

'Unhappy memories?' Honor guessed accurately.

'Yes,' David admitted.

Her directness, so very different from his own habit of caution and secrecy, could have been deemed offensive in someone else. In her, it seemed so natural and easy that he found it equally natural to reply openly.

'It isn't always easy being a parent,' Honor offered.

'It isn't easy being a child when you have a father as neglectful and selfish as I was,' David countered quietly. 'My children have little to thank me for and much to blame me for.'

'And do they? Blame you, I mean,' Honor asked him.

David shook his head. 'I don't know, but in their shoes...' He stopped and looked at her. 'This is getting maudlin and can't be of any interest to you. What exactly *does* this proper breakfast of yours consist of, apart from dubiously safe mushrooms?'

Honor laughed. She could recognise a closed door when she saw one, especially when it had been closed in her face with such determined, if gentle, politeness.

'There is nothing dubious about my mushrooms. Just wait until you taste them.'

'Mmm… What I'm worried about is whether I'll remember tasting them or if I'm going to wake up with a bad headache and then discover—'

'That I've used your body for my wicked female satisfaction,' Honor suggested with a grin that made her look like a girl.

A very sexy girl, David acknowledged as he leaned towards her and told her huskily, 'Now that I would resent.' As her smile faded, he added softly, 'Were you to take me to bed, I promise you that I would want to savour and remember every single second. I certainly would not need the encouragement of any aphrodisiac or magic spell to do so.'

Now what the hell had made him say something like that? Some kind of braggartly machismo, some kind of misguided desire to prove to her that he was a man…? What kind of *idiot* was he? With one sentence, virtually between one breath and another, he had completely changed the nature of their relationship, and in *her* shoes…

He held his breath, waiting for her to make a crushingly dismissive retort, or worse still, to tell him coldly that she had changed her mind about having him working and living at her house. Instead, she simply turned away from him, then walked over to the fridge and opened the door.

'The estate keeps me supplied with all my meat,' she told him calmly. 'The bacon's home-grown and home-cured. My cousin Freddy says I'm ruining the flavour of it by putting it in the fridge, but I'm not too happy about the efficiency of the drains here. I feel that I'd rather exchange a small loss of flavour for the advantage of knowing it isn't going to be contaminated by anything. In the summer, after a few days of hot weather, we seem to get an alarming number of flies.'

'The drains probably need rodding out,' David recited mechanically, hardly daring to believe that she had actually been gracious enough to overlook his indecorous comment. *Gracious*. It was an odd word to apply to such a thoroughly modern woman, implying some dowager-like Edwardian female of rank and fearsome hauteur. Honor's graciousness was much, much more than that—a subtle blending of gentleness, compassion, wisdom and strength, its strands as difficult to define and isolate as the notes of a beautifully blended perfume.

'Oh, and whilst we're on such unappealing subject matter, I feel I ought to warn you that I have my suspicions that the house might have mice.'

'Mice! I should imagine it does, out here in the middle of the countryside. A cat would soon get rid of those.'

'Mmm…that's what I thought, but so far, Jasper has proved to be either exceedingly inept or too well-fed to bother with them.'

'Jasper?'

'The cat…not mine…well, not exactly. He just sort of arrived. Since no one knows whom he belongs to, he and I have adopted one another. He'll be coming in soon for his breakfast. He always arrives about eight o'clock.'

'A cat that can tell the time. Well, plainly, he's far too intelligent to waste precious minutes catching mere mice,' David joked. As Honor walked past him and opened a cupboard to remove a heavy-duty grilling pan, he offered, 'If that's for the bacon, I'll cook that.'

'Thanks. I like mine crisp,' Honor informed him, handing over the pan without any protest or insistence that she should be the one to do the cooking.

She really was the most extraordinary woman, he acknowledged half an hour later as, the breakfast cooked, she disappeared into the hallway. She reappeared several seconds later with a copy of the *Telegraph*, which, she informed him, she always read whilst she ate her breakfast.

Most other women he knew of her generation would have insisted on cooking the breakfast *and* handing the paper over to him to read first. But instead of being chagrined by her behaviour, David actually found it refreshing and invigorating. It was as though she was subtly and indirectly informing him with her casual indifference to his traditional male role that only a very special sort of man, only a very special sort of *maleness* would impress and excite her.

A very special sort of man. Well, he most certainly wasn't *that*. He doubted that many women would find him attractive or desirable once they knew the truth about him and what he had done, and he couldn't blame them—

'Whatever happened in the past is past. We are living in the present. In the here and now. And live in it we must.'

David jumped a little as he realised that Honor had put down her paper and was watching him. How had she known he was thinking about his past?

'Are you sure you aren't a witch or at least a mind-reader?' he asked a little defensively before adding more openly, 'We may live in the present, but our pasts are a part of us. The things we've done make us the people we are.'

'Yes. But to dwell on past mistakes is to refuse to allow ourselves to learn from them, to grow and to move on,' Honor told him firmly.

'What about when our mistakes haven't just affected our own lives but also those of people close to us?' David pressed.

Honor looked thoughtfully at him. He was a man with a troubled conscience, no doubt about that.

'What about when we can't ask those people to forgive us because we know that what we've done can't be forgiven?' he asked her slowly.

'I don't know,' Honor admitted, shaking her head. 'I don't know, but if you—'

She stopped abruptly as the back door suddenly rattled loudly, making them both, but especially David, jump.

'It's just Jasper,' she reassured him, getting up to let the cat in.

'He needs a proper cat flap,' David said as the black cat stalked across the kitchen floor, then sat in front of the range and studied David assessingly before commencing to wash his paws. 'I'll make him one. You said you'd go through the

work you wanted me to do,' David reminded
Honor.

'Yes, of course,' Honor agreed, recognising
that he wanted to change the subject and was
probably regretting having said as much to her as
he had.

She was surprised at the extent of her own curiosity about him. He was a lean, attractive man,
yes, a very attractive and very virile man. His
body brought her own out in a rash of goose
bumps of sensual female appreciation, but...

But she was not in the market for a fling and
she certainly had no intention of being a confi-
dante or providing a comforting shoulder for him
to lean on. Why should she? Other people's trou-
bles and complicated lives were their own concern. She could only work best as a healer by
distancing herself from her patients and remaining
calm and unemotional.

'I'll take you on a tour of the house after breakfast,' Honor promised, wrinkling her nose as she
added, 'You're going to need an extremely large
note pad to list everything that needs doing.'

'I CALLED IN at the travel agency yesterday.
They've got quite a good deal going at the moment on flights to New York. I estimate it will be

cheaper for all of us to fly there first and then take a domestic flight to Philadelphia rather than attempt to fly direct. It'll take longer, of course, but as a treat I thought we'd stay somewhere like the Pierre overnight and after the wedding I thought we'd really go mad and spend a few days touring New England—'

'Caspar, there's no way I can go to America,' Olivia exploded, pushing away untouched the cup of coffee she had just poured herself. Upstairs, she could hear the regular household sounds of the girls getting ready for school. She had already been up for two hours. She had had some reading she needed to catch up on.

Caspar hated her working at home, but as she told him when they argued about it, her current workload meant that she had no option. It was all very well for him to say that when she worked at home it meant she had less time for him and the girls, but if she didn't, she would never get through everything.

She hated it when he pressured her and made her feel guilty. Sometimes it seemed as though she could never measure up to the standards imposed on her by the men in her life. Besides, increasingly lately, she felt that she desperately needed that extra hour to herself in the morning when the day belonged to her alone and the only needs she had to consider were her own.

Once, her only reason for waking up early in the morning had been so that she and Caspar could make love, but that seemed like a lifetime ago now. She couldn't remember the last time she had actually wanted to make love—wanted Caspar—and when Caspar did try to initiate love-making, it was resentment and anger she felt and not desire.

Just like she felt now?

As she experienced the draining mixture of anger, panic and despair swirling blackly through her, Olivia gritted her teeth. 'Caspar, I know you've managed to negotiate extended time out from the university for this trip, but you *know* I can't go with you. We've already discussed it and—'

'No. No, *we* have not discussed it,' Caspar interrupted her angrily. '*I* have tried to discuss it, Livvy, but all *you've* done is put a veto on the whole subject.'

Lifting her hands to her head in protest, Olivia reminded him, 'Caspar, I simply don't have time for another argument. I've got an appointment at eight-thirty and before then I've got to—'

'Oh…I'm sorry if our private lives are interfering with your busy work agenda,' Caspar interjected sarcastically. 'Forgive me if I forget from time to time just how important a person you are. A full partner in the family firm.'

As she listened to the angry sarcasm in his voice, Olivia's mouth compressed.

When Jon had talked over with her the issue of her becoming a full partner in the practice, he had insisted that she was not to feel that she would be under increased pressure to take on more work. So far as he was concerned, he had said sharing the partnership with her was simply a way of recognising the very important role she played in the firm's business.

But Olivia had not been able to see things that way. The euphoria of her love for Caspar and then the birth of their two daughters had, for a while, masked all the underlying pain and anxiety that she had carried with her from her childhood into adulthood. Just recently, though, with the tension between her and Caspar growing into a frighteningly dangerous rift and the pressure she was putting on herself at work, she was beginning to feel very close to paranoid.

Not that she thought about her feelings and her fears so analytically or even in any way acknowledged their cause. So far as Olivia was concerned, what was driving her on was quite simply necessity, although what that necessity might be she wasn't really able to name.

Now as she saw the very real anger in Caspar's eyes, the panicky feeling of alienation and pain that seemed to be growing between her and her husband made her react defensively. She immediately took Caspar's insistence on attending his half-brother's wedding as somehow saying that his blood family, his brothers, the *males* in his family, were more important to him than she was.

'I don't understand why you're so anxious to go to this wedding. After all, it isn't as though you and Bryant are close. You've told me yourself that when he was born you were already in high school and that the only time you ever saw him was when you spent duty vacations with your father and Bryant's mother. For heaven's sake,' she added irritably, 'if we attended every single one of your motley collection of siblings' weddings, christenings and other celebrations, we'd be spending over half our lives travelling.'

'Well, that sounds like a bonus to me,' Caspar informed her curtly. 'At least we'd see something of one another that way. Right now, with your spending virtually ninety per cent of your waking hours working—'

'Don't be ridiculous,' Olivia interrupted. 'You're exaggerating.'

'Am I?' Caspar asked coldly. 'I don't think so. Ask the girls what they think—if you dare.'

'That isn't fair,' Olivia protested fiercely. 'I spend as much time with them as I can.'

'As much time as you *can*, and how much time is that exactly, Livvy?'

Olivia bit her lip. It was true that just lately she had not been able to spend as much time with their daughters as she longed to, but it was in part for their sakes that she was pushing herself, that she was working as hard as she was. What kind of a role model would she be for them if she allowed them to grow up as she had done, believing that to be a female automatically meant that one was somehow of less worth as a human being? No! There was no way she was going to allow that to happen to *her* daughters. No way at all, and if that meant she had to work when she would much rather have been with them...

'You're just saying that because...because you're trying to put pressure on me over this wedding,' Olivia retorted angrily. 'I don't understand why it is you're so keen to go to it anyway. After all, it isn't as though you and your family have ever been particularly close, is it?'

'Not like you and *your* family, you mean,' Caspar countered furiously. 'And we all know just how close the Crighton clan is, don't we? Especially those of us who are on the outside of its charmed circle. *We* are your family, Livvy, me and Amelia and Alex, but sometimes—no, correction—*most* of the time now, you behave as though—'

'That's not fair and it's not true, either,' Olivia protested immediately.

'Isn't it?' Caspar challenged her. 'Have you any idea just how many people still refer to you as Olivia *Crighton*? No matter how much you try to deny it, Livvy, you're still held in thrall to the Crighton credo, to the Crighton way of doing things. Can you imagine how *you* would have reacted if I'd suggested that *we* didn't go to Louise's wedding, for instance…and she isn't even a sibling.'

'That's different. We've all grown up together. I see my cousins all the time. You haven't seen your half-brothers and sisters for years.'

'No, I haven't,' Caspar agreed quietly, 'which surely makes it all the more understandable that I should want to see them now. Remember how, when we first got married, Livvy, *you* were the one to preach forgiveness—a new start, a new way of integrating with and reacting to my family.'

'We *did* visit them,' Olivia insisted.

'I'm just not getting through to you, am I?' Caspar responded grimly. 'Well, perhaps *this* will get through to you, Livvy. I am going to be at my half-brother's wedding and so are my children. Whether my wife comes with us is, of course, up to you.'

As Olivia opened her mouth to protest and tell him exactly what she thought of his high-handed behaviour, she could hear the warning sound of the girls coming downstairs and she knew that it was too late to say what she was feeling. Instead, she forced her lips to part in a wide smile as the kitchen door opened and both girls came rushing in.

'Right, girls, breakfast, and then you've got ten minutes to collect all your gear together.'

'Oh, good, it's Dad's turn for the school run,' Amelia was saying happily as she tucked into her breakfast whilst Olivia quickly drank her now-cold cup of coffee and prepared to leave. 'That means we can go the long way round and drive past the field with the ponies in it.'

As she kissed both girls and headed for the door, deliberately avoiding going anywhere near

Caspar, Olivia could feel the pain and resentment inside her like a hot, hard lump that pressed painfully against her breastbone.

It wasn't Amelia's fault that those innocent words had underlined the differences between her and Caspar's parenting roles. Caspar, as a senior university lecturer, could arrange his working day to allow him a more leisurely start in the morning. It was different for her. She could just imagine what her grandfather would have to say if he found out that she was drifting into the office any later than eight-thirty. He would condemn her immediately for it. As she drove to work, though, she couldn't help dwelling on what Caspar had said. He hadn't meant it, she was sure. There was no way he would go to his Bryant's wedding without her. He was just trying to put pressure on her, to *blackmail* her. But he of all people knew how impossible it was for her to take any time off right now. As her husband, he ought to have been more understanding.

'WELL, THERE'S OBVIOUSLY at least one and probably more holes in the roof,' David warned Honor as they stood side by side surveying the large damp patches on the ceiling and walls of the bedroom.

'Yes. I'm afraid you're right, and it's even worse up in the attic,' Honor agreed.

They were on the last part of their tour of the house, and from what David had seen, there was enough work simply repairing the building's defective windows and roof to keep him busy for the next few months.

Once, a long time ago, in another life, another David would have looked at Honor in horror at the mere thought that he might undertake such work. He would not have had a clue where to start or how to go about it, because his father had brought him up to believe that any kind of manual labour was vastly beneath him. Even the children's bonfire behind the house every fifth of November had been put in place by the man they had in to do the garden.

Things were different now, of course, and in the years he had been away, he had learned, initially out of necessity, how to do such jobs. He had also, much to his surprise, discovered just how much satisfaction could be gained from teaching himself how to do them well.

Now his experienced eye quickly recognised the tell-tale signs of neglect in the fabric of the old house. He reckoned he could quite easily tackle most of the work himself.

'What I'd like to do is scout round a little to see if I can pick up matching materials so that the repairs can be as invisible as possible. When it comes to finding the right quality of hardwood for the window frames...' He paused and shook his head.

'My cousin may be able to help you there,' Honor offered. 'I'll give him a ring and arrange for us to go over.' She stopped as she saw the way David was frowning.

David didn't know Lord Astlegh personally, so he had no fear of Honor's cousin recognising him, but he had no idea whether or not the man knew any other member of his family and in particular his twin. The last thing he wanted right now was to meet anyone who was likely to recognise him through his likeness to Jon. This was one of the reasons that staying with Honor in her out-of-the-way house was so perfect.

'What's wrong?' Honor asked. 'You'll like him, I promise you.'

Honor's perceptiveness caught David off guard. She was far too intuitive, far too quick to pick up on his innermost feelings. Tiggy, for instance, would never in a million years have sensed what Honor had so easily discerned.

'It isn't so much a matter of my liking *him*,' David admitted wryly.

'You mean he may feel obliged to take on a paternal role and question your intentions towards me?' Honor laughed, shaking her head. 'I'm forty-four, and all other considerations apart, my cousin is so unworldly that he'd feel that *I* have far more experience in judging whether or not someone is to be trusted than he does.'

'Really!' David couldn't stop himself from giving her a tender look. He suspected that even if her life had held some pain, she had actually lived the kind of sheltered existence that meant that she had little or no idea to what depths of unpleasantness people could sometimes sink.

'Yes, really,' Honor confirmed firmly. 'My late husband was a photographer—perhaps not another David Bailey—but he was well-known enough in the seventies and eighties to attract commissions from glossy magazines that kept him in drink and drugs as well as gave him an endless supply of pretty models,' Honor said frankly.

'He had a bit of a thing about threesomes,' she added, 'and contrasts. Perhaps that was the artist in him. His favourite combination was one black model and one white. The reason I know is not just because he told me so, but because I saw the photographs—and so, too, very nearly did the girls! He wanted me to see what he was getting elsewhere that I refused to supply for him.' She gave David a brief smile. 'Sharing has never been my strong suit.'

'I'm sorry,' David apologised.

'There's no need to be. I'm not. It was a bad marriage, but I learned a lot from it—and it gave me Abigail and Ellen.'

'It wasn't your marriage I was apologising for. It was for my misjudgement about you—for pigeon-holing you as a woman who'd been pretty much sheltered from life's realities.'

As Honor held his gaze, David had to struggle to resist the temptation to close the distance between them. There was something so warm and inviting about her, something that...

A little hoarsely he told her, 'Although it's been very neglected, the house itself is well-built and a good size. With the land that goes with it, the property is sure to be a good investment and—'

'I could never buy it,' Honor interrupted him. 'My cousin is totally opposed to anything that means breaking up the estate, and I have to admit I can see his point of view. However, he *has* told me that I can have as long a lease on the house as I wish, so I've opted for one of ninety-nine years.'

'That should be long enough,' David agreed, smiling. 'Even if you are a witch.'

'Will you stop saying that?' Honor scolding him, laughing. 'I am not a witch.'

'Ah, but you would say that, wouldn't you?' David teased her back, his expression changing abruptly as his body registered the fact that she had turned towards the open bedroom window and the breeze was flattening her top against her body. 'I'm not too sure I can believe you,' he added huskily. 'I certainly feel as though you've cast a very special spell over me.'

'Oh?' Honor questioned, turning her head to look at him.

'I'm sorry, I shouldn't have said that,' David apologised gruffly.

'Why not, if that's the way you feel?' Honor asked him calmly.

'What I feel isn't... I shouldn't be talking to you like this,' David protested, pushing his hand into his hair. 'I don't have anything to offer a woman—any woman, but most especially a woman like you.'

Honor gave him a long, steady look before saying, 'Isn't that for *me* to decide?'

And then, before he could make any response, she turned and pointed to the damp patch on the wall. 'If you can cure this,' she told him briskly, 'then I intend to redecorate this room and move into it. I don't know why, but somehow I feel this is the right room for me. The whole place needs redoing, of course, but all this other work has to be done first. Then I intend to try to persuade Freddy to let me add on a glass house for my herbs.'

She glanced at her watch.

'Look, I've got to go and see a patient. Can I leave you to sort through everything we've seen and work out the best place to start? You're going to need some money to buy supplies. We can talk about that this evening.'

CHAPTER SIX

'ANYWAY, HOW DO YOU KNOW he loves you?'

'Because he said so,' Annalise told her tormentor quickly, flinching a little as the other girl tossed her newly styled, up-to-the-minute, oh-so-casually tousled mane of thick dark hair with its—according to her—'naturally' sun-streaked strands of rich warm honey.

'Oh, but he would say that, wouldn't he?' Patti gave Annalise a sideways look as she added coolly, 'All boys say that when they're in bed with you.'

Annalise could feel her heart starting to hammer too fast. They were in the rumpus room above the garage block of Patti's parents' newly built neo-Georgian-style mansion on the outskirts of the town. Patti—who could twist her father around her little finger—had persuaded her parents to allow the band to sometimes practise in the large, centrally heated room above the detached garages. Her father had grumbled that allowing them to do so meant that he would have to put off having the space fitted out as a snooker room and bar for his own use, but he had nevertheless agreed.

The band, who had practised there for the first time the previous evening, had declared that their new venue was far cooler than Mike Salter's auntie's barn. Annalise was miserably aware that Patti's motives in arranging for them to be able to play at her parents' place were far from as altruistic as she liked to pretend.

As a newcomer to the area and to the school, by rights Patti ought to have kept a low profile, but Patti, it seemed, wrote her own rules for social behaviour.

Her father had owned a small chain of supermarkets in the south of England, which he had recently sold for what Patti dismissively described as 'millions'. The reason he had moved his family up to Cheshire was because he was aware of the excellent business opportunities in the area. Like his daughter, Will Charles was a brash self-publicist with all the sensitivity of a rhinoceros hide.

Ever since her first weeks at school, Patti had made a beeline for, and been determined to become part of, the crowd around the band. Annalise had no doubts about the fact that Patti was secretly targeting Pete, her boyfriend. On the surface, Patti might claim that she wanted to be her friend; she might be besieging her with phone calls and invitations, but Annalise sensed that it wasn't *her* friendship she was after at all.

'Why do you have to do that?' Patti had demanded one evening when Annalise told her that she couldn't go out because she needed to help her father with the housework. 'Let your dad do it or find someone else. Has he got a girlfriend?' she had asked with a gleam in her eye that Annalise hadn't liked.

'No,' she had told her shortly.

'How do you know?' Patti had countered. 'He might have and not have told you about it. Men don't always. He's a man after all and he must need sex. All men do. I bet Pete is good in bed,' she had added coaxingly. 'You can tell me about it…I'm your best friend.'

'There isn't anything to tell,' Annalise had replied primly.

'Liar,' Patti had accused her promptly, rolling her eyes as she claimed, 'Pete is just so sexy. If he isn't getting it from you, then he's got to be getting it from someone else. And if he's going a bit short, *I* certainly wouldn't mind helping out!'

She had giggled, then added, 'Only joking. You know you're my best friend.'

Patti now gave Annalise a sharply assessing look, then frowned.

'I don't think that hairstyle suits you at all,' Patti told Annalise. 'Really, I'm not being unkind. I heard Pete saying the other day how much he liked girls with dark hair.' She tossed her own and shot Annalise a distinctly calculating glance. 'If he really loved you, he wouldn't say that, would he?' She stroked her hair. 'He told me that he really liked my new style.'

Annalise was beginning to feel sick. It was true what she had said to Patti about there being nothing to tell about her sex life with Pete. So far, all they had done was kiss. Pete had wanted to go further, to do more, but she had refused. She wanted to go to bed with him, to be completely and utterly a part of him, but her romantic soul yearned for something much, much more than the mundane, indeed almost casual, physical intimacy Pete was offering her. But it had been so hard to say no to him. She loved him so much.

In her imagination, loving him and being loved by him were so different from the anxious reality of being his 'girl'.

In her day-dreams they were two parts of a per-

fect whole and he loved her above and beyond
everything and everyone else in his life. In her
day-dreams he was just waiting for the day of her
eighteenth birthday to marry her and make her
his, and once they were married they would be so
happy together. Everything would be perfect; she
would feel so wanted, so loved, so safe.

She would never leave her children the way her
mother had done. No, she would never do that.
She longed for Pete to say the words she needed
to feel secure, but she had seen the way his glance
roved to other girls. She had seen, too, the way
they looked back at him, and her tender, vulnerable heart was already aching with the foreknowl-
edge of what it sensed was to come.

'I know a way to make anybody I want love
me,' Patti boasted, giving Annalise a crocodile
smile of competitive self-assurance.

Gravely, Annalise watched her. She shouldn't
really be here now. She ought to be at home, but
the band was coming round later, and if she
wasn't here, Patti, her 'best friend', would be
making up to Pete, coming on to him.

'I wonder what time Pete will get here?' Patti
was saying impatiently. 'He looked really fed up
last night and he wasn't talking to you much, was
he?'

Annalise said nothing, looking away from the
other girl. Sometimes Pete could be cruelly indif-
ferent to her. She tried not to mind, but when he
wasn't nice to her it hurt so much.

'My parents will be away at the weekend and
I'm going to have a party,' Patti informed her.

'I have to go,' Annalise said, getting up and
heading for the door as she realised how late it
was getting.

'But Pete will be here soon,' Patti told her, adding with a gleam in her eye, 'Still, if you must...
I'll look after him for you, shall I?'

Giving Patti a wan smile, Annalise opened the
door.

'ANNALISE, IS THAT YOU?' her father called out
as she let herself into the house.

'Yes,' she called in reply, her heart sinking a
little. She was later than she should have been,
she knew. She had hoped to get back before her
father came home from work. He didn't like Patti
any more than he liked Pete, and if he knew that
she had been with her instead of coming straight
home to do her homework, he would be annoyed.
To her relief, as she pushed open the kitchen door,
she saw that one of her father's friends, Hal, was
sitting at the kitchen table with him.

Hal had his own business building extensions and doing general property repairs. He had always had a bit of a soft spot for Annalise, and with a twinkle in his eye, he told her, 'My, but you're turning into a lovely-looking lass.'

Whilst Annalise blushed, her father frowned. 'Don't you go filling her head with that kind of nonsense. She needs to spend more time at her books than at her mirror.'

Hal laughed, winking at Annalise as he teased her. 'What's this I hear about you and Pete Hunter courting?'

'Courting!' Annalise winced as her father exclaimed, 'She's doing no such thing!'

Giving Annalise a sympathetic look, Hal told her father pacifyingly, 'I was just teasing the lass a little bit, that's all.'

DAVID GRIMACED as he looked at the list he had made of the materials and equipment he would need for the work Honor wanted him to do. It was going to be expensive, very expensive, and perhaps when Honor saw it...

Honor...

He wondered how much longer she was likely to be gone. The house felt empty without her. He had been thinking about her all day...imagining...

It was just because she was the first woman he had been in anything like close contact with for such a long time that he was reacting to her like this, he tried to reassure himself. She *was* very attractive after all and he was only human, only a man. Just how much of a man he was turning out to be around her was part of the reason he was feeling so bemused and on edge.

The afternoon had brought rain and dark, heavy clouds along with the threat of thunder.

He heard the sound of a car driving up to the house and his body tensed.

Outside, a car door slammed and then Honor was in the kitchen shaking raindrops off her hair and laughing up at him as she exclaimed breathlessly, 'It's pouring down out there. I got soaked just coming from the car.'

As he listened to her and watched her, a feeling of the most extraordinary tenderness swept over him. Very gently, he reached out his hand and brushed the raindrops from her face.

'You're wet. You should have worn a coat,' he told her absently, but it wasn't the dampness of her clothes that he was really thinking about, and the message in his eyes told her so. 'I've made a list of the materials and equipment you'll need.

It's going to be expensive,' he warned her a little huskily.

'Yes, I know,' Honor replied equally unsteadily. He really did have the most amazingly mesmerising dark blue eyes and she knew perfectly well that beneath the mundanity of their conversation something much more meaningful, powerful and potentially dangerous was taking place. A connection was being made between them at one of the deepest and most intense of human levels.

Men had flirted with her before, hinted and sometimes much more than hinted, with innuendo and *double entendre*, that they desired her, but none of them had ever had such a profound effect on her as David was now having. But she gave no hint of what she was thinking or feeling as she smiled calmly and moved away from him over to the table to pick up the list he had made and scrutinise it.

'I think we had better organise some form of transport for you,' she told him when she finished reading it. 'Presumably you can drive?'

He could drive, yes, and even possessed a current driving licence, but of course it wasn't in the name he had given her and neither did he have any insurance.

'I—'

'My car is insured for any driver,' Honor informed him. 'It's a hatchback and large enough for most of the smaller things you'll require. You can use it when you need to.'

Had she guessed that he was lying to her about his identity? But no, she couldn't possibly have done. It was just his guilty conscience making him think that she was deliberately avoiding looking at him.

'I...' he began, then stopped as thunder crashed in the distance.

'I'm getting hungry,' Honor told him when the noise had died away, 'and I've got some notes to write up after we've eaten. Oh, and I called to see Freddy on the way back and he seems to think the estate manager will be able to supply us with any bricks or wood we might need. He introduced me to him. He's a nice guy, an Australian, and new to the job.'

David hadn't realised that he had been holding his breath with anxiety. But if the estate manager was an Australian and new, he was hardly likely to recognise David.

As she spoke, she accidentally dislodged a herbal book she had been reading from the table. As David bent to pick it up, he read the Latin description of the plant on the page where it had fallen open, automatically translating it.

'You know Latin?' Honor asked him in surprise.

'A little. We...I...it was part of our school curriculum,' David stammered uncomfortably.

Honor frowned. She wasn't an intellectual snob, but an itinerant manual labourer who knew Latin was hardly the norm. To have attended a school where Latin was part of the curriculum also suggested that David must have attended a public school rather than a state comprehensive.

'Most people think of it as a very dry, dull language and associate it mainly with the law, but—'

'What makes you say that?' David interrupted sharply, so sharply that for a moment Honor frowned a little. He realised then that he was overreacting and offered gruffly, 'I've always thought of it more as the language of the church. It's lingua franca, so to speak.'

'Yes, I suppose you're right,' Honor agreed easily.

Why had her innocent mention of the law provoked such a strong reaction in him? He had described himself to her as a thief. If that was the case, he would no doubt have good reason to fear the law.

'IT'S GONE ELEVEN O'CLOCK. I'm going up to bed now. Can I leave you to clear up?' Honor asked David as she came into the kitchen.

He had spent the evening drawing up some detailed worksheets of all the jobs that needed to be done so that Honor could prioritise them.

'Yes, of course. I'll start making some phone calls in the morning to find out where we can hire the stuff I'm going to need to fix the roof at the best rates. The sooner I can get that hole sealed and the slates replaced, the better.'

Smiling, Honor walked past him and opened the kitchen door. He had paused several times in his work during the evening to watch her whilst she concentrated on her notes. She was so totally engrossed in what she was doing that she was oblivious to his perusal.

Even in the harsh light of the kitchen, her skin was as fresh and unlined as a girl's, but her expression had a maturity, a warmth, that a girl's could never have. She was one of the most natural and relaxed people he had ever met. There was nothing either contrived or artificial about her and, in some odd way, she reminded him very much of the priest. Was it because he could sense that, like the priest, she possessed the ability, the honesty and the compassion to see right through a person's outer shell to the inner soul? To see through that shell and not to judge what lay behind it? Not to judge him?

'YOU'RE VERY RESTLESS this evening,' Jenny commented to Jon as he paced the length of their sitting room. 'It's gone eleven. I'm ready for bed. Are you?'

'You go ahead. I'll be up shortly,' Jon told her. He grimaced, admitting. 'I do feel a bit on edge. I don't know why.'

'It's probably because the boys aren't back yet,' Jenny said soothingly.

'It was good of Guy to get them both holiday jobs on Lord Astlegh's estate.'

'Yes, it was,' Jenny agreed, smiling lovingly at him as she opened the door and headed for the stairs.

After she had gone, Jon went to stand in front of the window. Perhaps it was the storm outside that was making him feel so tense and edgy, as though…he was waiting for something. For *something*? For *what*?

He frowned as he remembered the conversation he had had with Olivia earlier in the day. They had been talking about Ben, and Jon had mentioned how concerned he was about his father's health.

'He misses your father very badly,' Jon had told her.

'*He* may do, but I certainly don't,' Olivia had retorted immediately. 'I never want to see him again as long as I live and if I did...' She stopped and said harshly to Jon, 'But you must feel the same way—after what he did.'

'Yes...at first,' Jon had agreed slowly. 'And I certainly can't condone his wrongdoing, but time passes. Wounds heal.'

'Mine haven't,' Olivia had countered. 'There's no way I could ever forgive him for what he did.'

The vehemence in her voice had disturbed Jon, but he had felt unable to pursue the issue. Olivia wasn't a girl any more. She was a woman. An adult...a wife...a mother...and a daughter?

Outside, the thunder rolled nearer. It was going to be a wild and stormy night.

WHEN DAVID WENT UPSTAIRS, all the lights were on on the landing. Honor warding off the demons of the dark? As he opened his own bedroom door, he could hear the thunder rolling closer.

IN HER BEDROOM, Honor heard the floorboards creak as David walked along the landing. Both her bedside lamps were on, their comforting glow dispelling the darkness of her bedroom. People found it difficult to understand her fear of the dark and even her grown daughters teased her a little for it, but she had never been able to shake it off. Tonight, though, she had something much more pleasant to think about, to go to sleep on... David was such a gorgeously sexy man.

'Mmm...' Smiling to herself, she closed her eyes as she reviewed with sleepy female appreciation just *why* she considered David to be so sexy, ignoring the increasingly loud rumble of the thunder as it came closer. Unlike the dark, thunder had never bothered her, not even when, as it had done just now, it seemed to be right overhead, but as the sound died away, the lights flickered and Honor froze. She sat bolt upright in bed, her mouth dry with dread as they flickered again and then went out.

No, please not that, she prayed, but it was too late. Too afraid to move as the darkness closed over her, Honor made a small keening cry of terror.

David wasn't sure at first just why he had woken up, only that some sixth sense had alerted him to the fact that something wasn't as it should be.

Lying fully awake in his bed, he looked searchingly around the shadowy darkness of his room and then realised what was missing—the thin bar of light from the landing that he had been able to see beneath his closed bedroom door. Which meant... Swiftly, he reached for the switch on his bedside lamp. Nothing. No power, no electricity, no light.

Without stopping to analyse what he was doing, or why, he pushed back the bedclothes, reaching for the heavy towelling robe Honor had produced for him earlier in the day. She had informed him that it was a gift from one of her daughters 'just in case you should have any male visitors'. 'I rather fancied at the time the male visitor Abigail had in mind was her then current boyfriend,' Honor had told him wryly. 'But they split up before the relationship got as far as bringing him home. I daren't tell either of them, but I must admit that I'm rather looking forward to the day they make me a grandmother—not that I'd want either of them to rush into motherhood without being very sure about what they were doing. Do you have any grandchildren?' she had asked him.

He hadn't been sure what to reply, but she had

saved him from the necessity of saying anything by smiling and apologising.

'I'm sorry. I'm prying.' And then she had tactfully changed the subject.

David opened his bedroom door and stepped out onto the dark landing. The house held that night silence that to some people was comforting and to others eerie. After living the way he had done virtually out in the open with none of the refinements of civilisation, any building with four stout walls and a roof to keep out the elements would have been welcoming. Still, David acknowledged that he actually liked Foxdean. Going round it with Honor, he had found himself sympathising with the house's plight and its surely undeserved reputation.

Halfway down the landing, he paused, listening as he caught a sound that had nothing to do with creaking floorboards or ill-fitting windows. There it was again, a muffled indrawn sound of terror. Honor!

Quickly, David hurried to her bedroom door and turned the handle.

The room, of course, was in darkness, but despite the storm clouds in the night sky, there was enough light from the sickle moon for a man used to the darkness of velvet tropical skies to make out the shape of the room's furniture and the huddled form curled up in a tight ball on the bed.

'Honor. It's all right. It's me,' he reassured her in a soft voice as he approached the bed.

She had turned her head towards him, but David wasn't sure if she had actually registered either his presence or his words.

'Honor.' As he reached the bed, he sat down on it beside her. 'It's all right. There's been a power cut.'

'David?' He could hear the relief in her shaky voice.

'Yes, it's me,' he told her comfortingly.

She looked directly at him and he glimpsed the shadows of her fear in her eyes.

'Thank you for coming. I was too terrified to move. Silly, I know—'

'It's not silly at all,' David hastened to correct her. 'If we're honest, most of us have to admit to a fear of one thing or another.'

Honor gave him a wan smile and asked, 'So what are you afraid of, then?'

She was recovering now. David saw it in her eyes, but he could see more than that. Much more...

He could see, for instance, the way the moonlight shadowed her skin, highlighting the tempting curve of her mouth and the way her hair lay against her throat. He could see, too, the smooth warmth of her bare shoulder and guessed that beneath the bedclothes she was totally naked.

His body stirred in reaction to his thoughts.

'What I'm more afraid of than anything else at the moment is being here with you,' he answered honestly. Just for a second he thought that her silence meant that he had offended her and that she was rejecting him.

Then he saw the glimmer of tears shining in her eyes. When he reached out protectively to cover her hand as it lay on top of the bed with both of his own, she told him quietly, 'Every year, we—my parents and my brothers—used to go up to Scotland to visit my grandparents. They had this huge old barracks of a house. Upstairs, there was a long gallery.' She made a small face. 'You know the sort of thing, all heavy family portraits hanging on the walls alongside a hideous collection of hunting trophies. We used to play there when it rained. At one end there was a large oak chest. My brothers used to tease me that it was really a coffin.' She smiled again. 'Of course it wasn't, but for some reason I actually believed them.

'They were both older than me and I suppose,

too, they resented having to play with a girl—they were at boarding school and so we didn't really have much contact with one another apart from the holidays. It sounds terribly archaic now, but then... Well, this particular holiday—I was quite young, only just eight and a very young eight at that. We were playing pirates. I was "captured" and they bundled me up in an old sheet... threatened to make me walk the plank, but instead, for some reason, I don't remember why, they decided to imprison me in the chest...'

As she talked, her speech had speeded up and he could hear the dry anxiety in her throat, but now it slowed right down as though she was finding it hard to speak at all. Her voice had dropped and become so low that David automatically moved closer so that he could hear what she was saying.

'It was just a boyish prank...they didn't mean... But something must have happened. Either they were called away or they just simply forgot about me.'

She had begun to shiver and her face was nearly the same colour as the pale white sheets on the bed. But despite her shudders, David could see the perspiration dewing her skin as she relived the terror of her imprisonment. David could fully understand why.

Just listening to her and imagining how she must have felt was making his own heart beat heavily and fast. If he had those two little wretches—her brothers—here right now…

Anxiety, anger and an aching need to take hold of her and tell her that she was safe, that there was nothing for her to fear, that he, David Crighton, would guard and protect her for the rest of his life, thundered down over him in an avalanche of feeling.

'What is it?' Honor asked a little bit breathlessly as his grip on her hand tightened.

'Nothing,' David denied, and then, shaking his head, admitted, 'Your brothers, I'd like to have skinned the pair of them.'

To his relief, Honor laughed, a deep rich chuckle that arched her throat and made him long to press his lips to her skin.

'Although as a mother I'm totally against any kind of violence towards children, you don't know how good it makes me feel to hear you say that,' she acknowledged frankly.

'When my grandparents' housekeeper eventually found me, everyone was so fed up all I got was a thorough telling-off for playing silly games and getting my clothes dirty. My brothers had gone out to have tea with a friend and had forgotten where they'd left me. They'd neglected to tell anyone of the fact that they'd locked me in the chest. Fortunately, the housekeeper who was looking for me to give me my supper heard the noise I was making and had a spare key.'

'Your brothers must have been mortified to think of what they'd done to you,' David said.

'Not really,' Honor told him, adding simply, 'We weren't that kind of family. You've got to remember,' she counselled him gently when she saw the expression in his eyes, 'that my brothers were both at boarding school. In those days, boarding schools, whilst not in the Tom Brown's school-days mode, were nevertheless quite tough forcing houses for what were perceived to be prized male qualities. I think my family was quite out of patience with me when I developed this ridiculous fear of the dark. Such experiences are supposed to make one stronger, not weaker.'

She sighed gently. 'I wasn't allowed to have a night-light in my bedroom and my father was almost obsessive about insisting that all the lights be turned off at night. I smuggled a candle and some matches into my bedroom and I can only think that I must have had a very kind guardian angel watching over me to keep me from accidentally setting the whole house on fire.'

'A candle...' Thoughtfully, David looked round the room, suddenly understanding the real purpose of the many decorative candlesticks he had seen dotting the house.

'Mmm...stupidly I took the one I normally keep up here downstairs with me the last time I had a power cut and forgot to replace it, so it's my own fault that I got in such a state tonight. I'm sorry that I woke you. It really is most undignified in a grown woman to make such a noise that she wakes up her house guest. You must think I'm an idiot.'

David paused and looked at her, savouring the luminous darkness of her eyes and the soft sheen of her skin, the tempting fullness of her mouth, the sleep-scented warmth she exuded, before telling her gruffly, 'What I think is...is immaterial...' He intended to say, since *I* am in no position to pass judgement on anyone, but instead, to his own bemusement, he heard himself admitting thickly instead, 'What I think is that *I'm* the one who's an idiot for coming in here when I already know how dangerously vulnerable I am to you and how very, very much I want to make love with you.'

'You do?' Honor responded almost whimsically, but there was nothing whimsical about the way she was looking at him.

'Yes, I do,' David agreed, and as she lifted the hand he was still clasping towards her throat, he leaned over and kissed her.

Honor made a soft sound of appreciation as David's mouth covered hers. The fear that had terrorised her had gone, but in its place was an equally dangerous emotion.

How long had it been since a man had made her feel like this...made her *want* like this?

Too long, her hungry body protested impatiently, but she wasn't an impetuous girl any more, Honor cautioned herself. She was a mature woman. Yes, she was, and as such, surely she was allowed to know what she wanted, to indulge herself a little, to be open and honest about her sensuality. After all, whatever she chose to do or not to do with this man was her business and hers alone. She wasn't accountable to anyone now. Her daughters, the primary reason why as they were growing up she had been so determined not to allow a man into her life, were now adults themselves. To them she no doubt seemed too ancient to suffer the aching heat of sensual desire, but the reality was...

The reality was that she wanted David with an

intensity that made it devastatingly easy to simply
lie here and permit herself to be lapped by the
voluptuous waves of their mutual need.

She knew already that he would be a caring,
tender lover, that his touch—his *possession*—
wouldn't be greedy or selfish.

Because of Rourke, she had witnessed, if not
personally experienced, most of the harsh realities
of what sex for sex's sake could be. It had perhaps
given her a jaundiced view of men, as had the
numerous attempts by her male acquaintances to
convince her that what she needed was to have
sex with them.

Not true. What she had needed, if she had
needed anything, was to love and be loved in return, but that had been a long time ago. Now she
was content to accept with mature wisdom that
love took many forms, that one could have as
much joy in the emotional and non-sexual love
one shared with a child or a friend as one was
likely to find with a lover.

No, she wasn't going to even attempt to persuade herself that the tension she could almost
feel pulsating between her and David was 'love'.

No. She would much rather respect and enjoy
the purity of the sexual intimacy and need that
was bonding them together than to denigrate it

and attempt to dress it in the shabby clothes of pseudo love.

'Mmm…that was nice,' she murmured softly when he lifted his mouth from hers.

'Only nice?' he whispered back equally softly.

Smiling, Honor offered judiciously, 'Better than nice…'

'Much better,' David agreed as he reached out to brush her hair away from her neck. 'Much, much better.'

Blissfully, Honor closed her eyes as he kissed the sensitive column of her throat. He was wearing the robe she had loaned him and she slipped her hand inside and delicately traced the line of his collar-bone.

'You're so tanned,' she told him dreamily.

Lifting his mouth from her skin, David laughed. 'It's dark…how can you tell?'

'I can feel it,' Honor insisted. 'Your skin feels warm and golden.'

As he nuzzled the tender spot just behind her ear, David smiled to himself, remembering how he and the others had crewed naked in the early stages of their voyage to bring the yacht back to Europe.

'*Your* skin feels like satin,' he countered. 'All

creamy soft.' As he spoke, he was edging the duvet away from her body.

Honor let him, her ego and her female pride
feeding off the look she could see in his eyes as
he studied her naked body.

Honor believed in moderation in all things. She
had never dieted or excessively exercised, but she
liked good healthy food and clean fresh air. She
liked, too, the sensation of using her body, of
stretching and enjoying it. In London, when the
girls were young, she had attended a regular yoga
class and she still followed the principles she had
absorbed then. Mainly, though, she suspected the
elegant shape of her body and the creamy, youth-
ful tone of her skin were due to good genes.

As he slid the duvet away from Honor's body,
David felt his throat tighten in awe.

Unlike Tiggy's, Honor's body was full-
breasted, warm-fleshed, curving in at her waist
and out again over seductively rounded hips, her
legs tapering to delicate, fine-boned ankles, so
fine-boned, in fact, that he suspected he could
probably circle them with the fingers of one hand.

Tiggy, oddly in a woman who had such a child-
ishly thin body, had quite thick ankles, or so she
had always complained to him. But then, Tiggy
had been obsessed about every aspect of her body,

constantly finding fault with it and relaying her findings to him.

In some intangible way, Tiggy's dissatisfaction and constant fault-finding with her body had made him feel that she was similarly dissatisfied with him and their marriage. Every time she pinpointed or highlighted another physical feature she found unacceptable, it seemed to him as though he was the one she was actually finding fault with. Her failure to achieve the perfect body was somehow reflected in *his* failure to be aroused by her.

There was no problem in his being aroused by Honor. Even before he had seen her naked, his body had been embarrassingly direct in its reaction to her.

Once, he would have been proudly vain of such a fact, but time and the priest, as well as his awareness of his own failings, had taught him better. He *was* pleased, of course, and in a way proud. To be able to so openly and vigorously display male desire must always be a source of pride to the baser part of a man's make-up, but his real pleasure, his real pride, came from knowing that Honor felt able to openly express *her* sexuality with him.

A little ashamed of the emotion he was feeling, he bent his head to conceal his expression from her, gently brushing the lightest of light kisses against the soft curve of her belly.

'Ohhh...' Honor breathed in voluptuous pleasure.

'Nice?' David teased her.

'I'm not sure,' Honor responded provocatively. 'Do it again.'

Laughing, David obliged, but neither of them were laughing a few seconds later as the bedroom echoed to the increasingly charged sound of their breathing.

'Take this off,' Honor whispered unevenly to him as she tugged at the lapel of his robe.

'Help me, then,' he whispered back, equally unsteadily, closing his eyes and shuddering as he felt her fingers on his naked body.

There was a waterfall not far from the house in Jamaica where the water fell so fast and from such a height that it was impossible to dam it and that was exactly the way he reacted to the sensations, the emotions, crashing down over him, through him, right now.

Honor tensed a little as she felt the raw hunger of his kiss and the seeking, probing thrust of his tongue as it parted her lips, but the arms he had wrapped around her were holding her safely and tenderly and her own body was as eager to return his passion as he was to give it. Delicious shudders of pleasure rushed dizzyingly through her body where he touched it—her back, her belly, her breasts. Heavens, how they ached, becoming swollen, provocative mounds of tempting female fruit, heavy and ripe with promise, luscious and succulent.

No wonder that David, having soothed the darkly burgeoning crest of her nipple with the tender stroke of his thumb, should bend his head and bite delicately into the provocation they offered. And no wonder, too, that she should enjoy the sensation of his mouth against her body so much so that she cried out in hot delight. Eagerly, she reached down her hand and urged him to touch and taste her more intimately.

A piercingly sweet thrill of emotion touched David at the deepest level to know that she wanted to give him such an exquisite pleasure.

The female heart of her, like her breasts, was lush and ripe, sweet tasting and sensually pleasurable to his tongue and lips.

As David caressed her, gently opening and exploring her with his fingers, Honor began to feel the first sharp contractions of her orgasm. There was no time to warn him or to urge him to penetrate her.

'Self-gratification' might be endorsed and even encouraged as a rite of passage of female maturity, but... But whilst physically satisfying, it lacked that very definite and irreplaceable special something, that sharp thrill of excitement and fulfilment that came with a partner.

Helplessly, she let herself be caught up in the increasingly urgent sensations of her own body, unashamedly enjoying them whilst she gasped her appreciation to the man who had incited them.

'I'm sorry,' she told David a little breathlessly as her pleasure subsided to a gentle ache, 'but it's been a long time and you were—'

'I *was*,' David agreed wryly, taking her words and using them to convey his own meaning to her, 'but unfortunately, I no longer am.' As he read the recognition of his meaning in her eyes, even before her gaze dropped to his body, he admitted, 'It's been a long time for me, too, and I'd forgotten, if indeed I ever knew, just how erotic and arousing it is to touch and taste a woman so intimately. Your pleasure was too much for my self-control.'

To his surprise, Honor started to blush. So much so that he could actually see the warm colour staining her skin despite the darkness surrounding them.

'I'm sorry,' he began to apologise. 'I didn't mean to embarrass you.'

'You haven't,' Honor assured him quickly. 'It was just... My late husband used to complain that I had much the same effect on him in bed as toast crumbs. I irritated him to the point where he just wanted to do what had to be done and get out of the bed as fast as he could. To be told now, when I'm the mother of two adult daughters and, in vulgar parlance, well past my sell-by date, that a man...a very attractive and sexy man, finds me so desirable that he can't stop himself from...' Honor gave a small, satisfied sigh. 'You have just made me a very happy woman.'

'I have?' David asked, unable to stop himself from expressing his own pleased pride at her praise. 'Well, I don't know how you're going to feel about this,' he began, 'but I rather suspect that before too much longer—'

'What I feel about it...what I feel about you,' Honor emphasised blissfully, 'is... No, come here and let me show you what I think and feel,' she murmured huskily to him.

David needed no second bidding.

CHAPTER SEVEN

'SO, WHAT ARE YOU TWO planning to do this weekend?' Jon asked Jack and Joss as they enjoyed a leisurely late brunch prepared with a good deal of teasing and laughter by Jack, who had insisted on showing off his newly learned domestic skills.

'You wait until you're off to uni,' he advised Joss defensively when his younger cousin had grinned to hear Jack earnestly discussing the recipe for a vegetarian casserole he was eager to learn to make with Jenny. 'When I get to college, it isn't going to be easy managing on a student grant and some of the stuff you hear guys eat...yuck!' He pulled a grim face. 'At least if I can learn to cook for myself, I'll know what I'm eating.'

She was so proud of him, Jenny reflected as the two boys argued amicably together. Yes, there had been that unhappy patch a little while back when poor Jack had been so confused and angry about David, but now, thankfully, he seemed to be over it. Jenny knew how much his decision to study law and follow Jon into the family practice had pleased her husband.

Their own son, Joss, was the kind of person whom everyone just naturally loved. Ruth had once declared that he was one of that rare breed of human beings who somehow bridged the gap between God and man. Although she had protested at the time that Ruth was exaggerating her favourite relative's attributes, Jenny had nonetheless secretly and proudly agreed with her. Joss *was* special, very special, but that didn't make the love she had for her other children, or for Jack, any less strong.

'To each according to his needs' went the saying and that was how Jenny felt about her love for her children. Sometimes one of them needed more love than the others, and Jack, like Olivia in many ways, had a special little bit of her heart that her own children didn't have because they didn't need it.

Olivia had been born after the stillbirth of Jenny's first child. Tania, Olivia's mother, had been overwhelmed and sometimes repelled by motherhood. Tania fretted about getting her figure back and refused to breast-feed the cross, hungry baby she was more than glad to hand over to Jenny who, despite her longing to have another child, had at that point still not conceived.

Jenny's tender heart had ached for Olivia when the child had been confronted by her parents' indifference and her grandfather's dismissal of her because she was a girl.

Jenny had been delighted when Olivia had married Caspar and gone on to have a family of her own, but since the birth of Olivia's second child, the bond between her and Jenny had not been so close. Jenny had put it down to the demands on Olivia's time, coupled with the presence of a loving partner in her life, which did away with Olivia's need to confide in her.

It was only natural and right that Olivia's closest confidant, the person she turned to most, should be her husband.

It was probably her age that made Jenny feel she had somehow almost overnight undergone a change of status. She was no longer a busy mother at the hub of her household and her extended family. It must be the empty-nest syndrome with a vengeance, she ruminated. Whilst the bond she had built with Maddy was one she cherished and valued, she still missed the earlier closeness she had had with Olivia whom, in many ways, she considered to be her eldest 'daughter'.

Some women of a certain age, *her* age, might think themselves ill-used when their mothering role came to an end.

She was determined that when Joss followed Jack to university, there was no way *she* was going to mope. No, instead, she intended to persuade Jon to think about semi-retirement. There were so many things she wanted them to have time to do together whilst they were still young enough to enjoy them.

'Is there any chance we can borrow your car tonight, Mum?' Joss asked Jenny.

'Maybe,' she agreed cautiously.

Although both boys had passed their driving tests and were competent drivers, Jenny and Jon had mutually decided not to provide either of them with their own cars.

'It doesn't matter how responsible they are, at bottom they are both still testosterone-driven young males. I've had to deal with the legal aspects of too many appalling tragedies involving hot-blooded young men and their cars not to be aware of what a potentially dangerous combination they can make,' Jon had told her.

Jenny had agreed wholeheartedly with him, and

although both boys protested and wheedled, Jon and Jenny had refused to give in. Jenny's small car was there for them to borrow—with her permission—but that was all.

'They'll drive just that bit more carefully in your car and that's a fact,' Jon had said to Jenny. '*And* they'll value their own cars all the more if they've had to work and save for them.'

Jenny smiled. Jon knew what he was talking about after all. Ben, his father, had given David a sports car for his coming-of-age, telling Jon dismissively that he didn't need his own car because, unlike David, he was still living at home.

Both Jenny and Jon had objected when Ben had also insisted on buying a fast car for their own son, Max, but Ben being Ben had delighted in overruling them and, of course, Max as he had been then had openly abused his grandfather's generosity.

'It isn't Max he's indulging, it's himself,' Jon had once exploded when his father's high-handed attitude to their parental authority had pushed him beyond the limits of his patience.

Jenny had said nothing, unable to refute the truth of what her husband was really saying—that Ben was buying Max's loyalty, and much more shamefully and hurtfully their son was allowing him to do so.

Not that they were likely to have *that* problem with either Joss or Jack.

Ben had never been close to either of his younger grandsons. Jenny suspected that the fierce intensity of the love he felt first for David and then for Max had exhausted and burned out his ability to love anyone else.

Jack had come to feel that his grandfather somehow blamed him for the disappearance of his father, whilst Joss, with his sunny nature, looked upon Ben with the kind of mature compassion that made Jenny reflect that in some way their roles had been reversed. In terms of human awareness and what made others tick, it was Joss who was the adult and Ben the child.

'What do you want to borrow the car *for*?' Jon now asked the boys promptly.

'We're going to a party,' Joss announced.

Jon's eyebrows rose.

'It's okay,' Joss was quick to reassure them. 'We'll drive safely.'

Jon and Jenny exchanged looks and Jenny gave her husband a brief nod of her head.

'Very well, then,' Jon consented, and Jenny had

her reward when she saw the proud, pleased look in Jack's eyes as he thanked them.

'Whose party is it?' Jenny asked Jack curiously an hour later as he walked through the garden with her, helping to deadhead the last of the late-summer roses. In this sheltered part of the garden, they had managed to last until the autumn gales had battered them the night before.

'Patti's,' Jack responded promptly. 'Her family has only recently moved to Haslewich. Joss and I bumped into Mike Salter last night and he invited us over. He was on his way to her place to practise with the band. Mike plays keyboard for them.'

'Mike Salter,' Jenny repeated. 'That's Guy's sister Frances's son, isn't it?'

'Uh-huh,' Jack agreed without elaborating any further. He didn't think that Jenny would particularly care for Patti or her parents if the comments he had heard about them were anything to go by. It wasn't that Jenny was a snob. Far from it. But Jack had gained the impression that there was something a little bit too materialistic about both Patti and her father. He especially hadn't liked the way she so openly, and in his mind, unfemininely displayed her sexuality.

That pale little blonde, Annalise, whose boyfriend Patti was so obviously and aggressively determined to hijack, didn't stand a chance of competing with her. Not if the sultry, assessing looks Pete Hunter had been giving Patti were any indication.

Jack knew which of the two *he* preferred. Heavy make-up, too-short skirts and overt displays of sexuality didn't hold very much appeal to him.

Not that he really had time to be interested in *any* type of girl right now. He was determined to work hard at university and get a good degree. It was important to him not just to make Jon proud but to refute the look he had so often seen in his grandfather's eyes.

He might not, unlike Max, ever make Queen's Counsel and he certainly didn't share Joss's easy learning skill and flair, but as Jon had very warmly assured him, he did have the potential to become a very good lawyer.

'There's a lot more to the law than courtroom dramatics,' Jon had told Jack during one of their heart-to-hearts. 'An awful lot more.'

And Jack had taken comfort from Jon's gentle words after the unkind cruelty of his grandfather's dismissal of him as a son unworthy of a man like David.

It had been on the tip of Jack's tongue to retort that far from being the wonderful human being his grandfather believed, his father was actually a liar and a thief, but he had fortunately managed to restrain himself. His own memories of his father were vague and shadowy. David had never seemed to have much time for him although he had never been actively unkind to him. When Jack tried to talk to Olivia, his sister, concerning his curiosity about his father as a man—after all, she had had the opportunity to view their father through the eyes of an adult—she had told him curtly that she didn't want to discuss the subject.

It was no secret in the family how much Ben longed for David to return, but Jack wasn't sure how *he* would feel if he did.

It was Jon whom he turned to for advice and support…and for love.

'COME ON. WHO'S GOING to know? Your dad and his kind are out. Wouldn't you like me to take you upstairs and undress you and—'

'No.' Annalise tried to sound firm, but she knew her voice was trembling. Her body was trembling, too, but not with excited desire. No. What she actually felt was horribly afraid and nervous, all the more so because she could sense not just Pete's impatience with her refusal to have sex with him, but his boredom with her, as well. She'd become all too aware of just how much time he was spending with Patti and how triumphant the other girl looked.

'You're not real, do you know that?' he derided her bitterly now. 'Why are you so keen to hang on to it anyway? No one wants a virgin—it isn't cool. You should be grateful to me. I'd be doing you a favour.'

Annalise felt acutely sick. She knew that what he was saying was true. The crowd the band went around with was openly mocking about girls who hadn't had sex.

'Imagine not knowing what it feels like when a boy really makes you come,' Patti had said to her only a few days ago, closing her eyes and smiling a secret and, to Annalise, very enviable smile. 'They just don't know what they're missing, do they? Has Pete ever gone down on you?' she had asked casually.

Annalise's heart had missed a beat as she floundered for the right degree of insouciance.

'All my boyfriends have done it for me,' Patti had boasted. 'That's a sure way of telling that they love you. What else have you done?' Patti had asked her, fortunately not waiting for a reply to her previous question. 'My last boyfriend gave me twenty out of ten for the way I gave him head,' she had bragged. 'You should have seen him. He was really big. I bet Pete is, too, isn't he?' she had demanded with a sideways smirking look at Annalise's pink, hot face.

'Have you ever done it with more than one boy—or another girl?' Patti had continued. 'I went to this party once. It was cool, everyone doing it with everyone else. They'd got this stuff. You put it in your drink and it really turns you on…mind-blowing.'

'Drugs…?' Annalise had asked nervously. 'But—'

'Yeah,' Patti had agreed, changing the subject with lightning speed, demanding, 'Did you ever see your folks having sex?'

Numbly, Annalise had shaken her head.

'I've seen mine. I found this video. It was a scream. No wonder my dad is always telling my ma that she's got a fat bum. Not that he's got much room to talk.' She had pulled a face. 'Yuck. I couldn't do it with a fat old man, could you? No way. I like boys with fit, strong, horny bodies…just like your Pete's.'

'Okay, then, don't bother,' Pete announced, the

wheedling tone of his voice giving way to angry dismissal.

'Where…where are you going?' Annalise asked unsteadily as he dropped her hand and turned away from her. They were now in the shopping precinct, their regular meeting place on a Saturday afternoon. Pete liked to go to the local music store and listen to all the latest releases.

'Why should you care?' he responded sulkily. 'You don't want to go to bed with me, so why should I stay here with you?'

Annalise sucked in her breath on a sharp sob of despair. It was happening already, just as everyone had predicted. He was going to leave her…dump her. She didn't think she could bear the humiliation of it. He would tell everyone that she was still a virgin and they would all make fun of her…especially Patti.

But there was no way Annalise could give in to his urging. No way she could allow herself to be branded like her mother, because no matter what Pete might say, in the real world, the adult world, things were different. She had only to listen to her father to know that, and besides… A tiny quiver of fear slicked through her. Despite all she had heard, all Patti's boasts and enthusing, she just didn't feel that she wanted…

Ducking her head so Pete wouldn't see the betraying tears sheening her eyes, she wondered despairingly what he would say if she were to tell him that she was frightened, that she was afraid that having 'it'…doing 'it' would hurt.

Perhaps there was something wrong with her. Perhaps she wasn't quite like other girls…perhaps she was…horror of horrors…*abnormal* in some way.

Now, as she watched Pete being absorbed by the group, she hunched her shoulders and started to walk quietly away.

She was dreading tonight's party. For one thing, she didn't have anything to wear…at least not anything like Patti was going to be wearing. And for another… Her mouth went a little dry at the thought of what the evening might hold.

There would be drink, lots of it, according to Patti, and probably drugs. But the band would be playing and that would give her an excuse to sit somewhere on the sidelines. As Pete's 'girl' she was naturally excused from getting involved in the horseplay indulged in by the others. Pete was the 'boss', the 'top guy', and as his girl she was considered untouchable by anyone else. Thankfully.

But was she still Pete's girl? What had happened to the boy who had kissed her so sweetly and lovingly at the school dance last term? Pete had seemed so tender then...so caring. But that was before he had become involved with the band. Now everything was different, she acknowledged sadly. Now *he* was different.

AS THEY WALKED across the town square together, having come from Ruth Crighton's home, which was close to the church, Joss nudged his cousin and asked him, 'Isn't that the girl who was at the band practice the other night?'

Screwing up his eyes against the sharpness of the autumn sun, Jack followed the direction Joss was indicating.

Annalise was walking away from them, her body tight and hunched over. She looked lonely and pensive.

'I think so,' Jack agreed noncommittally.

'She's pretty,' Joss announced unexpectedly. 'Much prettier than that other one.'

'Pretty?' Jack questioned.

'Yes,' Joss confirmed, adding with insight, 'Other people might not see it yet, but that's just because she can't see it herself.'

'Uh-huh. You wouldn't be thinking of chancing your arm, not to mention other parts of your anatomy, with the boss's girl, would you?' Jack teased.

'Nope. She's not my type,' Joss returned loftily, adding with a grin in his cousin's direction, 'but I reckon she's yours!'

A passer-by tut-tutted as the pair of them started scuffling together, much as they had done when they were younger.

On her way home, Annalise stopped off at the restaurant owned by Frances Salter and her husband. They had given her holiday jobs in the past and she was hoping that they might have some more work for her now.

'Well, we could do with an extra washer-up,' Frances allowed cheerfully after Annalise had made her stammering request, ignoring the way her son was shaking his head at her behind Annalise's back. 'When do you want to start?' she asked the girl. 'Tonight?'

Blushing a little, Annalise shook her head. 'No…I…there's a party tonight. But I could do tomorrow lunch-time,' she offered eagerly.

'What do you mean we could do with an extra washer-up?' her son asked reproachfully once Annalise had gone. 'We've only just bought a brand-new, state-of-the-art dishwasher.'

'I know that,' Frances Salter agreed. 'But I just

can't help feeling sorry for her. She doesn't have the easiest of lives. Her father...' She paused and smiled at her eldest son. Her own family life was so happy that she felt that somehow she had to acknowledge her own good fortune by helping others out whenever she could.

She was always being teased by her family for not being able to turn anyone away. Every down-and-out for miles around knew they could always get a hot meal at her restaurant.

'I'm just paying my dues' was all Frances would say when her family asked her why she did it.

'CASPAR, HOW LOVELY to see you,' Maddy exclaimed as she opened her front door. 'Come in.'

'I'm not calling at a bad time, am I?' Caspar asked as she ushered him and his two small daughters inside, calling to her own children to come and see who had arrived.

'Not at all,' Maddy assured him. 'Max isn't here, I'm afraid. He's playing golf.' She wrinkled her nose. 'And I suspect there could be a slight delay at the nineteenth hole! How's Olivia? It seems ages since I last saw her,' Maddy continued as she led the way into her comfortable kitchen and the two girls were carried off by their cousins to inspect their toys.

'She's...she's very busy.'

Maddy, who was filling the kettle with water to make them both a drink, turned round to look at him, alerted to the fact that something was wrong by the cool tone of his voice.

'She *is* busy,' she agreed quietly. 'Jon and Jenny have both mentioned how hard she's working, and the fact that Katie has been taking some days off won't have helped, either.'

'Has she?' Caspar commented lightly. 'I'm afraid that Olivia and I don't have enough time together to discuss things such as other people's schedules. Hell,' he said in a much more forceful and explosive voice, 'we don't even have enough time together to discuss our own... I'm sorry,' he apologised as he looked across at Maddy. 'I didn't mean to let off steam like that, but—'

'It's all right,' Maddy reassured him. 'I can understand your concern. I've been rather worried about Livvy myself recently. But if you're planning a holiday for the two of you—'

'Not for the two of us,' Caspar interrupted grimly. 'Olivia refuses even to talk about it. She says she's got too much on... My half-brother, Bryant, is getting married,' Caspar started to explain. 'He's invited us to the wedding and I think we should go—as a family. Olivia seems to have other ideas. Of course, I appreciate that my people aren't Crightons,' he added sarcastically. 'And there's no way we could ever be described as close-knit, but this is the second time she's found a reason not to visit them and I'm beginning to run out of excuses for her. I'm even starting to wonder if it's having to spend time with my folks she's so against or having to spend time with me and the girls.

'I don't understand her, Maddy. She wanted children so much and yet she hardly has any time for Amelia and Alex and she certainly has no time for me.'

'Caspar, I *know* how much she loves all of you,' Maddy tried to reassure him again.

'Do you? So did I—once! Or at least I thought I did, but it seems that I was wrong. It isn't just that she's off sex,' he added rawly and frankly. 'I might be a man, but that doesn't mean I can't appreciate the depressive effect having a family and a full-time career can have on a woman's libido.'

'Much the same effect as it can have on a man's libido under the same circumstances,' Maddy pointed out gently, immediately defending her sex. 'But not feeling like having sex doesn't mean not loving someone.'

'No, but refusing to even discuss attending my brother's wedding does... I'm sorry,' he apologised again. Rubbing the back of his neck wearily, he tried to relieve the tension that had been building up in him ever since he had given Olivia his ultimatum.

He had never dreamed that it would come to this, that Olivia would absolutely and totally refuse not just to discuss the matter, but to speak to him at all. He swore she would have slept at that damned office of hers if she could. He'd certainly been tempted to stay safely out of the way in his university rooms these past couple of days and probably would have done so if it hadn't been for the girls.

'Olivia's changed, Maddy. She doesn't...she isn't the person she was.'

Perhaps not, but Caspar had changed, too, Maddy suspected. She found it worryingly ominous that Caspar was referring to Livvy as 'Olivia'. Almost as though he were deliberately trying to distance himself from her.

Her heart sank a little. She liked both Caspar *and* Olivia and didn't want to side with either one of them against the other.

'Perhaps you should try to talk to her again, Caspar.'

'Talk!' He grimaced. 'Olivia doesn't have the time, and when she does we just go over and over the same old ground—the same old grievances. I've tried to suggest we take time out together, but Olivia says I'm trying to pressure her and make her feel guilty. Yeah, I guess I am overreacting a little, but sometimes it feels like I just don't matter to her any more. I know my own family background could have been a role model for a book on dysfunctional families, but they *are* still my folks, and now that we've got the girls, I just kinda feel I want to mend a few family fences—for their sakes.'

'Tell Livvy that,' Maddy suggested gently. 'Sometimes we expect our partners to understand everything we're thinking and feeling without having to be told, but unfortunately, it doesn't always work that way.'

'It isn't just me that Olivia doesn't have much time for any more. It's even happening with the girls,' Caspar went on. 'Your kids are so lucky to have a mother like you, Maddy. You're always there for them.'

Maddy gave him a rather perturbed little smile. 'I *know* how much Livvy loves her children, Caspar,' she told him firmly. 'I know how much she loves all of you.'

'WASN'T THAT CASPAR I just saw turning out of the drive as I came in,' Max commented to Maddy half an hour later as he walked into the kitchen.

'Mmm…' Maddy acknowledged. 'He's worried about Livvy. He thinks she's spending too much time at work and apparently she's refusing to take time off to go to America to attend his half-brother's wedding.'

'I wouldn't get too involved there if I were you, Maddy. Married couples should sort out their own differences, and besides, if any man's going to be crying on my wife's shoulder, it's going to be me.'

As she looked up from the sauce she was making, Maddy teased, 'You aren't getting jealous, are you…not of Caspar?'

'Not of Caspar,' Max mimicked back. 'No. Then whom *should* I be getting jealous of?'

'No one,' Maddy protested.

As he watched her, Max wondered what Maddy would say if she knew just how jealous and insecure he actually sometimes felt. He hadn't forgotten how close he had come to losing her or how determinedly she had held him at an emotional distance even after they had been officially reconciled. Nor had he forgotten, either, how he had deliberately planned for her to conceive their third child, knowing that the emotional claim of the new life she was carrying, as well as those of the two children they already had, would prevent her from leaving him. He had told himself he was buying time and it had worked.

Those months of Maddy's third pregnancy had brought them together in a closeness that Max had vowed to cherish for ever.

But that didn't alter the fact that Maddy *had* planned to leave him. He knew how many other men envied him his marriage and his wife and he couldn't blame them. The old Max, the Max he had once been, would, no doubt, had he been one of those friends, have set out very resolutely to seduce a woman like Maddy for no other reason than it amused him to do so. Max knew he wasn't the only man to think like that. There were others and Maddy had a dangerously tender heart. He wasn't suggesting that Caspar was like that, no, but right now Caspar was feeling aggrieved and vulnerable, and Maddy…

'No, I'm not jealous,' Max told her with a

smile. 'I'd just rip apart any man who tried to take you away from me.'

Although she protested and shook her head at him, Maddy couldn't help but be inwardly flattered. It was rather nice to know that one's husband felt so possessive about one and it was especially nice for her, Maddy admitted, but she hadn't been in the habit of saying so recently to Max. Maddy had learned to be a little more sturdy and a lot more independent than the girl she had been when she first married him. But now she abandoned her feigned indifference and admitted, 'I like it when you get all possessive about me. It makes me feel—'

She wriggled and protested as Max crossed the kitchen and took her in his arms. 'You make *me* feel horny,' he told her trenchantly. 'Forget supper. I want to eat *you* and then—'

'Max,' Maddy said, laughing. 'The children...'

'No, I don't want to eat them,' Max replied mock seriously, relenting as he suggested, 'Give them their supper and let them watch that wretched video they've been going on about and then you and I—'

'Max...' Maddy warned.

'I'll go out and get you your favourite take-away,' he promised. 'It's Saturday night. Married couples always have sex on Saturday night.'

'No, they don't,' Maddy protested. 'Most of them have it on Sunday morning.'

'Mmm…' Max lifted his mouth from the warm curve of her throat where he had buried it. 'Well, we can do that, as well. I don't mind,' he offered obligingly.

PROPPING HIS HEAD UP, David leaned over to look down into Honor's sleeping face. Even in her sleep she was smiling. What was she dreaming of—him? He grimaced a little at his own vanity and then wondered if she would still be smiling if she knew the truth about him. Inevitably, they had spent what was left of the night together after he had insisted on going downstairs to find some candles. She had protested a little at the waste when he had lit them all after placing them round the bed.

'No?' he had queried softly. 'It will be like making love on an island becalmed in a dark sea.'

And as she had told him huskily later, there had been something almost magical…and mystical… about making love with one another in the flickering candlelight.

They had had breakfast in bed, giggling together like two children as they argued over who was responsible for the toast crumbs.

He had licked honey off her skin and she had...

David closed his eyes as he remembered the way she had touched and tasted him. In reality, they hardly knew one another, but there had been an honesty, a purity, about their coming together that had elevated it way above anything cheap or carnal.

It was both pointless and unfair to compare what they had shared with what he had had with Tiggy, but that didn't stop him knowing that all the real intimacy, the real sharing, the real loving, had been in Honor's arms...in Honor's body.

'We haven't used any precautions,' he had reminded her earlier this morning when she had touched him lovingly, whispering her desire for him. 'Or...'

'No.' She had shaken her head, laughing a little. 'At my age, I doubt that they're necessary. I've got two grown-up daughters,' she had reminded him. 'And as for safe sex—since neither of us has had a partner for a long time...'

'I have *never* had a partner,' David had told her honestly. 'A wife, yes, but a partner...no.'

'I used to wonder what I had done wrong, why fate wasn't sending me a man who would really love me,' Honor had told him dreamily. 'But that was before I learned how important it was to love myself.'

'And since then?' David had whispered as he nibbled gently on her ear lobe.

'Since then, I haven't needed anyone else's love,' Honor had replied honestly.

She had talked to him openly about her life, her past, but he had not been able to be similarly honest with her.

There was no real point, he reminded himself. Their time together could only be brief, their relationship transitory, and once she knew the truth she was bound to reject him. Who could blame her? But as he looked down into her sleeping face, David knew that he would have to tell her even though he couldn't really understand the compulsion that was driving him to do so. Just as he didn't understand why he had felt that he must come home.

What was he going to do now that he *was* here—spend the rest of his life skulking in the shrubbery at Queensmead?

'Honor...'

Reluctantly, she opened her eyes.

'There's something I have to tell you,' David began.

CHAPTER EIGHT

'CASPAR. WHERE ON EARTH have you been?'

Caspar's mouth twisted as he sent Amelia and Alex upstairs to get changed before turning to confront Olivia.

'Do you really care?' he challenged her angrily. 'It's five o'clock on a Saturday afternoon, for heaven's sake, Olivia. You left this house before eight this morning and—'

'I was back at half past one,' Olivia defended herself. 'But you weren't here. Where were you?'

'I took Amelia to dancing practice. She goes every Saturday—remember?'

'That only lasts an hour,' Olivia pointed out.

'I went to see Maddy,' Caspar told her quietly.

'To see *Maddy*…' Olivia stared at him in confusion and then started to frown as he refused to meet her eyes. 'Oh, I see,' she guessed. 'You went to see Maddy to cry on her shoulder. To complain about me.'

'She's concerned about you, Olivia. We all

are,' Caspar stated grimly. 'Everyone can see what you're doing to yourself and this family.'

'Can they? Are you sure about that, Caspar, or can they only see it because you've described it to them? What are you trying to do to me?'

'I'm not trying to do *anything* to you. It's what you're doing to yourself that concerns me. This paranoia you've developed about your work—'

'Paranoia?' Immediately, Olivia stiffened. 'What are you trying to say? That I'm mad... deranged...?'

'Don't be ridiculous,' Caspar protested.

'But that's what paranoia is, isn't it?' Olivia pressed. 'A form of madness. I work because I have to, Caspar.'

'You *have* to? Why?' he demanded sharply.

'Well, one very good reason is that we need the money,' Olivia defended herself. 'You know that. We couldn't have bought this house on what you earn as a lecturer. We run two cars. We live well, and you're the one who's insisted on the girls' having so many out-of-school activities. They all have to be paid for.'

'So it's *my* fault that you have to work. Is that it? It's *my* fault because I'm not a good provider...because I don't earn enough—'

'I said no such thing,' Olivia interrupted

sharply. 'Look, Caspar, *you* were the one who started this argument. You're just behaving like a spoiled, petulant child because I won't go to your brother's wedding. What I still can't understand is why you're so keen on going. You've admitted you're not close. According to you, you can't even remember all their names and—'

'God, Olivia, that was years ago. Yes, I *did* still feel sore about my childhood when I first came over here, but since then we've had the girls and now…' He made a brief, helpless gesture with his hands. 'This isn't a dress rehearsal. This is life…real life. It's time for me to make my peace with my family, my father—'

'Your father!' Olivia's mouth twisted. 'What is it about you men that makes you stick together…forgive one another anything? Ben would welcome my father back with open arms given the chance, and even Jon… I thought that Jon felt like I did…that he would never, could never, forgive my father, but the way he talks about him sometimes now it's almost as though—'

'As though what? As though he misses him? Olivia, they *are* twins.'

'Yes, and he's *my* father,' she returned fiercely. 'But that doesn't stop me hating him.'

Caspar started to frown. 'Look, why are we

talking about your father? It's my family we were discussing. You know, Olivia, sometimes I think you're obsessed by David. Yes, he did something very wrong and yes, I can understand how bad that must make you feel, but to keep dwelling on it the way you're doing—to keep digging it up, exhuming it—'

'I'm doing no such thing. It doesn't need exhuming. It's there, Caspar, there in front of me every day. How do you think I feel, knowing that other members of the family, that Uncle Jon and Max and the others *all* know what my father did, that they're probably watching me just to make sure—'

'Now I know you're beating yourself up over nothing,' Caspar broke in sharply. 'What the hell is this, Olivia? If you think that dragging up the whole trauma of your father's fraud is going to sidetrack me from wanting to go to the wedding, if you're trying to play for the sympathy vote—'

'You just don't understand, do you?' Olivia exploded, her face white and her eyes nearly black with temper. 'You just don't understand *anything*. I am *not* going to your brother's wedding and you can go and complain about me as much as you like to Maddy, because I'm *not* changing my mind. I *hate* men,' she cried furiously. 'You're all the same…you all want your own way regardless of what or whom you damage to get it—Gramps, my father, Max, you—'

'I'm not listening to any more of this,' Caspar told her tersely. 'I'm not responsible for what your father did or for the fact that Max is your grandfather's favourite. *None* of it's my fault!'

'Oh, God,' Caspar seethed as Olivia rushed past him and slammed the door behind her.

A LITTLE HESITANTLY, Annalise looked from the open kitchen door of Patti's parents' home into the hallway behind it, which was crammed with an excited press of teenagers.

'Are you sure your parents won't mind us being here?' she asked Patti uneasily. 'There's a lot of people I don't recognise. They could be gate-crashers.'

'So what? The more the merrier,' Patti drawled, giving a sultry pout in the direction of Joss and Jack Crighton as they came in.

'Why did you invite those two?' Annalise hissed at her.

'Because they're sexy,' Patti responded.

Annalise gave Jack a longer look, remembering the pity she had seen in his eyes the previous evening.

'Patti, I don't think we should be here,' she repeated to the other girl, wincing as she heard the high-pitched, excited scream of laughter coming from one of the other rooms, followed by the appearance in the doorway of an obviously very drunk girl with a bottle in her hand. 'Who is she?' Annalise demanded anxiously.

'Dunno,' Patti admitted. 'She came with a gang from Chester.'

'Chester!' Annalise protested. 'How did *they* know about a party here?'

Patti gave a careless shrug. 'Word gets round.' She went over to drape herself against the body of the thickset youth who had just walked in. 'Here, Toby,' she demanded. 'Aren't you going to kiss me?'

As he obliged, Annalise looked away. The all too sexual way in which Patti was pressing herself against Toby Horley's body and the cheers of the onlookers calling out a variety of openly suggestive comments were making her feel very uncomfortable.

She had come early to help Patti prepare for the party and now, as she searched all the new arrivals, she wondered why Pete was so late. The other members of the band were here. She could, of course, ask one of them where Pete was, but for some reason she felt reluctant to do so.

'Mmm...not bad...' Patti drawled as Toby released her.

'If you liked that, wait until you find out what I can *really* do.'

Annalise heard his boasting as he slid his hand very deliberately the length of Patti's body and let it rest between her legs. Squealing with laughter, Patti moved provocatively towards him, her expression suddenly changing as she saw what Annalise, who was too preoccupied, still hadn't seen.

'Pete. Look what Toby's doing to me,' Patti purred.

'Lucky guy.' Annalise heard Pete's response as she turned round just in time to see the admiring look he was giving Patti's skimpily clad body.

'Pete.'

Why did her own voice sound so hesitant and nervous? Perhaps Pete hadn't heard her and that was why he was ignoring her. Or perhaps—her heart thudded painfully—perhaps he was still angry with her about this afternoon.

'Pete...' she tried huskily again.

'I need a drink, doll,' she heard him saying to Patti as he kept his back to her. 'Where is it?'

'Come with me and I'll show you,' Patti responded, laughing as she ignored the cheers of the group that had gathered around her. 'It's this way,' she told him, taking hold of his hand and smiling up into his eyes as she led him away from Annalise.

It was a long time before Patti and Pete came back, and when they did, Annalise saw with sickly apprehension that Patti's lipstick was smudged.

She waited until she could see that Pete was on his own and then went over to him, touching him uncertainly on his arm and enduring the humiliation of being ignored by him for several minutes before he finally turned to look at her.

'What do you want?' he asked her truculently.

Annalise could smell the drink on his breath and she recoiled slightly from it. He was swaying, his eyes hot and glazed, and he smelt of something else, as well, something her deepest feminine instincts told her was the scent of another woman. Patti? Even so...

'I thought that you and I...' she began hesitantly, but he cut her off before she could finish.

'Well, you thought wrong, didn't you, babe?' he sneered arrogantly. 'It's *over*. What there was of it...which wasn't very much. I need a real woman…one who knows what it's all about. Go back and play with your dolls, little girl.'

It was over. He had dumped her and soon everyone would know. Hot tears of shame and anguish scalding her eyes, Annalise stumbled towards the front door. She couldn't stay here now. At the door she turned round. She could see Pete standing with Patti at his side. He was openly caressing her breast as she leaned against him, and as though Patti sensed that Annalise was watching them, she turned and gave her a triumphant look.

Half-blinded by her tears, Annalise stumbled out into the night.

'COME ON, I THINK it's time we made tracks.'

Joss looked questioningly at Jack.

'I thought you *wanted* to come,' he protested.

The party was a good deal more rowdy than Jack had expected. There was an atmosphere here that he didn't trust or like. He winced as he heard the crashing of glass from somewhere inside the house.

'Let's get out of here,' he urged Joss. 'I smell trouble.'

Joss, who had only come out of curiosity, nodded his head amicably. It took Jack several minutes of careful negotiating to extricate Jenny's car from the carelessly parked vehicles around it, but miraculously, he eventually managed to do so.

'I don't envy whoever's going to have to clear up back there tomorrow,' he said, shuddering as they drove down the dark lane that led to the main road.

'It was a bit wild, wasn't it?' Joss agreed.

'A bit!' Jack lifted his eyebrows. 'My guess is that the whole house is sure to end up trashed. Half the people there weren't from around here.'

'I certainly didn't know them,' Joss acknowledged. 'I tell you what I did see, though. Patti and Pete. Did you?'

'Yes, I did,' Jack said tersely, cursing as he suddenly had to swerve to avoid the girl who stepped blindly out onto the road in front of them. Braking, he stopped the car and wrenched open the door, yelling as he got out angrily, 'What the hell are you trying to do? Kill yourself?'

As she recognised Jack's voice, Annalise knew then that her humiliation was complete. Stiffening, she turned away from him, refusing to say anything, praying for him to just go away.

'Jack,' she heard Joss Crighton calling from the passenger seat of the car, but instead of turning away from her, Jack came up and grabbed hold of her arm, forcing her round to face him.

'Answer me, dammit,' he demanded. 'Are you...?' He stopped the moment he saw her face and her tears.

'Let me go,' Annalise demanded, mortified. He was the *last* person she wanted to see her like this.

Jack looked at her and then at the empty road. It was a good three-mile walk to Haslewich, and to leave her here alone at this time of night...a girl and in such a distressed state...

'Get in the car,' he told her abruptly. 'We'll give you a lift back to town.' When she refused to move, he told her impatiently, 'Come on. You *can't* stay out here. It isn't safe.'

Curious to find out what was going on, Joss got out of the car and came across to them, his voice warm with sympathy as he recognised Annalise and asked her in concern, 'What is it? What's wrong?'

'What the hell do you think's wrong?' Jack answered him shortly. 'You saw what was going on back there.'

'Oh, yes, of course,' Joss affirmed.

It had started to rain and heavily, and Annalise began to shiver as it penetrated her thin dress.

'Get in the car,' Jack repeated.

'Yes,' Joss added gently. 'Come back to town with us.'

Annalise wanted to refuse. Her pride demanded that she refuse, but suddenly, there was a burst of noise from the house behind them and the sound of car engines being started up and revved. She trembled a little to think of being found walking on her own by some of the drunken youths she had seen at the party.

'You can't be thinking of going back there,' Jack remonstrated, misinterpreting the anxious look she was giving the youths. 'You must be mad. What for? You saw what was happening. He doesn't—'

'Want me,' Annalise supplied for him, tight-lipped.

Jack looked away. 'He doesn't deserve you,' he had been about to say.

'Come on, let's get in the car,' Joss suggested, giving her an engaging smile. 'I'm getting soaked.'

Somehow or other it was much easier to accede to Joss's suggestion than it had been to Jack's demand.

'Where is it exactly you live?' Jack asked her as he drove down Haslewich's main street a little later.

'Oh, you can drop me here in the main square,' Annalise told him swiftly.

'Oh, it's no bother to take you home,' Joss assured her warmly. 'Is it, Jack?'

'None at all, once we know where home *is*,' Jack agreed grimly.

Tersely, she gave them her address. She could see how much Jack Crighton despised her and no wonder. No doubt, like Pete, he would have preferred to be with Patti.

They were outside her house now, but to her mortification as she got out of the car, so did Jack.

'What are you doing?' she asked him in a stifled voice as he came to her side.

'Seeing you safely to your front door,' he informed her curtly. 'It's considered the polite thing to do...to see a girl home safely.'

'That's if you're out on a date,' Annalise retorted. 'And we're...' Quickly, she looked away, telling him ungraciously, 'You didn't have to bring me home, you know. I could have walked.'

'You could have,' Jack agreed, adding, 'Look, don't take it out on me just because—'

'Because what? Because Pete dumped me?' she challenged him furiously.

'You're better off without him,' Jack blurted out, then wished he hadn't said anything as he saw the tears welling in her eyes. 'If he has any sense...' he began and then hesitated.

Shakily, Annalise found her key and opened the door, fleeing inside before Jack could say anything else. Now her humiliation was *totally* complete. He had seen her tears, known just how she felt.

Slowly, Jack made his way back to the car.

'She was very upset,' Joss commented as Jack restarted the car.

'Yes,' Jack said grimly. 'She was.'

AUTOMATICALLY, DAVID turned his head and ducked slightly out of view to avoid being seen by the driver of the car on the opposite side of the road as he turned into the lane leading to Foxdean. It was unlikely that he would be recognised, not by a casual passer-by at this time on a Sunday morning, who probably, like him, was going to buy the Sunday papers.

'Oh…freshly baked croissants *and* the Sunday papers. Wonderful…' Honor had enthused. 'I can't think of any more enjoyable accoutrements to a blissful Sunday morning in bed. Well, at least I *couldn't*!' she amended with a twinkle of naughtiness in her eyes.

'I'll go and buy the croissants and papers,' David had volunteered.

'And I'll make the coffee,' Honor had offered.

This harmony that seemed to flow so naturally between them made David feel that he had been given one of life's richest gifts, richer even in some ways than the surprising intensity of the sexual urgency they were sharing.

The previous day's storm had died away and the sky was fresh and clear, a low mist lying over the fields.

In Jamaica, Father Ignatius would already have been awake for several hours, making the most of the coolest part of the day.

David yearned to be able to talk to Honor about him, but he didn't know how she would feel about the work they had done. Sometimes even the most intelligent and educated people expressed fear and distaste when they learned the manner of sick people the priest was caring for. David had seen it in their faces when he had accompanied Father Ignatius to Kingston to attempt to persuade those with wealth or power to do something more than simply tell him that he was doing a wonderful job.

AIDS, leprosy, untreatable cancer—David had seen them all and, had his own reactions not initially been dulled and muted by the apathy of his own self-pity, he suspected he might very well have turned away in revulsion, too.

He could still recall the way he had reacted—

the way he had felt—when he had found Tiggy indulging in one of her orgies of eating and then the period of self-mutilation that would follow it, when the bedroom and bathroom and sometimes the whole house seemed tainted by the smell of her self-induced sickness.

He had seen and smelled far worse than that since then. He had choked back tears sometimes of anger and sometimes of pain but most often of anguish for the suffering of the afflicted, knowing that no matter what they did, it was impossible to save them.

'We all have to die,' the priest would tell him.

'To die, yes...but *not* like this,' David remembered protesting. He had known full well that the 'herbal' concoctions the priest made up for those who were in the last throes of their agonising illnesses were nothing less than the powerful narcotic drugs that were so readily available on the island. They were used for recreational purposes by those who could afford them, and even in medicinal form they were still too expensive for the poor to obtain.

It had seemed to him this morning, as dawn broke across the sky and he lay beside Honor in the bed that she had told him gently she wanted him to share with her, that there was something rather extraordinary and ordained by fate about the fact that she and the priest shared a common bond of wanting to help and heal others. They would like one another, he knew, and probably have so much to talk about together that he might well be excluded and forgotten by both of them.

He had wanted to tell her so. But then he remembered the other morning. When he had wanted to tell her the truth about himself, she had stopped him, smiling gently as she placed her fingers against his mouth and shook her head.

'No,' she had told him. 'No confidences, no confessions. Let's just enjoy what we have.'

And then she had reached out and touched him, and everything but the need she was fostering in him ceased to exist.

They had spent the rest of the day in leisurely companionship, working harmoniously together as she showed him how to harvest the herbs she was gathering, laughing as she taught him the correct way to collect them, offering him tantalising snippets of information about them as she did so.

Then later when it grew dark, they had made a meal together and afterwards talked about her plans for the house.

The house David had shared with Tiggy had been decorated in whatever style was currently 'in' and David had been too busy living the life he believed was the one he wanted to bother having any input into it. Significantly, or so it seemed to him now, he had never thought of the house as 'home'.

Home was... Home was a house like Jon and Jenny's, filled with warmth and love.

But when Honor started to talk about her plans for decorating Foxdean, David had discovered that he was as eager and enthusiastic to express his own ideas as she was hers.

'It seems that we both share a love of strong colours,' Honor had acknowledged at one point. 'My daughters both think I'm mad to even consider painting the sitting room a deep ochre. They think it's too dark as it is.' She smiled reminiscently. 'Abigail is frighteningly organised and tidy. She lives in one of those loft spaces where everything is white, wood or chrome.'

'And your other daughter?' David had asked her.

'Well, she's living in a rented flat at the moment. She's a bit undecided about where her future lies. She's thinking of changing her job, which could entail a move, maybe even abroad.'

'I think ochre would look wonderful,' David approved.

A long time ago when he was a child, he had been given a box of paints as a Christmas present by Aunt Ruth. Jon, he seemed to remember, had been given seeds. Knowing what he now did as an adult, he could see that Ruth had probably been trying to encourage them both to develop different sides of their personalities. Ruth was both a keen gardener and artistic. He had loved those paints, enthusiastically creating huge, bright sunbursts of colour, but when his father had seen what he was doing, he had become angry.

'Painting! Arty rubbish! That's for girls,' he had told him, and David had put the paints away, truculently repeating to Ruth the words his father had used when she asked if he was enjoying them.

And yet in Jamaica he had often itched for canvas to be able to capture the vibrant brilliance of the colours all around him.

'This poor house has been left cold and unloved for so long that it needs warm colours to bring it back to life,' Honor had said.

'Yes.' In David's mind's eye he could see the north-facing room where Honor had dumped boxes of books, which, she had informed him, would have to stay there until she had shelves made for them, painted in a warm terracotta.

'I want to decorate the stairs with a huge mural,' Honor had continued. 'All lovely glowing colours.'

'A Tuscan scene,' David had said, smiling. He had seen such murals in some of the villas where he had worked abroad, but Honor had shaken her head.

'No. What I've got in mind is something...' She had paused and screwed up her eyes in concentration. 'Something unique and special. Only I'm not sure just what.'

'How about copying some of the illuminated scripts that monks used to paint in their herbals?' David had suggested. 'The colours they used were wonderfully rich and you could create your own personal monastery garden with all the herbs you—'

'Oh! That's a wonderful idea,' Honor had interrupted him excitedly. 'Yes, that's exactly what I want. Now why on earth didn't *I* think of that? Oh, you are *so* clever.'

Her almost childlike enthusiasm had made David laugh, but at the same time he had been both thrilled and flattered that she had so obviously liked his suggestion.

They had spent the rest of the evening going through some of the older herbals Honor had collected, jotting down ideas, and then at bedtime

Honor had turned to him and very calmly and directly said, 'I'm going up now. I doubt that we're going to have a power cut tonight now that the storm's passed, but you'd be very welcome to share my bed—if you want to.'

She had left the room without waiting for his reply. He had caught up with her when she was halfway up the stairs.

'The way you make me feel, I'm not sure if I can make it as far as the bedroom,' he had confessed frankly before kissing her possessively.

Driving back along the empty roads through the mist-wreathed Cheshire farmlands, David reminded himself of that old maxim: 'Never look a gift horse in the mouth.' In other words, some situations did not profit from over-analysis or too close an inspection.

Once when David had asked the priest in exhausted anguish why people who were so innocent of any crime were punished with the ravages of dreadful and surely needless pain at the end of their lives, he'd admitted he didn't know.

'All I do know is that such things seem easier to bear if one has faith, beliefs, acceptance—call it what you will—if one accepts what is instead of seeking to find an explanation for it.'

To some, such an attitude of mind was a weakness; to others, it was a strength. David wasn't sure any more which side of the argument he favoured. All he *did* know was that on this misty autumn morning as he drove towards a house where a woman of almost magical enchantment waited for him, he was happier, more at peace, more fulfilled than he had ever been in his entire life. Perhaps Honor was right to insist that they live simply for the day. Why complicate or spoil things?

As he parked the car outside the house, he reached over to pick up the bag containing the croissants. They had been fresh from the baker's oven when he bought them.

COULD THERE BE a more perfect way to spend a lazy morning? Honor wondered happily as she heard David return.

She had had an idea for the décor of the potentially elegant dining room she wanted to discuss with him.

He had looked a little bemused the previous evening when she had commented on what was his very obvious artistic streak. She had to admit she had felt a little bit curious then about the circumstances of his life and why he was not just surprised by her recognition of his talent, but almost seemingly embarrassed and ashamed. Still, she did not intend to allow herself to become too curious about him. He was simply someone who was passing through her life and that was exactly what she wanted. She was perfectly happy as she was. She didn't need or want the complications of a committed relationship. She had so many plans, so many things she wanted to do. Selfish things, perhaps, to others, but surely she had earned the right to do what *she* wished, to be the person she had firmly pushed to one side so that she could be a daughter, a wife and a mother.

Her healing was very important to her. There was so much she still had to learn that she didn't want to feel she had to consider someone else's views and feelings if, for instance, she should decide to study more intensively or maybe even travel.

She had no fixed plans; that was the beauty of being where she was in her life right now, of being *who* she was. Yet there was no denying the extraordinary rapport she had with David or the unexpected pleasure of their shared intimacy.

It had felt totally wonderful to wake up this morning to find his body curved protectively around her own, the strength of his arm comfortingly warm where it lay across her, holding her.

'Coffee smells good,' David told her appreciatively as he came into the kitchen.

Honor didn't respond. She had her nose pressed blissfully up against the bag of croissants he had handed her.

'THIS REALLY WAS an excellent idea,' David told Honor later as he bent his head to lick some flakes of pastry off her skin.

'Mmm…it was, wasn't it?' Honor agreed lazily as she reached up and wrapped her arms around his neck, arching her body up to the tender ravishment of his mouth.

THERE HAD BEEN a good family turnout for church this morning, Jenny reflected as she discreetly guided Ben out into the thin sunshine. She had to admit that she and Jon didn't attend Sunday services as often as they should although barely a week passed without her walking through the churchyard and pausing for a few minutes by the small grave of her first-born child. She no longer felt the sharp, unbearable grief and despair she had experienced when she lost him, but there was still sadness…for Harry as well as for herself, for all that might have been.

'David was christened here,' Ben told her unnecessarily as they walked slowly towards the gate. 'You could see then what kind of man he would be. He never cried...not once.'

Jenny stiffened a little at her father-in-law's unspoken but implied criticism of her own husband.

'Laurence and Henry were his godfathers—and Jon's—not that either of them ever did very much for him. When David came back from London, they should have by rights offered him a place in chambers, but of course they were jealous that he would outshine their own boys.'

As she listened to him, Jenny forbore from pointing out that the reason Henry Crighton had not offered David a place in chambers was perhaps because David had been dismissed from his in London under something of a cloud.

'This family isn't the same without David,' Ben continued to grumble as Jenny guided him towards the car. 'He knew how to do things. People admired and respected him. He had a presence...an authority. He should have been a QC, you know. He would have been if it hadn't been for that wife of his.'

Jenny, who had heard the same boast allied to the same complaint a hundred or more times before, simply said nothing.

David had married Tania in the same spirit that

he had done almost everything else in his life—because it had seemed the easiest thing to do. At the time it had also given David the kind of boost to his ego that Ben had taught him was his rightful due.

'It's Jon's fault that David isn't here with us now,' Ben suddenly claimed, changing tack.

Jenny stopped in her tracks.

'That isn't true,' she told him with firm dignity. If anyone other than David was responsible for what had happened to him, then it was Ben, but there was no point in saying so. Ben was an old man and frail, but even so, she was not going to stand there and let him criticise her beloved Jon.

'Oh, you would say that,' Ben returned angrily. 'None of you really appreciated David—not even his own children.'

Jenny had had enough. She was the last person in the world to want to hurt another human being or to encourage an argument, but Ben really was being very unfair.

'No, Ben. You're wrong,' she corrected him determinedly. 'If anything, it was David who didn't appreciate *us*.'

'What are you saying?' Ben cried out fiercely. 'David was my son. I knew him better than anyone else. He—'

'*Jon* is *also* your son,' Jenny pointed out pithily.

'Oh, Jon,' Ben dismissed him impatiently.

To Jenny's relief, they had reached the car. She had no idea just what she might have said if the conversation had continued.

'Problems?' Max asked his mother sympathetically as Maddy helped Ben into the car.

'Not really,' Jenny assured him. 'I should be more patient with him, but it makes me so cross when he puts your father down. I know he's in a lot of pain, but sometimes...'

'Maddy's got this herbalist woman coming to see him tomorrow. Oh, which reminds me, I want to have a word with Dad. There's some land coming up for sale on the other side of town and I'm thinking about buying it.' When Jenny raised her eyebrows, he explained, 'It sounds a horrible thing to say, I know, but Ben isn't going to live for ever and ultimately that means that Maddy and I are going to have to look for somewhere else to live.'

'But I thought it was agreed that Ben would leave Queensmead to you and Maddy,' Jenny protested with a small frown.

'Well, yes, he did promise me Queensmead once I became a QC, but he's been dropping a lot of hints recently about believing that the house should ultimately be David's. By rights, of course, it should go to Dad, but Gramps still has this thing about David coming back. Maddy said that when she mentioned to him the other week about some alterations she wanted to make, he told her quite sharply that she had to remember that we are only tenants there. Despite what he promised me, he said that it's a Crighton tradition that the house goes to the first-born son.'

'But that's not fair,' Jenny protested. 'Heavens, you and Maddy have spent a fortune on the house. You pay all the bills and—'

'And the house belongs legally to Ben,' Max reminded her. 'He's like a bear with a sore head at the moment, Ma, and capable of doing any-thing, which includes leaving Queensmead to just about anyone. In his defence, I have to admit that it can't always be easy for him, having three small children running around.'

'Without the care Maddy gives him he'd have to go into some kind of sheltered accommodation. He could never live on his own,' Jenny pointed out.

'Mmm…well, Maddy and I have agreed that there's no use in getting in a state about it. We've already agreed that even if he did leave Queens-

mead to me, we'd have it valued and make sure
that all the grandchildren got an equal share of
that value.'

'Oh, Max, no one would expect you to do that,'
Jenny told him.

'Maybe not,' Max acknowledged quietly, 'But
I'd certainly expect it of myself.'

AS HE TURNED into the narrow street with its mixture of medieval, Tudor and Georgian buildings,
Jack began searching for the door he wanted, examining the houses until he saw the one he was
looking for.

It had been dark when they dropped Annalise
off last night, but he still recognised it.

When he woke up this morning, the last thing
on his mind, the last *person* on his mind, had been
her. But then Joss had persuaded him into going
to church. As boys, they had both sung in the
choir, and although Jack was loath to admit it,
there was something comfortable and familiar
about the age-old ritual of being inside the ancient
church with its unique scent of damp stone, wood,
velvet and flowers.

Whilst Joss was talking with his sister Katie,
her husband Seb and their delightful—if quite a

handful—twin sons, Jack had seen his chance and slipped away.

The street was empty. A little hesitantly, he approached the house and rang the bell.

Annalise jumped nervously as she heard the doorbell ring, her hopes soaring that maybe Pete had had a change of heart and come round to beg her forgiveness.

Her father, fortunately, was out and her two brothers were squabbling heatedly over the computer.

Quickly pulling the clip out of her blonde hair, she smoothed it down with trembling fingers and hurried to the door. When she opened it to see Jack standing on the doorstep, the excitement faded from her eyes.

'What do you want?' she demanded ungraciously.

Shrugging dismissively, Jack told her tersely, 'Nothing. I just happened to be walking past, so I thought I'd call and see if you were all right.'

'All right? Why shouldn't I be?' Annalise challenged him defensively.

It was bad enough that her visitor wasn't Pete, but for it to be Jack Crighton and for him to remind her of her humiliating loss of face last night made it ten times—no, a hundred times—worse.

Annalise was just about to close the door on him when there was a wail of protest from the living room followed by a loud crash.

Immediately fearing the worst, knowing what her brothers were like, Annalise hurried down the hallway and into the room, unaware that Jack had followed her. She saw in dismay that the crash had been caused by something being thrown at the fish tank, which now had a large jagged hole in it. Water and fish were flooding onto the chair and carpet until, above the boys' protests that it was not their fault, she heard Jack saying crisply, 'One of you go and get a bucket and keep away from that broken glass.'

'A bucket won't do any good,' Annalise protested.

'Yes, it will,' Jack told her calmly as he made his way towards the tank. 'The hole's less than halfway down, and if we can patch it up temporarily, we can lift the tank up and put it in the bath. That way, if the glass does give way, at least the fish should be safe.'

Before she could say anything, one of her brothers, Teddy, rushed in with the bucket, and Jack deftly used it to catch the growing flood.

'The fish are all over the floor…dying!' the boy said in panic.

'Here, you hold this,' Jack instructed Annalise, moving to one side so that she could take the bucket from him. He knelt down on the floor and carefully picked up the squirming fish. 'No. Don't you touch them,' he warned Teddy firmly. 'You might cut yourself on the glass,' he went on to explain as he carefully slipped the rescued fish back into the now nearly half-empty tank.

'Will they live?' Teddy asked anxiously when Jack had rescued the last of them.

'We'll have to see,' Jack answered calmly, adding, 'If you've got some newspaper and a roll of cling film, we can fix the hole whilst we carry the tank upstairs.'

Half an hour later, with the fish tank safely placed in the bath, Jack shook his head at the boys' offer of a game on their computer.

'Sorry, but Aunt Jenny will be wondering where I am. Look,' he suggested, 'I think there might be a tank in the garage at home. If we've still got it, I could bring it round and you could use it until you get another one.'

'Did you used to have fish?' Teddy asked.

'Yes, we did,' he replied.

'What happened to them?' the younger of the two boys, Martin, asked with interest.

'My mother didn't care for fish, so I had to get

rid of them,' Jack told him briefly. 'Fortunately, Aunt Jenny said that Joss could have them.'

'But...' Annalise began, then bit her lip. She had been about to say that she assumed that he had always lived with his aunt and uncle.

'Look, if I can find the tank, I'll call round with it tomorrow evening after work, if that's okay with you. With any luck, the cling film should hold until then.'

'Well, if you're sure it's no trouble...' Annalise accepted a little reluctantly.

As Jack had calmly repaired the damage to the fish tank and while they had carried it upstairs, she had tried to visualise Pete doing what he had done, but she knew that there was just no way Pete would have bothered to involve himself in their small family drama.

It still made her heart ache with sick misery to think that everyone would know by now that he had dumped her. She would have to face her classmates all too soon.

'Come on, you two,' she urged her brothers now. 'I've got to go out to work and you have to tidy up your rooms...'

'You work?' Jack frowned. 'I thought you were still at school.'

'Yes, I am,' Annalise agreed, telling him curtly,

'but some of us have to work, as well, you know. We don't all have rich families.'

The look Jack gave her made her flush uncomfortably.

'Where are you working?' he asked her.

'For my aunt, Frances Salter. They own the restaurant in town.'

'Oh, she's Guy Cooke's sister, isn't she?' Jack asked.

'Yes,' Annalise said. 'But if you're thinking that because I'm part Cooke that that means...' She stopped and turned on her heel. 'I'll show you out.'

As he followed her, Jack made to catch hold of her arm, demanding quietly, 'What did you mean...what you just said?'

'I didn't mean anything,' Annalise denied, shrugging, but she could see from his expression that he wasn't going to be fobbed off. 'There's a thing they say in town about Cooke girls that... that they're easy,' she burst out, red-faced. 'And if you're thinking that I—'

'Now just a minute,' Jack said, putting out his free hand to stop her from opening the front door whilst he held her arm with the other. 'You're the one who mentioned it, not me. I...I had no idea that you *were* a Cooke and even if I had... Is that why you think I've come round here? Because I…because I'm looking for someone easy? I'm not that desperate for sex,' he declared loftily. But to his bemusement, instead of looking relieved, Annalise's eyes immediately filled with tears, her hands bunching into small, anguished fists.

Trying weakly to strike him, she exclaimed passionately, 'It isn't my fault that I'm not sexy…or that I don't…that I haven't… I hate you,' she cried out to Jack's astonishment. 'I hate you.'

What on earth had he done? All he had said was that he hadn't thought of her as being easy and she was behaving as though he had somehow insulted her, when in fact…

'Hey, come on,' he told her gruffly as he reached out to grasp her flailing hands. Tears were pouring down her face and her whole body was shaking. Her hands, her wrists, were so small and fragile, her bones so delicate and fine. 'Please don't cry,' Jack begged her huskily. 'I didn't mean…'

Somehow without meaning to do so, Jack discovered that he was holding her in his arms, pressing her wet face against his shoulder. She was crying in earnest now, deep, racking sobs.

'I know what everyone believes, but it isn't

true,' she wept against his shoulder. 'And when Pete tells them, they're all going to be laughing at me.'

'When he tells them what…that he's given up a girl like you for someone like Patti? It won't be you they'll be laughing at,' Jack assured her positively.

Annalise lifted her head from his shoulder and gave a small hiccup. 'You can't mean that,' she said blankly. He was lying to her, she knew. No boy could possibly prefer her to a girl as sexy and experienced as Patti.

She really had the most gorgeous eyes, Jack decided a little giddily. Maybe so, but she was far too young for him, he told himself sternly. He was nineteen and she…

'How old are you?' he asked her huskily.

'Eighteen,' Annalise lied promptly, then when she saw the look he was giving her, admitted reluctantly, 'Seventeen, but I'll be eighteen in March.'

Eighteen in March, but she'd be a very young eighteen, Jack could tell, which meant that a man who became involved with her would be taking on a serious responsibility—making a serious emotional commitment—because she certainly deserved much better than what Pete Hunter was giving her. Much better, Jack warned himself grimly, and that meant, no matter what message his body was giving him and no matter what her relationship with Pete might have been, that she was strictly off limits so far as he was concerned. He had his education to think about; he couldn't afford to get emotionally involved.

'You shouldn't be running around with people like Hunter,' he told her sternly. 'And if I were your father—'

'My father!' Annalise's eyes widened.

'Well, your brother,' Jack amended.

It made his blood run cold to think what might have happened to her at last night's party. Didn't her family realise what kind of risks she was taking? When Olivia's girls, his nieces, were that age, there was no way he wouldn't have something to say if *they* started getting themselves tied up with bad'uns like Pete Hunter.

After he said goodbye to her, Jack was struck by the awesome, heavy responsibility that being a man involved.

CHAPTER NINE

'I'VE GOT TO SEE a potential new patient today,' Honor told David as they ate breakfast.

'Well, I'm going to make a start on stripping back the rotten roof timbers where the slates are missing to see just how extensive the damage is and then when I've done that I'll walk over to Fitzburgh Place and see the estate manager. It might be an idea for you to look into the question of that generator we were both talking about,' he added thoughtfully.

'Mmm...' Honor agreed. 'It's probably time to update the central heating, too, as we discussed.'

After talking over Honor's plans for the house for another half an hour, she announced that if she didn't go upstairs and get dressed she was going to be late for her appointment.

'I'll see to these,' David offered, indicating the breakfast things on the table, then, as Honor stood up and leaned across to kiss him, she reflected that they were so comfortable with each other, so compatible, that an unknowing observer might have assumed that they were a couple of long-standing.

'I DON'T CARE *who* this woman is. I'm *not* seeing her. Herbalist…hocus-pocus, if you ask me,' Ben grumbled when Maddy told him that Honor was coming to see him.

'Well, you're the one who's in pain,' Maddy agreed calmly, 'and if you don't think—'

'She won't be able to do anything,' Ben persisted, but Maddy could see that he was speaking less aggressively.

'Well, no, perhaps she won't,' she acknowledged cheerfully, 'and I must admit that Dr Forbes thought I was being silly in consulting her—'

'Forbes said that?' Ben interrupted her. Smiling to herself, Maddy looked away, busily dusting the already dust-free surface of his desk. The antagonism that Ben felt towards their long-suffering local GP was no secret to her.

'Well, he seemed to think that there isn't any reason for you to be experiencing pain,' Maddy continued sunnily.

'He thinks that, does he?' Ben roared. 'And just how the hell would he know? It isn't his ruddy body, is it? What does this woman say?' he asked Maddy suspiciously.

'Well, she said she would have to talk to you first, but she seemed to think she might be able to do something to help,' Maddy replied cautiously.

'If she starts thinking I'm going to drink some filthy concoction...'

To Maddy's relief, she saw a car coming to a halt outside the house. Ben really was becoming increasingly difficult.

'Problem?' Max asked her a few minutes later when she stepped into the hallway and closed the door to Ben's study behind her. 'I did warn you,' he added as he collected the post and started to sift through it.

He was spending the day working at home and Maddy knew that his father was coming over to see him to discuss his plans to buy some land.

Personally, she would hate to have to move from Queensmead, especially into a brand-new modern house, but at the same time she fully accepted that Queensmead belonged to Ben.

'You did,' Maddy agreed as she went to open the door. 'Please come in,' she welcomed Honor warmly. 'This is...'

As she turned round to introduce Honor to

Max, she realised that her husband had conveniently disappeared.

'It's this way,' she said instead, guiding Honor towards Ben's study. 'I'll introduce you to my grandfather-in-law and then I'll leave the two of you alone together. He normally has his tea and biscuits at eleven, so—'

'So if I need help before then, I'll shout,' Honor responded with a smile.

Ben Crighton was every bit as difficult as his daughter-in-law had warned, Honor acknowledged, but she could also see that he was in a lot of pain. She suspected it was not so much caused, as he believed, by his hip-replacement operations but by the fact that prior to them he had perhaps not been using his body properly. Whilst she could offer him no outright cure, a carefully balanced diet underpinned with various herbs and creams could make a significant improvement, not just in lessening his discomfort but also in increasing his mobility.

'What kind of diet?' Ben demanded suspiciously. 'Not expecting me to live on some kind of vegetarian mush, are you? A man needs red meat.'

'Carnivores need red meat,' Honor counselled him firmly, 'and when they can't catch it and kill it, they die. Human beings are rather more fortunate.'

She saw to her amusement that that silenced him, but she suspected it wouldn't be very long before he launched another offensive against her. She glanced discreetly at her watch. It was almost eleven o'clock. Before she went any further, she could do with talking to Maddy Crighton to see what alterations could be made with immediate effect to his diet.

'Go and tell Maddy that it's eleven o'clock,' he told her rudely. 'I want my tea.'

Calmly, Honor stood up just as the door opened and Maddy came in carrying a tray.

'About time,' Ben greeted her belligerently.

'I thought you might like to have your tea in the kitchen with us,' Maddy told Honor with a smile.

'Us?' Ben questioned, frowning.

'Yes. Jon's here. Max wanted to see him.'

'Huh, some son. Doesn't even bother to tell me he's coming round or to come and see me even though this is *my* house. If it had been David...'

Hastily, Maddy guided Honor out into the hallway. 'I'm sorry about that,' she apologised. 'Ben can really be dreadfully rude at times. Jon is my father-in-law, by the way, and Ben's son. Da-

vid…was…is his twin brother,' she told Honor
by way of explanation. 'Do you think you can do
anything to help?' she asked anxiously as she led
the way to the kitchen.

'I hope so,' Honor confirmed cautiously. 'But
to what extent I *can* help depends very much on
your grandfather-in-law.'

'Oh dear,' Maddy sighed. 'I rather thought you
might be going to say something like that. He
flatly refuses to take the pills our GP prescribes
for him and—'

'And he's told me that there's no way he in-
tends to give up red meat or have his food mucked
about with, or drink some hocus-pocus stuff that
will probably kill rather than cure him,' Honor
added.

'Oh dear, he said *that* to you, did he?' Maddy
sympathised as she pushed open the kitchen door
and called out, 'Max, Gramps has been truly hor-
rid to Ms Jessop.'

As Honor followed her into the kitchen and saw
the two men standing together by the table, she
came to an abrupt standstill.

'Honor, are you all right? You look rather
pale,' she heard Maddy commenting anxiously.

She stared at the man who, for a split second,
she had actually thought was the same man she

had been sharing her home with for the past few weeks—the same man she had been sharing her bed, herself, with. *No!* Not the same man—almost but not quite. There were some differences, the sort you might naturally expect in adult identical twins. Twins—David was this man's twin brother, which meant...

Disciplining her rioting thoughts, she acknowledged the introductions Maddy was making. Jon Crighton, son of Ben, her reluctant patient, and brother of David. Hadn't Maddy said the name with a distinct note of disapproval and sharpness in her voice almost as though just saying it brought a bad taste to her mouth?

During the years of her marriage, both for her own survival and for the sake of her children, Honor had learned not to betray what she was feeling. She was glad of that self-discipline now as she immediately forced herself to produce a smile and shake her head, reassuring Maddy, 'I'm fine.'

It was incredible just how alike the two men were, but when he shook her hand, she knew immediately that, were she blindfolded, she would know which of them was which simply by touch alone.

Even so, she couldn't quite stop herself from

asking as Jon released her hand, 'You have a twin brother?'

'Yes,' Jon agreed with a smile.

'And therein lies the crux of Gramps's main problem,' Maddy admitted ruefully, casting a quick look at both Jon and Max before explaining, 'I know from what you said to me when we spoke on the telephone that you believe in a holistic approach to treating your patients, and because of that...' She paused and took a deep breath. 'We've agreed that we should perhaps fill you in on a little of our family history.'

Honor listened attentively as Maddy sketched out the events leading up to David's disappearance and the effect his absence was having on his father.

'Ben misses him dreadfully,' Maddy explained, 'and I think that if anyone were to tell him that David isn't going to come back, he would just give up.'

'No, he wouldn't,' Max said robustly. 'He would simply refuse to believe it. Personally, I don't think that David ever will come back.'

'Not even though he has a family here?' Honor asked quietly. 'A daughter, you said, and a son, as well as his father and—'

'A daughter and a son whose lives he walked

out of,' Max reminded her sharply. 'Neither of them would welcome him back, especially not Olivia. She will *never* forgive him for what he did.'

Silently, Honor digested what he was saying. It was an odd sensation sitting here with David's family, listening to them talk about him. The man they had described, though, was a stranger to her. His shallowness, his conceit, his selfishness, all of which came through so strongly in what they said about him, were not aspects of his personality that she could recognise.

Where was his humour, his humility, his humanity, the warmth and compassion *she* had sensed so clearly in him?

'This money you say he took...' Honor began, but Jon shook his head somewhat impatiently.

'The money isn't the issue,' he exclaimed, surprised at how much the family had opened up to this woman who, he believed, genuinely wanted to help his father.

'Dad,' Max protested. 'Of course it is.'

'No, it isn't, not now,' Jon denied. 'Yes, what he did *was* wrong, very wrong, but that is between him and his conscience. Thanks to Ruth's generosity, a potential disaster was successfully averted.'

'Look,' Max told him, 'if anyone should be defending Uncle David, it should be me. After all, it was always *me* he favoured over and above Olivia, even though she was his daughter.'

'He was just repeating the lessons he learned from our father,' Jon said. 'Sons are of more value than daughters.'

'And some sons are more valued than others,' Max cut in drily. 'You needn't do him any favours, Dad. After all, when did he do any for you? He knew when he walked away from the mess he'd caused that you'd be the one left carrying the can.'

'*He* probably didn't see it that way,' Jon chided Max gently. 'Whatever his weaknesses, David was never knowingly malicious.'

'Do you miss him?' Honor heard herself asking Jon.

'I don't miss his actual presence,' Jon admitted cautiously as though he was weighing his words. 'We were never close either as children or adults.'

'No, Gramps saw to that,' Max interjected and was silenced by a brief shake of Jon's head.

'But what I *do* miss is some sense of knowing that he's there. It's hard to explain, but it's as though…as though in an odd way that some part of *me* is incomplete. Yet my life has never been more fulfilled or fulfilling.'

'You've never said anything about this before,' Max said in a slightly chagrined voice.

'I've never really thought about it much before,' Jon reassured him, 'and to be honest I don't really know why I feel the way I do now. Perhaps it has something to do with a conversation your mother and I had a little while back about the closeness of twins.'

Turning to Honor, he told her wryly, 'We had been discussing Ben's health and his desire for David's return, and Jenny suggested that I might try to contact him telepathically. We have twin daughters of our own, and as she reminded me, they *do* have a way of somehow knowing when one of them needs the other. Mind you, *they've* been like that since they were children. David and I never were.'

'Are you trying to say that you've been taking what Ma said seriously?' Max asked him in some astonishment, exchanging stunned looks with Maddy. 'You never said—'

'Because there wasn't anything *to* say,' Jon responded, adding in exasperation, 'It isn't as though I've been sitting around willing David to make some kind of telepathic contact with me. It's just…well, I just can't help thinking about him.'

'He won't come back,' Max insisted again. 'There wouldn't be any point. His marriage is over. Tania has divorced him. Jack is far happier with you and Ma than he ever was at home. Olivia makes no secret of the fact that she never wants to see him again. Who, apart from Gramps, is there for him to come back for? And if Gramps knew what he's done, how close he came to destroying the family reputation that he's so obsessive about, I doubt even he'd welcome him!'

'I think you're wrong, Max,' Maddy intervened gently. 'Parental love is very strong, very forgiving.'

'Yes, it is, as I have good cause to know,' Max agreed, looking warmly at his father. 'But Gramps doesn't love Uncle David. All right, all right, I know,' he conceded when both Maddy and Jon started to object. 'But think about it. It's true. What Ben loves so single-mindedly about Uncle David is the fact that to him he's the twin brother he himself lost. I doubt if he's ever actually seen David as he really is or if he'd want to.'

Jon gave a small sigh as he listened to Max. Little as he liked to admit it, he suspected that his son was probably quite right.

'Well, be that as it may,' he commented quietly, 'I think we've probably bored Ms Jessop enough already with the sorry tale of our family history.'

'I'm not bored,' Honor said truthfully. 'But I can see what you mean,' she confirmed to Maddy, 'and I agree that your grandfather-in-law's health is quite likely being affected by his emotional unhappiness.'

'So given that we can't bring David back for him, is there *anything* you can do to help?' Maddy asked.

'I'll do what I can,' Honor replied, standing up. She desperately wanted to be on her own, to digest what she had just learned. David had lied to her about his surname. David Lawrence...it had suited him somehow.

LORD ASTLEGH'S estate manager was just as helpful as Honor had told David he would be, inviting him to take whatever he might need from the estate stores.

'I was told to tell you that Lord Astlegh's happy for his cousin to have whatever she might need,' he told David. 'In the old days he'd have been able to send down a team of men to put the house in order, but we just can't afford to carry that kind of workforce these days. When we do need extra men, we hire them in.'

'Ms Jessop has been talking about updating the house's central heating system,' David told him, 'and she wants to open up the original fireplaces.'

'Does she? Well, we've got some original radiators that were ordered when central heating was first put in the Place and never used. Are you planning to do the work yourself?'

'It all depends,' David said. 'I'm certainly not a qualified plumber, but she was telling me that there's some kind of problem getting men to work on the property.'

'Yes, I believe so. I'm not from round here myself, so I don't know that much about it, but I understand that Lord Astlegh had trouble himself in the past getting anyone local to work there.'

'One thing she does need,' David confided, 'is a generator. The power supply to the house is liable to interruption.'

'That shouldn't be too much of a problem,' the manager assured him. 'In fact...what kind of car have you got? If it's an estate—'

'I didn't come by car. I walked,' David answered promptly.

'You walked!' The other man looked surprised. 'OK, well, I'll check out a generator for you. I've got some fencing to take care of close by the house this week and I'll bring it for you then.'

'Excellent,' David said, thanking him.

Ten minutes later as he walked back towards the cart track, he took a detour through the recently established workshops Honor had told him about, curious to see what had been done. It had occurred to him that if there was a cabinet-maker amongst them, he could ask for some replacement window frames to match the originals.

As he crossed the cobbled courtyard, two boys emerged from one of the units, both of them tall, but it was only one of them whom David really saw. Stiffening, he stared. His heart stood still and he could scarcely breathe. Shock coursed through his body like icy water, immobilising him.

Greedily, he drank in every tiny detail of his son whilst at the same time retreating out of their line of sight. In a series of flashbacks he compared Jack as he was now with the child he had been. He ached to go over and hold him in his arms, to run his hands over him—flesh of his flesh—his child, his son. Tears scalded his eyelids. How could he ever have been foolish enough to throw away the love they could have shared?

Jack had grown taller since his visit to Jamaica and broader, too. He was laughing at something the other boy had said. Jon's youngest, Joss, David guessed. They looked similar enough to be brothers, Jon's and his own features stamped distinctively on their faces.

As he watched, David saw Jack punch Joss playfully on the arm, shaking his head as though in denial of something Joss had said. They were walking towards him and David cursed a little, moving deeper into the shadows.

'OK, so I took her the fish tank. She wasn't even there. She was still at work. So what,' he heard Jack saying.

'So what? Why did you go round in the first place if you don't fancy her?' Joss demanded with a grin. 'You said yourself that she was the one you preferred.'

'I might have said that, but that doesn't mean... Come on, I'm starving. I hope that Aunt Jenny has some of her game pie for lunch.'

To David's relief, they changed direction and began moving away.

Jack...his son... A fierce shock of raw emotion speared through him. He hadn't any right to Jack's recognition. He hadn't any right to anything. After all, what had he cared for Jack's right to his love and protection, his fathering, when he had walked out of his life? Nothing. Nothing at all, but it still hurt like hell having him so close, knowing he could have reached out and touched him.

HONOR HAD no other appointments. It had been her intention to stop off in the town on her way back from seeing Ben Crighton and collect some paint charts so that she and David could look at them. Now, though, paint charts were the last thing on her mind.

As she reached the entrance to the lane that led to the house, she stopped the car on the roadside. Then coming to an abrupt decision, she restarted the engine and drove past. She couldn't go back yet. She had too much to think about.

'There's something I have to tell you,' David had said, but she had stopped him. Neither his past nor his future were any concern of hers, she had told herself. All she wanted, all she needed, was the here and now. When it was over, when the unexpectedly fierce fire of passion they had lit between them burned itself out, she would be quite happy to see him move on.

She owed him no loyalty, no compassion, no support. There was a lay-by ahead and Honor pulled into it, stopping the car again, her mind a mass of confused thoughts.

It wasn't David's 'crime' that concerned her. Financial fraud, theft... It was dishonest, yes, deplorable, maybe, but there were worse offences, far, far worse.

'He won't come back,' Max Crighton had said, and Honor had seen in their eyes that they all shared his belief.

But he *had* come back. Why? Not for financial gain, Honor would stake her life on it. Then *why*? To see a daughter who, by all accounts, hated him? To see his son who apparently was much happier living with his uncle? To see his father...his brother...?

Why should she care? Why *did* she care?

Caring was the one thing she had resolved not to do. Caring led to complications and she didn't want complications.

This is ridiculous, she told herself crossly. You've known the man hardly any time at all. You're forty-four years old, too old to believe that falling in love is anything more than a trick of nature designed to ensure the continuation of the species. The problem was that mankind had decided to try to improve on nature and turn what was designed to be simply an urge to mate into something it was never intended to be. She was beyond the mating stage, way beyond it. Love, real love, had nothing to do with the urgency of sexual desire. It involved knowing someone, and knowing another person required time and dedication. It also required a certain degree of selflessness and commitment, neither of which she had any desire to give.

She didn't *have* to get involved, she reminded herself. She could turn the car round and drive back to Foxdean and just say nothing. The Crightons had no idea that David was here, living with her, and David didn't know who the patient was she had been going to see today.

But then, as she drove down the lane, she could hear Jon Crighton telling her almost in bewilderment, 'I just can't help thinking about him.'

'JUST BE CAREFUL,' Annalise warned her brothers. 'We don't want that fish tank damaged. After all, it isn't ours.'

She had been out when Jack Crighton had come back with the tank. They had asked her to stay on at the restaurant and she had told herself that she had no reason to want to see him again. Why should she have?

When she eventually got home, the fish had already been installed in their new tank.

'Jack did it,' the boys had told her.

'Nice lad,' her father had commented gruffly.

Annalise had said nothing. She hadn't told them, either, that when she stepped out of the back door of the restaurant, Jack had been there waiting for her.

'What are you doing here?' she'd demanded sharply.

'I thought I'd walk you home,' Jack had told her.

Walk her home?

'I'm not a child,' she had begun belligerently.

As they crossed the town square, she'd seen a couple of girls from school walking in the opposite direction. When they spotted her with Jack, they had stared at them.

'What's wrong?' Jack had asked her as he noticed the anxious glance she gave them.

'They'll tell everyone at school they've seen me...us,' she had told him crossly.

'So...is that a problem?' Jack had asked her unperturbedly. His lack of concern fuelled her growing anger.

'Maybe not for you,' she said, 'but now they've seen us together, they're going to think...'

She stopped, compressing her lips, but he guessed what she had been about to say, grinning as he teased, 'You mean they're going to think that we're seeing one another?'

'Yes. I don't know why you're smiling,' she choked angrily at him.

'No. Perhaps it's because *I* rather like the idea,' Jack told her.

He rather liked the idea!

She didn't know where to look, her anxiety increasing as she wondered just what it was he thought he was going to get from her. He was nineteen and heading off for university. He had probably slept with loads of girls. He probably thought she'd slept with Pete, too. Perhaps he did think it was true what they said about Cooke girls and he was just looking for some easy sex whilst he was at home. Well, if he thought *she* was about to give it to him...

And it was then she saw them...Patti and Pete. They were just getting out of Pete's car and Patti was clinging possessively to his arm.

A hot tide of angry chagrin washed over her, and without weighing the consequences of what she was doing, she turned impetuously to Jack and told him, 'You can kiss me if you want to.'

Kiss her? Jack was bemused. What on earth had made her say that? Then, out of the corner of his eye, he saw the other couple. He didn't know whether to remonstrate with her or laugh. But as he looked at her and saw the aching despair in her eyes, he knew he wasn't going to do either.

As he leaned over her, shielding her from any onlookers, he slid his hand against her neck, stroking her throat like a lover and saying softly, 'When I kiss you, it won't be out in the street. It will be somewhere private, *very* private, and it will be very special.' His voice grew thicker and slower. 'When I kiss you...'

He stopped speaking and lifted his hand to brush away the tears brimming from her eyes.

'You're too young...you're much too young,' he groaned, and then he was holding her tight. Shocking quivers of sensation were running through Annalise, making her feel dizzy and making her want to stay pressed up against him for ever.

But he was already releasing her, and as she peeped over his shoulder, she saw the exhaust fumes from Pete's car as it raced noisily out of the square.

He had left her outside her front door without saying anything about seeing her again, but as her brothers talked excitedly about his visit, she wasn't really listening to what they were saying.

Instead, she was hearing Jack saying softly to her, 'When I kiss you...'

When he kissed her... She closed her eyes, swaying slightly.

CHAPTER TEN

HONOR DROVE SLOWLY down the car track. For the first time since moving in, she was reluctant to return to the house.

She didn't want to get involved in thinking about the situation. It was too complicated, too demanding, and she had had enough of inner emotional warfare, of being pulled one way by her heart and another by her head.

Not even to herself did she like admitting how much her realisation of what Rourke really was, or how foolish she had been to love him, had hurt her. It had taken her a long time to make herself see Rourke as he really was and to accept that the man she believed she loved was simply a figment of her imagination.

If she had learned one thing from that experience it was not to trust her emotions, and yet, here she was, already letting her heart try to wheedle her round over David Lawrence. No, not David Lawrence, she corrected herself. His name was

David…Crighton. A stranger's name…and he was that stranger.

She had reached the cottage. She stopped the car and got out slowly. She might be wrong, she told herself. His resemblance to Jon Crighton might simply be a fluke. There *could* be other members of the family she knew nothing about.

When she opened the kitchen door, he was standing with his back to her, examining a piece of wood.

'Hello, David Crighton,' she said quietly, and watched as he froze, then very slowly put down the wood and turned to face her.

'You know who I am,' he said, and she could hear the tremor in his voice, see the shock in his eyes.

'Yes,' she replied quietly. 'You have a twin brother named Jon, a nephew named Max, a grumpy father named Ben. Oh, and you have a daughter and a son…and two grandchildren.'

David let her finish in silence and then sat down at the table, his head in his hands.

'You know everything,' he said thickly.

'Most of it,' Honor agreed quietly.

'I *was* going to tell you. I *should* have told you.' He stood up and turned away from her.

'You won't want me here now,' he said determinedly. 'I'll get my things....'

Silently, Honor watched him. He was right. It would be better for them both if he left. He wasn't gone very long and when he walked back into the kitchen she gestured downwards to the table without looking at him.

'There's the money I owe you for the time you've been here.'

'But I haven't done anything,' she heard him protest.

'Take it.' She paused and then asked, 'Why have you come back? Your family...' She stopped.

'I don't know,' David admitted. 'Father Ignatius said that I should.'

'Father Ignatius?' Honor questioned.

'It's a long story,' David told her, 'and I won't bore you with it. I'm sorry for—'

'Taking me to bed?' Honor supplied with a small twisted smile.

'No, *never* for that,' David denied. 'I could never be sorry for experiencing something so... No, I'm not sorry for that,' he repeated as he headed towards the door.

Honor didn't turn round as she heard him go. Her throat ached and her eyes were dry even though the tears were there. Foolish, stupid tears, the kind of tears that might have been permitted in a girl but which were surely ludicrous in a mature woman.

He would be out of the garden and in the lane by now. Which way would he go? Towards Haslewich or...

Suddenly, she was running towards the door, flinging it open, flying breathlessly into the lane and down it.

He had gone a lot farther than she had expected and she had to call his name twice before he stopped walking and turned to look at her.

'You're going the wrong way,' she told him huskily. 'Haslewich—'

Immediately, he shook his head. 'There isn't anything there for me. I shouldn't have come back.'

There was no bitterness in his voice, only an aching pain that made her own heart tighten.

'Don't go,' she said softly, reaching out to touch his arm.

'You don't mean that,' he insisted flatly.

'Yes, I do,' she contradicted.

And then she reached up on tiptoe and kissed him fiercely.

'You shouldn't be doing this,' David groaned

against her mouth. 'And I shouldn't be letting you.'

'Come home,' Honor urged.

'*Home.*' He gave her a crooked smile.

'Yes. Home…' Honor repeated.

For a moment she thought he was going to refuse. She held her breath and then to her relief he turned round.

HONOR YAWNED and looked at the clock. It was gone three in the morning. She couldn't believe that she and David Laurence Crighton—he had told her his full name—had been talking for so long.

He had told her everything, sparing nothing, and more than once her eyes had been wet with tears, not just for him but for the other players in his story, as well. Poor unhappy Tiggy with her eating disorder and her fractured life, his brother Jon, his children Olivia and Jack.

'I would like to meet him,' she had said when he told her about Father Ignatius.

'I would like you to, as well,' he had answered, wrapping his arms round her and holding her tightly against his body. 'He's taught me so much, given me so much, helped me discover a true sense of my real self. I have so much I want to say to them all, so many wounds I need to heal.

'I saw Jack today,' he had revealed to her unexpectedly. 'He was up at your cousin's, working there, I think. Jon's done a fine job.'

'He's your son, David,' Honor told him gently.

He shook his head. 'No. I fathered him, but that's all. Him and Olivia. Poor girl. My father was very unkind to her and I made matters worse.'

'Your father has a lot to answer for,' Honor said.

'No. Blaming him is too easy. I could have, should have, been stronger. I've hurt so many people, Honor, and I don't know... It might suit my own needs to blame my faults on my father—' he paused and looked at her '—but there comes a point in people's lives when they have the freedom to make a choice, to acknowledge the influences that have shaped them and to either accept or correct them. It's called growing up, becoming mature,' David continued drily. 'I knew what my father was doing, but I liked the boost it gave to my ego. I looked upon it as my right to do and have everything I wanted. Are you sure you know what you're doing, asking me to stay here?' he finished softly.

'I think so,' Honor responded with confidence.

'Your family won't like it,' he warned her. 'Your daughters…' He paused and searched her face, his own gaze stark and bleak. 'Or are you anticipating that what's between us will be short-lived and over—that you'll have dismissed me from your life before—'

'No!' Honor interrupted quietly but with such vehemence that the intensity of her own denial shocked *her* a little. She hadn't been thinking about her family or the future when she had run after David and persuaded him to come back. She hadn't even known until just now why it had been so vitally necessary to stop him leaving, but suddenly and gloriously, she did.

'Don't look at me like that,' she heard David groaning as he reached out to hold her. 'I don't deserve it, Honor. I don't deserve *you*.'

'As your priest friend would say, "Isn't that for a higher authority to decide?"' she chided him huskily. 'I want you to be here with me, David. I want you to stay.'

She wasn't going to say the words, 'I love you'. What did they mean anyway in this modern world where their currency had become so tarnished and cheapened? Besides, they were far too banal and unimaginative to express what *she* was feeling.

'It must be fate,' she told him thoughtfully instead. 'Our karma. *You* must be *my* fate, David,' she amended with emotion.

'How could someone so wonderful as you deserve a fate like me?' David whispered unsteadily in return. 'You deserve a prince amongst men, Honor, a knight in shining armour. You deserve a man of courage and strength and virtue.'

'*You* have courage and strength,' Honor began, but he stopped her, shaking his head and placing his finger tenderly against her lips.

'Don't say it,' he begged. 'Both of us know it isn't true.'

'It is true, David,' Honor insisted seriously. 'The truth is what is happening now, this moment. Maybe in the past it wasn't true, but you have been courageous enough to come back. You have shown strength.'

'And virtue?' he asked drily.

'Aren't your motives in returning home virtuous?' Honor reminded him.

'I don't know,' David admitted starkly. 'What *have* I come back for?' He shook his head. 'I really don't know.'

'Sometimes life can be like a bend in a river,' Honor offered comfortingly. 'When you approach the bend, it isn't always possible to see what lies around it, so it's necessary to traverse it with faith and hope.'

'*You* are my faith and hope,' David said thickly.

Tenderly, Honor reached out and touched his face, her eyes misting with tears when he took hold of her hand and slowly kissed each of her fingers…and then her palm…and then her wrist…and then…

'I HAVEN'T TOUCHED a woman since Tiggy and I split up. I haven't wanted to,' David confessed later as Honor lay in his arms. He was holding her as close to his body as he could, as though he couldn't bear not to have her there. 'And for a long time in our marriage…I wasn't…I didn't… The way I feel about you isn't like anything I've ever felt before. I can't categorise it. Whatever else I might have damaged or tarnished, I want you to know that what I feel for you is the very best of me, Honor.'

'I do know it,' Honor reassured him.

His obvious concern for her, coupled with his bemusement over the strength of his feelings, made her feel very protective towards him.

His past, with its pains and failings, was his past and personally she considered there was something much more laudable about a man who had made his mistakes and honestly regretted them than a man who denied ever making any.

Abigail and Ellen would be appalled, of course, considering her behaviour both impetuous and foolhardy. They would remind her that as a woman of considerable financial means she was an automatic target for men of a certain type, freeloaders who were looking for women to batten on and take advantage of, but Honor knew that David just wasn't like that.

'Tell me about meeting him today,' David suddenly asked her gruffly, almost as though he was embarrassed to reveal the hunger she could hear in his voice. 'What did he look like…what did he say…? Did he mention me or—'

'Your father?' Honor asked. 'He—'

But David stopped her, shaking his head as he said quickly, 'No. No. I meant Jon. You said he was there at Queensmead.'

Jon, his brother…his twin. *Now* Honor knew why he had come back even if David himself didn't yet realize it.

'Yes, he was there,' she affirmed. 'He…' She paused. 'I liked him,' she told him simply. 'He has a wonderful rapport with his son.'

'His son.' David frowned. 'Which one? He has two, Max and Joss.'

'Max,' Honor replied. 'It was Max I saw him with at Queensmead.'

'Max?' David fought against his own envy. 'Max and Jon never used to get on. As a boy, Max was closer to me than he was to Jon.' As he saw Honor's expression, he fought back his feelings again. 'I know that Jon and Max have a much better relationship now. I'm glad for them both. It was my father, really, who used to say that Max should have been my son and Olivia Jon's daughter.'

Honor didn't say anything. She was quietly digesting what she had just learned.

David's relationship with his twin brother was obviously very important to him. She had heard the anxiety in his voice when he asked about him, but she also suspected that he would refute anything she might say about Jon's being the cause of his return.

Well, that was understandable enough. She had seen with her own girls how very difficult it was for an elder child to admit to needing a younger sibling. Perhaps subconsciously David had always felt that Jon was the stronger of the two despite their father's determination to have it otherwise.

Possibly because of that, David had once welcomed the rift their father had created between him and his twin, using it to keep his feelings at bay.

'Jon won't want to see me, of course,' she heard David announcing tersely. 'In his shoes, I would feel exactly the same, so I can't blame him. You say they told you that Aunt Ruth repaid the money I took,' he added, closing his eyes. 'I still have nights when I wake up sweating with fear over that, not wanting to accept that I actually did it, dreading being discovered, but at the same time almost wanting to be.

'I only meant to borrow it…just a little money…just for a while. I'd got this hot investment tip, some shares, but the market…' He gave a small shrug. 'I'd been so sure I was going to make a killing that I'd already spent my profit, and then when the share price dropped, not only was I unable to repay the money I'd taken, but I was thousands of pounds in debt, as well. That's how it started. I "borrowed" more to repay the bank. Tiggy and I were living way above our means, but trying to preach economy to her was like… Well, she just didn't have a clue. Of course, I can see now what I couldn't see then, what I didn't *want* to see then, that she had an addictive personality and that, through my own selfishness, I drove her...' He stopped. 'I can't make excuses for myself and I'm not going to, just as I can't expect Jon to listen to me.'

'I believe it may be easier than you imagine,' Honor told him calmly. 'They were very open about how much your father is longing for your return. I think that for his sake if nothing else...'

'Exactly how ill is he?' David asked her quietly.

'Physically, he's really quite strong, but spiritually...' Honor shook her head. 'He's nearing the end of his life, David, and he's carrying a very heavy load of emotional pain.'

'Because of me?'

'No, because of himself,' Honor said firmly. 'In his physical state, a happier person, a man who allowed himself to love both his sons generously, could live another decade, but your father... He wants you back, but he wants you back as the image he created.'

'You remind me more and more of the priest,' David told her. 'He said much the same thing to me. Perhaps I shouldn't go back. Perhaps I should stay away—keep out of their lives.'

'Stay hidden away here at Foxdean with me.'

Honor laughed. 'Well, *I* certainly don't object to that.'

'You do realise, don't you,' David asked soberly, 'that I have nothing—that my only possessions are quite literally the clothes I stand up in, that I can never support you financially in the way you have every right to expect?'

'Money isn't important. Not to me,' Honor reassured him. 'You can mend the hole in my roof and repair the fabric of my home. You can also repair the hole in my heart and the damage to the fabric of my emotions,' she added huskily.

'Money may not be important to *you*, but in the eyes of the world—'

'The eyes of the world aren't important, either. It's what I see with *my* eyes that matters,' Honor told him.

'And what do you see?' David asked with just enough hesitancy in his voice to let her know how important her answer was to him.

'I see *you*, David,' she answered gravely. 'I see a man whose humanity and strength warms my heart, not to mention what your less esoteric and rather more physical attributes do to my body and for my more carnal desires.' She laughed, lightening the emotional tension she could feel emanating from him.

'So it isn't love you feel for me at all, it's lust?' David asked teasingly.

'Mmm...' Honor tipped her head to one side and pretended to consider the matter. 'I should say it's an excellent blend of both,' she announced eventually, adding in a husky voice as he moved to draw her up against his firm, hardening body, 'a very excellent blend.'

'OLIVIA.'

'Yes,' Olivia responded tersely as she turned away from Caspar, cradling the cup of coffee she was holding defensively in front of her.

'I've booked flights for New York.'

'Flights?' Olivia questioned, her stomach muscles clenching. The last thing she needed was another fight with Caspar. She had had a bad enough day without that.

The wife whom she was representing in a particularly complicated divorce case had burst into tears in the middle of their appointment this afternoon, confessing that she didn't really want to divorce her husband after all. Then, after going without lunch and rescheduling all her appointments, she had managed to rush off early enough to pick up Amelia from her dancing class. The teacher had taken Olivia to one side and told her quite coldly that Amelia had outgrown her existing practise clothes and shoes.

'She has? But why on earth didn't she say something?' Olivia had asked the teacher in irritation.

'Perhaps she felt she couldn't,' the other woman had replied even more coolly. 'I understand that you don't have a lot of time to spare.'

Smarting under the teacher's implied rebuke, Olivia had had to drive into Chester, which was the nearest place she knew where the shops would be open late enough for her to buy Amelia some new things.

'Yes,' Caspar replied shortly. 'We fly out a weekend before the wedding and we'll fly back a fortnight later, so—'

'We?' Olivia demanded ominously. Her heart was thumping furiously and she was beginning to feel tense and sick.

'Yes, *we*,' Caspar repeated curtly. 'I've booked seats for all four of us.'

'You can't take the girls,' Olivia warned him. 'I—'

'I don't think you were listening, Olivia,' Caspar interrupted her grimly. 'I said that I've booked seats for *all* of us.'

'You know I can't go. We've already had this

out and I don't want to talk about it any more,'
Olivia said. 'If you have to go, then you have to
go, but I'm not going with you.'

'Then the girls and I will just have to go alone.'

'You aren't taking them without me,' Olivia
insisted furiously.

'They are my children just as much as they are
yours, Olivia, and I *am* taking them with me.
Whether or not you come with us is your choice.
I shan't alter the flight arrangements. There will
be a seat for you if you change your mind.'

'FANCY GOING INTO CHESTER this evening?'

Jack hesitated before shaking his head and telling Joss, 'Er, no, I can't…I've got something else
planned.'

'Something else? What else?' Joss asked, his
curiosity growing as Jack shook his head again,
his face colouring a little.

'It's nothing.'

'Nothing…?' Joss began and then stopped.
'This "nothing" wouldn't have anything to do
with Annalise, would it?' he guessed, grinning
widely when he saw from Jack's expression that
his guess had been right.

'I told the boys I'd go round and check up on
the fish,' Jack told Joss defensively.

'Check up on their sister, more like,' Joss countered.

'YOU LOOK TIRED. What's wrong?' Max asked Maddy as he walked into the kitchen. He dropped his briefcase onto one of the chairs and started to frown at the weary anxiety in his wife's eyes. 'Has the old man been playing you up again?'

'He has been a bit fractious today,' Maddy replied.

'Where is he? In the study?' Max asked, heading for the door.

'Max,' Maddy pleaded, 'don't. Don't say anything to him. He doesn't mean to be difficult and I can understand that the children must seem very noisy and a bit of a nuisance to him at times. This *is* his home after all.'

'Is that what he's been saying to you?' Max demanded sharply. 'Queensmead may be his *house*, Maddy, but *you're* the one who's turned it into a home. If he's been upsetting you—Maddy,' he protested with concern as she suddenly started to cry. 'My darling girl, what is it? What's wrong?'

As he crossed the kitchen and took her in his arms, holding her tightly, Maddy started to cry in earnest—deep, racking sobs that tore at Max's heart. Whatever his grandfather had done to upset her, he, Max, was going to make sure the old man made reparation for it with no allowances being made for his age.

'Maddy. Maddy, please, tell me what's wrong. If looking after this place and Gramps is too much for you, just say so. We'll move somewhere smaller. What do we need with a damn great barn like this anyway? A decent-sized modern house with four bedrooms and—

'What on earth is it?' he demanded as Maddy suddenly started to shake in his arms. Anxiously, he held her just far enough away from himself to be able to look down into her face. When he did so, instead of still crying as he had expected, she actually seemed to be laughing—if a little hysterically.

'We can't,' she was saying tearfully. 'Four bedrooms wouldn't be enough. Not now. We...'

'We...what?' he began, and then stopped as he saw the faint flush of colour staining her face and the almost bashful look in her eyes.

'I'm pregnant, Max,' she told him. 'I...I should have guessed, I suppose, but with being so busy and things never having gone quite back to normal after Jason's birth, I didn't...I wasn't... But

I had to go for a regular check-up today and when I was there—'

'You're *pregnant*?' Max repeated, bemused. 'But—'

'We weren't planning for another, I know,' Maddy interrupted him, 'but...well, I wasn't... you didn't...and...' Blushing like a schoolgirl, she told him simply, 'When you touch me, I forget about being a sensible married woman and mother and I...Max, stop looking at me like that,' she scolded him breathlessly, then gave a small squeak of protest as Max pulled her determinedly against him. He started to kiss her, one hand splayed against her back, the other resting tenderly on the small swelling of her stomach.

'Another baby,' he whispered. 'Oh, my God, Maddy. You know what this means, don't you?' he demanded as he swung her round in his arms, his eyes alight with love and laughter.

'Mmm...we won't be able to move to a smaller house,' Maddy answered wryly.

'No, worse than that,' Max told her, bending his head to whisper in her ear as he said jokingly, 'First Jason and now this baby. Everyone's going to know we just can't keep our hands off each other.'

'Oh, Max.' Maddy laughed in protest. 'You—'

'I what?'

'You're teasing me, but are you sure you don't mind?'

'Mind? Why should I mind? *You're* the one who's going to be carrying it—for nine months. All *I* have to do is look proud and accept everyone's congratulations. Mmm…I wonder what it is about knowing that your wife…your woman…is having your child that makes a man feel so very much a man. Something deep-rooted and atavistic, I suppose.'

'Whatever it is, it's something totally non-PC,' Maddy added drily.

'Mmm…maybe. Anyway, that does it. I'm not having it.'

'Not having what?' Maddy asked him, perplexed.

'I'm not having Gramps upsetting you. You can't be expected to care for him and four children, as well, Maddy,' he told her gently. 'I feel bad enough about the situation as it is.'

'But I like living here at Queensmead,' Maddy protested. 'And most of the time he isn't so bad. He just gets grumpy because he feels so afraid and alone at times.'

'I'll have a word with Ma, I think. It's a pity we can't trace David. If Gramps changes his will and leaves Queensmead to David, we're going to be in one hell of a mess.'

'If we could trace him, I wonder if he would let us buy it from him,' Maddy said quietly.

'Does it really mean that much to you?' Max asked her.

'It's our *home*, Max, and it's a part of your heritage as a Crighton. So much of your family's history is here.'

'Well, if Gramps doesn't change his will, everything will be all right, but if he leaves it to David... Look, I don't want you worrying about that...I don't want you worrying about anything!' He grinned at her. 'Can I tell the folks or is it something you want us to keep to ourselves for the moment?'

'You can tell them,' Maddy responded. 'In fact, I suspect that your mother has probably guessed that I'm pregnant. She came round the other week when I was being sick and hinted then that there might be a baby in the offing. I was so sure that she was wrong that I denied it. I owe her an apology. Max, what are you doing?' she demanded as he took the oven mitts she had just picked up.

'I will sort out supper. *You* can rest,' he declared masterfully.

'Oh, Max, you can't, not in your suit,' Maddy

protested, but nevertheless she allowed him to have his way.

DETERMINEDLY BLOTTING OUT the sight and voices of Jack and her brothers, Annalise bent her head over her homework. Her heart had thumped so heavily when she opened the door to Jack half an hour ago that she had automatically put her hand up to try to steady it.

Even her father was showing an unfamiliar excitement about the new life the fish had taken on under Jack's expert care.

Irritably, Annalise frowned as she forced herself to concentrate, but she couldn't help registering and following the husky sound of Jack's voice. He really had a rather sexy voice if one was impressed by such things and, of course, she wasn't. No, she was off boys for good. She still dreaded going to school each day. Everyone knew about Pete dumping her by now. Automatically, her body stiffened, her head lifting proudly.

'Having problems?'

She gasped as she realised that Jack had moved away from the fish tank without her knowing and that he was now standing behind her looking down at her work. Ineffectively, she tried to cover what she was doing, but it was too late. He had already read it.

'It isn't one of my best subjects,' she told him defensively, her face beginning to crimson a little.

To her surprise, instead of taunting her, he said quietly, 'You're doing fine,' he added gently, 'but if you do it this way, I think you'll find it a bit easier....'

She'd never felt she was any good at maths even though the teacher had encouraged her to take it for her A levels. The ease with which Jack deftly analysed and answered the—to her—complex problem she had been tussling with left her feeling bemused and breathless. Or was that more because of the way Jack was leaning over her as he wrote in her notebook than because of his mathematical skills?

'What do you hope to do when you finish your A levels?' Jack asked.

'Er...I'm not sure yet,' she responded. It was her secret, private dream to go to university and take an arts degree, but that would cost money—money she already knew her father didn't have. She suspected she would have to look for a job instead and perhaps take some more practical qualifications at college.

She was already taking a basic computer skills

course at school and building on that seemed a sensible idea; the local motorway network combined with EU grants made the area popular with multinational industries. Several of them had their head offices outside the town, including Aarlston-Becker, which had an excellent record for taking on and training school leavers.

She didn't want to discuss any of this with Jack Crighton, though, and she certainly didn't want to tell him of her secret dreams of developing her artistic skills and eventually using them as a means of earning her living. So she simply shrugged dismissively and said nothing, earning herself a small look of rebuke from her father.

'She's got to get through her exams first,' her father told Jack grimly, 'and that means spending more time studying and less messing around with her friends.'

'Oh, Dad,' Annalise couldn't stop herself from protesting defensively.

'Well, don't try to tell me that you wouldn't have been given extra homework if you hadn't fallen behind,' her father pointed out sharply. 'I'm not that stupid.'

Mortified, she flushed and bit her lip. It was true that she had fallen slightly behind with her maths, but that was because...

'Maths has never been my best subject,' she reminded him.

'Maths can be very unforgiving,' Jack commented thoughtfully. 'It doesn't allow for any shadings or imaginative interpretations. It's either right or wrong and because of that people sometimes feel apprehensive and nervous about it. If you're really having a problem with it, perhaps I could help,' he offered, looking not at Annalise but at her father, much to her furious chagrin.

Who did he think he was? She might not have his brains, but there was no way she was going to have him standing over her as though—

'Well, if you're sure you wouldn't mind,' she heard her father saying.

'Dad!' She began to protest in consternation, but it was too late. He and Jack were already discussing times just as though *she* wasn't capable of deciding anything for herself.

Annalise started to grind her teeth, but she had to wait until Jack got up to leave before she could vent her feelings on him in the privacy of the hallway as she opened the front door for him.

'Why did you have to say that to my dad about giving me some extra tuition?' she fumed. 'I don't need...' she began, then hesitated as she saw the way that Jack was looking at her. He was studying her mouth as though…as if… Nervous excitement began to flood through her. Her mouth had gone dry and her lips… Instinctively, she tried to wet them with her tongue and then flushed a deep, mortified scarlet, the scalding sheet of colour firing her skin as Jack took a step towards her and grasped her upper arms.

He was stronger than she had imagined and up this close he seemed so much bigger, taller and broader, so much more excitingly male. The hot, hungry glitter she could see in his eyes was making her feel dizzy and—

She tensed as she heard her father calling her name. 'I've got to go,' she objected shakily. 'I…oh…' she gasped as Jack leaned forward and pressed a hot, hard kiss against her mouth. 'Oh…' she gasped once more, flustered and flushed as he stepped back from her.

'I'll see you tomorrow,' he told her thickly.

He was walking away before she remembered that she had intended to tell him not to come round.

Why had he kissed her like that? Why had he…? She gave a small shiver of sharp excitement. What was happening to her? She couldn't be falling for Jack Crighton. She didn't even like him and besides…

After she shut the front door, Annalise leaned back against it and closed her eyes. What was falling in love, loving someone? She had thought she loved Pete. When he had singled her out for attention, he had made her feel so good, so proud, so able to hold her head up high at school. But he had made her feel so bad when he started to pressure her for sex, then criticise her and get angry with her.

Jack had made her feel angry when she first met him and she was also aware of the disparity in their social circumstances. The Crightons were wealthy, well-known and highly respected in the town, whereas her family... What did Jack want from her? The same as Pete? The panicky feeling inside her started to grow.

When he moved up close to her, something that was both exciting and frightening began to happen to her, something that confused and worried her. She didn't know if what he made her feel was love, but she knew that it was dangerous. Someone like him could only want one thing from someone like her, and she knew what that thing was—sex! He would try to coax her into bed and then he would go off to university and forget all about her.

She licked her still-dry lips. They burned where

he had kissed them, and with her eyes closed she
could almost imagine she still felt him doing it.
She shuddered wildly. When he came round tomorrow, she would be all on her own. Her father
would be out and the boys would be at a friend's.

Should she tell her father what she thought Jack
was really after? If she did, he would soon put a
stop to his visits. Was that really what she wanted
or...? Shakily, Annalise made her way back to
the living room.

CHAPTER ELEVEN

'THAT LOOKS A LOT BETTER.'

From his position on top of the ladder where
he was working on the window frame he had just
repaired and replaced, David smiled down at
Honor who was standing below looking up at
him.

He was enjoying working on the house, and if
he was honest with himself, the satisfaction he got
from working with his hands was far greater than
any he had ever received from working in the
legal world.

As he finished what he was doing and made his
way down to where Honor was waiting, he smiled
a little to himself, imagining his father's reaction
to what he had just thought.

'My cousin's just been on the phone,' Honor
told him as she linked her arm through his and
they strolled back to the house together. 'He's invited me over for dinner on Saturday evening.'

'Will you go?' David asked as he opened the kitchen door for her.

'Will *you* come with me?' Honor countered.

David gave a small sigh.

It was some days now since she had discovered his real identity—harmonious love- and laughter-filled days that had flown by. Days when Honor had lovingly refuted every suggestion he made that she might grow bored with his sole company. Nights when, after they had made love and she was asleep, he had lain there wondering what the future held.

'Honor…' he began hesitantly, then stopped as he saw the quick sheen of tears in her eyes before she looked quickly away from him.

'I know,' she said brightly—so brightly that if he hadn't seen her tears, he would have been completely deceived. 'I'm being foolish and thoughtless. Of course you can't go. He's bound to have other dinner guests and one of them could well recognise you and—'

'Honor,' he said gently, and this time she did look at him, her uncertainty showing in her expression as she searched his face for some clue as to what he might be going to say. 'This isn't going to work,' he told her heavily. 'I can't continue to hide away here like a recluse and I can't expect you to.'

'You've changed your mind. You're going to leave.' Her voice was totally steady, but her face was paper-white and her eyes...

There had been times in the years since he had left home when David had disliked, even despised, himself, but that self-hatred was nothing to what he felt now. He was hurting Honor, hurting her badly, and that was the last thing he wanted.

He saw her swallow, then to his disbelief heard her saying rustily, 'Would it make any difference if I said that I was willing to come with you? I could, you know. After all, there's really nothing to keep me here, not—'

'But you love this house. You've said so.'

'I love it, yes,' she agreed, turning her head away from him, but he could hear the emotion in her voice. 'But I love you more.'

'Would you really do that for me?' he asked gruffly.

'Yes,' she said simply.

'Then you're a fool,' David responded harshly. 'Can't you see what would happen if I agreed, if I *let* you? We'd end up living like two fugitives, constantly running, paranoid about being discovered and the paranoia would kill what…what we feel for one another. No. Besides,' he added a little shakily, 'I've had a better idea.'

She was standing like someone about to ward off a devastating blow and he ached to reach out and snatch her into the protection of his arms, to keep her there, holding her, *loving* her, but he couldn't…not now…not yet.

'I can't let you live like this, Honor. You deserve more…better. You need a man you can have openly by your side, a relationship that other people recognise. I've made up my mind.'

Honor held her breath, the ache of it… She couldn't bear to lose him, not now, but she couldn't keep him against his will, either.

'I'm going to ring Jon, tell him I've returned, ask if he'll see me…if we can talk.'

Honor stared at him, her eyes brilliant with feeling.

'Don't look at me like that,' David warned her thickly, groaning under his breath as he gave in to the temptation to reach out and hold her. 'Come here and let me…oh, God, Honor…Honor…'

He could feel the quivers of emotion running through her as he kissed her hungrily. They were almost clumsy in their mutual need for one another. His hand cupped her breast, warm and already belovedly familiar. Her hands touched him, stroking him, holding him, shaping him.

They made love greedily, desperately, almost as though in shared acknowledgement of the final burning of the bridges they had left as a safety measure between them. They were gone now in their mutual commitment to one another, their mutual recognition of the intensity and depth of what they felt.

'Would you really have done that for me...given up this house, this place?' David whispered against Honor's mouth as he kissed her.

'Everything...*anything*...' Honor promised recklessly.

'It won't be easy,' David warned her later as she lay curled against his side, the late-afternoon sunlight highlighting the warm curves of her body. She had a woman's body, not a girl's, and she was totally matter-of-fact about its warm ripeness, laughing at him tenderly when he had told her how beautiful he found her.

'Nature's very clever,' she had responded drily. 'As she increases the wrinkles, she decreases our ability to see them!'

'I'll have you know that my eyesight is perfect,' David had replied in mock outrage.

'Uh-huh,' Honor had teased back flippantly. 'So perfect that you were holding the newspaper two inches away from your nose to read the headlines this morning.

'Are you sure you want to ring Jon?' she asked him more soberly now. 'I took the medication and the diet I prepared round for your father this morning when I went out to do the shopping. He seemed to be a little better.'

She paused and then looked at him briefly before starting to trace a complicated pattern on his bare chest with her fingertip.

'There were two other children there, two girls, not Maddy's. I think they might have been your grandchildren.' She winced a little as she felt his grip on her tighten.

'Livvy's children?'

Honor nodded. 'Yes.'

David closed his eyes. 'Livvy was so angry with me when she found out about her mother's bulimia, and with good reason. I should have done something about it, got professional help for her instead of just trying to pretend it wasn't happening. What do the children look like?'

Pausing a moment, Honor told him judiciously, 'Not a lot like you. They're both dark...but there's something...'

'Caspar's dark…if it's him she married.'

'Yes, I heard Maddy referring to him… something about a wedding in America.'

'Yes, Caspar is American. Livvy brought him home with her just before—'

'You don't have to do this,' she repeated and meant it.

'Yes, I do,' David corrected her. 'It's what I came for after all. If Jon refuses to see me, then—'

'It won't make any difference to me,' Honor said quickly.

David shook his head and told her softly, 'Yes, it will. What if Jon and the rest of the family decide they've had enough of shielding and protecting me? What if they decide to go public about what I did? I can't put you through that, Honor, being branded the wife of a liar and a thief.'

The *wife*! Honor's heart thumped against her ribcage, but she didn't say anything other than a shaky 'Let's take one step at a time.'

HALF AN HOUR LATER, they were back downstairs. As David walked into the sitting room and stared at the telephone, Honor paused in the doorway before saying quietly to him, 'I'll be in the kitchen if...if you need me.'

'No,' David said without hesitation. 'No. Please stay. I want you to be here with me.' When he held his hand out to her, she walked unsteadily towards him and took hold of it. He had no need to check the number. He knew it off by heart, but his hand still trembled as he punched the buttons.

'PHONE,' JENNY CALLED OUT automatically as she finished cutting away the edge of the pastry from the pie she was making. 'Phone, Jon,' she repeated a little more loudly, then, dusting her floury hands against her apron, she sighed and started to move towards the kitchen telephone.

'I'll get it,' Jon told her, reaching it first.

'Grr...' As he picked it up, Jenny made a mock angry face at him and went back to her pie.

Maddy and Max had called in unexpectedly ten minutes earlier on the way home from Chester and, in the way of such things, their arrival had been quickly followed by that of Katie and her husband Seb and their twin sons who were dropping their house keys off with them before driving north for a few days' holiday in Yorkshire.

Absently, Jenny registered Jon's conversation

as she opened the oven door and placed the pie inside.

'Yes, it is,' she heard him saying quietly, followed by a raw, husky 'Yes, I know—God, I'd recognise your voice anywhere!' Which, for some reason, made Jenny stand stock-still.

On the other end of the line, David's hand gripping the receiver was damp with sweat. 'Is that Jon?' he had asked even though he had recognised his twin's voice immediately, and when Jon had answered yes, he had told him, 'It's David....'

Jon's acknowledgement had brought a lump of emotion to his throat and for a few seconds he was unable to say anything else. At his side, Honor squeezed his arm reassuringly.

'I'd like to see you Jon...talk to you.'

As he waited for his brother's response, he was shaking so much that he could hardly hold the receiver.

There was a long pause, long enough for him to wish he hadn't made the call, long enough for him to guess that Jon was going to turn him down.

As THOUGH BY some mystical force, the other members of their family who had been in the sitting room suddenly seemed drawn to the kitchen, walking in chattering and then falling silent as they sensed, like Jenny, the import of what was happening.

'Where are you?' they all heard Jon ask. Although none of them, bar Jenny, had heard the earlier part of his conversation, all of them tensed and waited in silence, watching Jon being gripped by emotion.

'I'm...I'm not very far away,' David responded huskily.

'Could you...could you come here?' Jon asked.

Honor, who had heard his question, nodded her head vigorously.

'Yes. Yes, I could,' David agreed. 'When—'

'Now,' Jon told him fiercely, 'now!' and put down the receiver.

He turned to look at Jenny.

'That was David,' he said quietly. 'He's...he's coming round. Right now!'

His face was white, but the emotion Jenny could see burning in his eyes disturbed and dismayed her far more than his shock.

'David!' the others were repeating with varying degrees of disbelief.

'*Uncle* David?' Katie asked.

'Dad...?' Jack demanded sharply.

'Yes,' Jon answered them all before saying to Jenny, 'I think I need a drink.'

'Where…what…why…?' everyone was asking.

'I don't know,' Jon told them, shaking his head. He was feeling oddly light-headed and perhaps drinking alcohol wasn't the sensible thing to do. He was suffering from shock, of course, and no wonder, and yet should he really be so surprised? After all, hadn't he…? But no. *That* wasn't the reason David had come back. It *couldn't* possibly be.

'Jon, did David give any indication of when he would be here?' Jenny was asking him, and his heightened sensitivity told him that she was apprehensive and on edge.

'No. He didn't…I didn't… Oh, God, I don't believe this is actually happening after all this time,' he cried out through his tears. 'He's here at last. David…David! What if he should change his mind?' He paced the room anxiously. 'I should have gone to him. He'll be anxious, nervous, afraid—I should have told him.'

As she listened, Jenny found it hard to control her immediate instinct to protect her man, her Jon! David had hurt him very badly in the past and yet here he was almost transmuted with joy at the thought of seeing him again.

AT FOXDEAN, Honor was telling David encouragingly, 'It will be all right. He wouldn't have agreed to see you if... I'll drive you there,' she insisted firmly.

'No. I can manage,' David protested unconvincingly.

'No, you can't,' Honor corrected him.

'TURN LEFT HERE,' David directed. Obligingly, Honor did so. Ahead of her she could see the outline of a house.

'I'll drop you off at the gate and then I'll drive back here to wait for you,' she told him.

As they reached the house, the security lights came on and illuminated the interior of the car and David's taut face. The sharpness of the light bleached the colour from his skin, oddly leaving him looking not older but younger.

'It *will* be all right,' she repeated, and kissed him on the mouth almost maternally.

THEY ALL HEARD the front doorbell ring, but none of them moved.

'Jon...' Jenny urged.

'I'll go,' Max offered, but Jon shook his head.

'No...no...' he said shakily.

Maddy touched Max's arm and told him gently, 'It's your father David wants to see.'

'Yes, because he knows that Dad's always been a soft touch. If he asks for money, Dad...' Jenny saw from Jon's expression just how unwelcome and how unpalatable he found Max's suggestion.

Jon started to move towards the door. Jenny looked round her kitchen. Joss and Jack were standing together, Katie was with her husband and sons, and Maddy was beside Max, his hand resting protectively over her stomach. They had broken the news of Maddy's pregnancy to Jon and Jenny the previous day.

Jenny had felt immensely pleased, but now all the anticipatory pleasure and excitement she had been experiencing had been swamped by shock and dread. She didn't want David to be back. She didn't want Jon to retreat into the person he had been before David's disappearance. She couldn't bear to see him suffer again as he had done before, when his father was constantly ridiculing him and decrying everything he did whilst praising David to the sky. Most of all, she didn't want to acknowledge what the look she had seen in Jon's eyes meant.

She heard the front door open and her body stiffened. Wasn't *she* enough for Jon? Wasn't *her* love, *their* family enough? Was there always going to be a part of him that didn't belong to her, a part of him that belonged exclusively to David and their twinship? It hurt and frightened her to think that he had never once told her that he was truly missing David, that she had not known how much he wanted his brother back.

Jon took a deep breath as he opened the door. 'David…'

'Jon…'

'Come…come in.'

Somehow, as he stepped back into the hall, Jon managed to prevent himself from holding out his arms to his twin—from letting him know how important this meeting between them was to him. Slowly, he told himself as he held back. Don't swamp him, panic him, alienate him. Don't burden him with your love—your need. Had David seen how much his changed appearance had caught him off guard? He had been expecting to see the David who had disappeared years ago, but the man whom he was ushering towards his study, whilst physically his own double, somehow just wasn't the David he had visualised.

Could he really be taller or was that simply a trick of the light? Certainly he was slimmer, fitter, more muscular. His skin was tanned, making his teeth look impossibly white and his eyes intensely blue.

'I wasn't sure you would agree to see me,' David was saying huskily to him as they walked into his study. 'In your shoes—'

'No. I'm glad you're here. Dad…' Jon cleared his throat as his emotions threatened to get the better of him. After all, why should he mind now that David had always been their father's favourite? 'He hasn't been very well.'

'Yes. I know,' David acknowledged.

'You know?'

'Yes. Er…there's someone…a friend…' David hesitated. 'I don't want to talk about Dad, Jon. Not yet. There are things I need to say to you first, important things, the first of which is…' David took a deep breath. 'I haven't come here to ask for your forgiveness or even your understanding. Why should you give either to me? I don't deserve them. I haven't done anything to warrant them. Far from it. But what I *do* want to do is tell you how much, how very much, I regret all the ways I've let you down. All the ways I've been so shamefully weak and self-serving, all the times I put my own needs before yours, all the times I stood back and let our father…'

He paused as Jon made a dismissive, anguished gesture with his hand.

'No, it isn't easy to talk about,' he agreed as though Jon had actually spoken. 'And like I've said, I'm not asking or expecting you to forgive me for my greed or the destruction of the bond I should have valued and cherished.'

'Our father...' Jon began thickly, but David shook his head.

'Our father may have been a victim of his own childhood, but that's no excuse for me. Just as soon as I was old enough to realise, I knew that everything he gave me came with a price and that you were the one who was paying that price. You were the whipping boy, Jon, and I let you be. I can never ask you to forgive me for that...nor can I forgive myself.'

'David, *why* have you come back?' Jon interrupted him starkly. David looked at him and then shook his head.

'I don't really know. I just felt...' He shrugged.

'That Dad needed you?' Jon suggested.

'No,' David owned truthfully, his voice low. 'No, I came back, Jon, because I needed *you*.'

For a moment they just looked at one another and then David saw the tears in Jon's eyes.

Without the least hesitation or uncertainty, he

made the first move. The old habits of behaviour, the upbringing their father had given them that said that boys, *men*, never showed their emotions, had been swept away by what he had witnessed and experienced working alongside the priest.

Jon's body felt familiar in his arms, almost a part of himself. 'I've missed you,' David told him gruffly.

Jon held him tightly. He had no words for what he wanted to say or the emotions he was experiencing. How often as a child, a boy, a young man, had he longed for this, for David to be like this. How often had he had to steel himself against the pain of David's rejection and his own awareness of how lacking in closeness they actually were.

'I've thought about you—often,' Jon said huskily.

'And I you,' David admitted. 'I love you, Jon. I've missed you so much!' Before Jon could overcome his shock at David's emotional openness or respond to him, David was continuing, 'In Jamaica I dreamed about you, and that was when the priest—'

'The priest?' Jon questioned.

'It's a long story,' David returned ruefully.

'Max and Jack went to Jamaica to look for you,' Jon told him.

David grimaced. 'Yes, I know.'

'Dad's been longing for you to come home. It's virtually all he ever talks about—even more than Max making QC.'

'*Max* is a QC?'

'Yes. He works from Chester with Luke, Henry's son. He's living at Queensmead. His wife has been looking after Dad. He and Maddy are here at the moment as it happens and so, too, are Katie and her husband and children.' He paused, then said gruffly, 'I'm so glad you've come back.'

Simple words, but they meant so much.

'Dad's a fool. *You* were always the better one of the two of us. That hasn't changed,' David responded.

'I don't know what your plans are,' Jon continued quietly, 'but so far as the partnership is concerned...' He took a deep breath. There was no easy way of saying this. 'You are my brother, David, and as such you'll always be welcome in my home and in my life, but—'

'But there's no place for me in the partnership,' David finished grimly for him. For a long moment he held Jon's gaze, then admitted honestly, 'How could there possibly be after what I did? For years I traded on your professional qualifications, letting other people assume that *I* was the one who was the fully qualified solicitor, happily allowing *you* to cover for me and shield me. Not just allowing but expecting it as my right. I was a liar and a thief, Jon, and I was damn lucky not to be caught and sent to prison. I understand that Aunt Ruth paid back the money I stole.'

These were spoken declarations, but inwardly at another deeper level, the brothers were communing with one another emotionally, the love flowing between them like a fast spring tide breaking down all barriers in its way and carrying away the debris, the hurts, of the past. The simple touch of Jon's hand on David's arm was all they both needed to break off their conversation and look into one another's eyes.

'Yes, she did,' Jon confirmed. 'I wasn't sure I should allow her to do so, but—'

'That isn't why I came back—money, material possessions.' David gave a small shrug. 'In Jamaica...' He hesitated. 'I understand that I've got two grandchildren.'

'Olivia's girls, yes.' A shadow crossed Jon's face as he reflected on Olivia's likely reaction to her father's return. He had recently been watching her more closely, following Jenny's concern, and he had to admit that Jenny was right to be worried. Still, every time he tried to talk to her, Olivia fobbed him off, keeping him at a distance.

'There's a lot we need to discuss,' David was saying. 'But I should go…there's someone waiting for me.'

'Someone?' Jon queried. 'Who?'

'A friend—Honor,' David told him lightly. 'I think you recently met her.'

There were so many questions Jon wanted to ask him, but he was still in a state of shock, not just over David's unheralded arrival but also because of the changes in him. The emotions he was feeling were akin to those he had felt at the birth of his children: Joy, disbelief, a humbling sense of the miracle of human life, an overwhelming feeling of love he couldn't articulate, a sense of a prayer being answered for the safe deliverance from danger of those he loved, coupled with a determination to love and protect them in return. David—Jon's heart filled with joyous love for his brother.

'Jack's here,' Jon told him. 'I think he'll want to see you.'

'Will he?' David responded. 'I saw him the other day up at Fitzburgh Place. I remember him as a little boy, but he's a young man now.'

'He's a fine boy, David,' Jon assured him.

'Yes—thanks to you,' David replied simply.

'He's *your* son,' Jon insisted as Honor had done.

'Maybe, but you are the one who raised him, Jon, and when he reaches maturity and looks back, it will be you he thanks for everything he has learned, for making him a man, not me.'

In his mind's eye David could still see Jack as he was one day in the kitchen with Tiggy, the mess caused by her binge eating in evidence all around her. Jack's face had been white and set as he looked with accusing eyes from his mother to his father.

'Will any of them *want* to see me?' David asked heavily.

'I'll go and fetch Jack' was all Jon could say.

'WHERE IS HE? What did he want? Has he gone? You didn't give him any money, did you?' Voices clamoured for answers.

As Jon walked into the kitchen, the air was thick with questions, but Jon ignored them all, going over to Jack and saying gently, 'David, your *father*, would like to see you, Jack, but he'll understand if you don't...if you feel...'

Jack hesitated. It was over an hour since David had arrived, an hour during which they had all remained in the kitchen looking at one another in between disbelieving and often angry snatches of conversation.

'God, he's got the nerve of the devil,' Max had fumed. 'And if he thinks I'm going to stand by and let him treat Dad the way he used to…'

'I don't know how Olivia is going to react to this,' Katie had remarked uneasily to her husband.

'Uncle David. I can't take it in,' Joss had murmured, shaking his head.

Of all of them, only Jenny had remained silent, her face bleached and set, something about her expression making Jack feel tense and hurt inside. He had wanted to go over and hug her, but he had been wary of doing so in case she pushed him away for being his father's son. Now Uncle Jon was back in the kitchen delivering the news that his father wanted to see him.

Just for a moment Jack was tempted to refuse. Not out of malice or self-righteousness, but because, quite simply, he was afraid.

Of what? Of having a father who was a liar and a thief or seeing in his father's eyes that look of dismissal and impatience he could remember so well from his childhood.

Instinctively, he squared his shoulders. Living with Jon and Jenny had taught him a lot about the importance of respect—for other people and for himself. If David, his father, didn't have that respect for him, then that was his loss, Jack told himself firmly.

'He's in my study,' Jon said as Jack followed him out into the hallway.

Outside the study door Jack paused. 'Come with me,' he begged Jon.

Jon hesitated and then nodded his head. 'If that's what you want.' He felt just as protective of Jack as he did his own children, just as ready to respond to his vulnerability and need.

In the study, David was standing looking out through the uncurtained window. Jon could see the defensiveness in the tense set of his shoulders.

'David, here's Jack,' he announced.

As his father turned round, Jack caught his breath. He looked so different, more like his Uncle Jon than Jack remembered, his face so much leaner and pared down with none of the heavy jowliness that Jack recalled. He looked a lot slimmer. Beneath his shirt Jack could see the outline of his muscles. The Jamaican sun had bleached his hair a few degrees fairer at the sides where Jon's was plain English grey, but the similarity between them was still strikingly evident. So much so that for a second Jack caught his breath.

It must, of course, always have been there, but as a child he had taken it for granted. Certainly he could not remember ever having been quite so sharply aware of it.

'Jack,' David was saying, his smile slightly forced and his tension showing.

'David,' Jack responded unbendingly. He wasn't going to call him 'Dad'. He couldn't.

Silently, they measured one another up. Jack was nearly as tall as his father and uncle and would, with maturity, perhaps even be a little taller, like Max, but as yet his body still had a hint of youthfulness about it.

There were years of questions he wanted to ask his father, but he had his pride and facing him was the man who had walked out on them—his mother, his sister and him. Here was the man who had never shown any real paternal interest in him, the man who... Did he have *any* idea what it felt like to wonder why you weren't loved, to question what it was about *you* that made you so unacceptable to your own father? But his parents' failings weren't his responsibility. He knew that. He and Jon had discussed these things at length.

'Jack,' Jon demurred with just a hint of reproach in his voice, but David quickly interrupted him.

'No, he's right, Jon. I don't have any right to
call myself his father and he does well to remind
me of that.' He turned back to his son. 'You've
been lucky, Jack,' he told him drily. 'The parenting you've received from Jon and Jenny, the parenting skills you will have learned in turn from
them, are a very special gift and they're certainly
skills you would never have received from me.

'Of all the things I've done that I feel most
ashamed of, my wilful abdication of my role as
your and Olivia's father is the second most important on my list,' David told Jack openly.

'The "second"?' Jack questioned him sharply.
'What's the first?'

Their glances met and clashed and David could
see in Jack's eyes how little he liked or trusted
him. Well, he deserved no less.

'The first is my inability to see what a precious,
irreplaceable gift I was given in the shape of my
brother.'

He sounded so genuine, but Jack wasn't sure
he was convinced. He *wanted* to believe him, but
what if it was just a trick, a ploy?

'You don't have to believe me, Jack,' David
was telling him as though he'd read his mind. 'It's
my task to win your trust and your faith, not yours
to give it. All I'm asking for is a chance to begin

that task. With Jon's agreement, I hope to stay in the area.'

'At Queensmead?' Jon asked sharply.

David smiled. 'No, I have other plans.'

'Gramps is talking about leaving Queensmead to you,' Jack informed him baldly, 'but Max and Maddy live there and by rights—'

'Jack!' Jon protested with a frown.

'Queensmead is the last place I would want to live in or own,' David acknowledged frankly. 'My memories of it are not ones I want to cherish.'

'You say that now,' Jack challenged him a little mulishly.

Despite his wish that Jack hadn't raised such an emotive subject, Jon couldn't help but feel touched and warmed by his nephew's obvious and unexpected championing of Max with whom he had always had a slightly strained relationship.

'I say it because I mean it,' David told Jack mildly but firmly. 'I haven't come back planning to claim some imagined inheritance, Jack, and if my father is intending to leave Queensmead to me, then I can assure you that I shall tell him that if he does, it will immediately be handed over to its rightful inheritor—Max. Unless...' He turned to Jon with a questioning look.

'I don't want it,' Jon interjected quickly. 'My memories of it are even less fond than yours, although I have to admit that Maddy has made it into a very comfortable home.'

'Then if you haven't come back for Queensmead, why have you come back?' Jack asked him bluntly.

'I...' David began, but this time it was Jon's turn to defend David.

'That's enough, Jack,' he said firmly. 'Your father doesn't have to dot all his i's and cross all his t's to explain his reason for returning home. It's enough that he's here.'

It might be enough for his uncle Jon, but it wasn't enough for him. Not by a long chalk, Jack decided fiercely.

'I can guess what you're thinking, Jack,' David answered sombrely, 'and I don't blame you. In your shoes I would probably be even less inclined to give me the benefit of the doubt. I know of only one other person as saintly as you, Jon,' he told his brother with a wry smile. 'The priest— and even he—'

'The priest? Who is he?' Jack demanded curiously.

Briefly, David explained.

'You worked with him nursing the sick?' Jack

exclaimed in such obvious amazement that David grinned.

'An unlikely task for reparation for my sins, I know,' he agreed. 'But nevertheless that is exactly what I did, although at the time it wasn't so much my sins I was thinking of as my empty belly. No work, no food…that's what the priest told me.'

As he saw the faint beginning of respect for his father dawning in Jack's eyes, Jon felt a pang of loss but quickly quelled it. Jack needed to be able to heal the rift with his father, to be able to question and understand the forces that had motivated David and he needed to hear them from David himself. If no other good came out of David's return, then the benefit it would be to Jack was incalculable—he was at such a very vulnerable stage in his life.

'Is that the time?' David suddenly remarked. 'I'd better go. Honor will be waiting…wondering…'

'Honor…' Jon began, but David was already looking towards the door and didn't seem to have heard him.

'I'll see you out,' Jon offered. As they reached the front door, David turned to his brother. Wordlessly, they embraced one another.

'I'd better tell Dad that you're back,' Jon reminded him.

'Yes,' David agreed. 'And there's Olivia...'

Olivia. Jon's heart sank. He started to warn David, then stopped, suppressing a sigh. But what had to be said had to be said.

'Olivia...things haven't...things aren't easy for her at the moment. She's under a lot of pressure and she... Don't expect too much,' he advised David cautiously.

From where she was parked on the lane, Honor could see the house and she watched tensely as she saw the yellow rectangle of light that was the open front door. David was standing with his back to her, talking with his twin. As Honor watched, she saw them embrace and a small, soundless breath of relief eased the constriction in her chest.

'How did it go?' she asked David anxiously as he opened the car door.

'I talked to Jon and Jack,' he told her. 'Jack was angry with me as he has every right to be and—'

'Jon—how was Jon? What did *he* say?' Honor interrupted.

'Jon was Jon,' David said quietly. 'He was more magnanimous than I deserve. He said he missed me,' he added emotionally.

'Did *you* tell him how much you've missed him?' Honor asked gently.

David gave her that slow, sweet smile that turned her heart over. 'Yes,' he admitted. 'I did.'

Suddenly, more than anything else in the world, he needed the security of her love. He wanted to take her home and make love with her, lose himself in her, with her, ease the suffering he was feeling—and causing—in the balm of her acceptance.

'It isn't going to be easy,' he confided. 'Jon said as much himself. Jack seemed to think that I've come back to claim Queensmead.' He shook his head sadly. 'I can't blame him for thinking of me as someone avaricious and self-serving. After all, that's just what I was. But at least it doesn't look as though I'm going to be drummed out of town—' he smiled wryly '—even though I might deserve to be.' He hesitated for a moment.

'Will you tell your family…your daughters…about what I did?' he asked. Honor looked judiciously at him as she started the car and turned it.

'Would it bother you if I did?'

'For your sake, yes,' David acknowledged, 'but then, if they were to hear the story from someone else… I suspect they'll be reluctant enough to accept me as it is—a vagabond of no fixed abode with no means of financial support.'

'You aren't a vagabond, you're a Crighton,' Honor corrected him in amusement. 'You have a fixed abode, namely Foxdean, and as for your financial support... Would it offend your male pride very much if I told you that *I* have more than enough, and to spare, to support us both and that I am more than happy to do so?'

'There's so much we can do, David,' she declared enthusiastically without waiting for him to respond. 'The house—but that's just the beginning. I need a partner, not just in my bed but to share everything, my life. The herbs I can grow here barely scratch the surface of what nature has provided. I want to travel...learn...and I want you with me. Will you come?'

David wasn't answering her. Anxiously, Honor looked at him. Did he perhaps think her foolish with her excitement, her plans, her hopes, that were in many ways so wildly idealistic, at least as far as her daughters were concerned?

'David...' she began uncertainly.

He stopped her, shaking his head and saying, 'My turn first. Yes, I'll come. Will *you* marry me?'

'*Marry* you, David?'

He had mentioned it before, but she hadn't been certain that he was serious.

'If I accept, you realise that the girls are going to want us to sign a prenuptial agreement, don't you?' she half teased him.

'I don't care *what* I have to sign just as long as I have you,' David told her softly. 'I don't want your money, Honor. I want *you*.'

'I'd like to be married on a mountain top,' she murmured dreamily. 'Somewhere high and spiritual, somewhere remote and peaceful. Just us and our vows to one another.'

'I know the very place,' David promised her.

'In Jamaica,' she guessed.

'In Jamaica,' he agreed.

'JENNY, WHAT'S WRONG?'

Quickly, Jenny shook her head. 'Nothing,' she denied. 'It's just been a very eventful day.'

'Yes, I know,' Jon said as he sat on the side of the bed, pausing in the act of removing his socks.

His back was to Jenny, who was curled up on her own side of the bed facing away from him so that he couldn't see the fear in her eyes.

'Did I tell you how different David looked? He *is* different, Jen,' he enthused. 'I could see it, feel it. It's odd, you know, but I've never really believed very strongly in all this intuition that's supposed to exist between twins, but tonight... now...'

Jenny's heart sank as she listened to him. It was happening just as she had feared...dreaded. Already he was back in thrall...back under David's spell.

'You only spoke to him for a little over an hour, Jon,' she reminded him. 'And he hasn't really explained why he's come back. Oh, I know what he told you, but how do we know that's the truth?'

'Jenny!' Jon expostulated. 'At least *try* to give him the benefit of the doubt. What's wrong?' he persisted. 'It's not like you to be so antagonistic. You're normally the first to counsel compassion and forgiveness.'

What could she say? She didn't want to remind Jon that David had already come close to ruining their marriage and destroying their love, not once but twice. When he left, it had been as though a dark cloud had lifted from their lives.

'I can't believe how easy it was to talk to him. How *close* I felt to him,' Jon was explaining.

Jenny bit the inside of her mouth to prevent herself from crying out in protest. She felt as though David was coming between them, as though somehow *he* was more important to Jon than she was.

'I'm going to have to tell Olivia what's happened, of course.'

'She won't like it,' Jenny warned him.

'Not initially,' Jon agreed. 'But I'm sure she'll feel differently when she's seen David and spoken to him.'

David...David...David. Jenny was already tired of the sound of his name. Why...why did he have to come back?

CHAPTER TWELVE

'JACK...JACK...' Frowning, Jack turned in Annalise's direction.

'I'm sorry,' he apologised. 'What did you say?'

He had arrived as arranged, but far from his trying to smooth-talk her into bed, Annalise discovered that he seemed oddly preoccupied, his thoughts very much elsewhere. On another girl? she wondered jealously.

'What is it? What's wrong?' she demanded.

'My father's come back,' Jack said simply.

'Your father?' Annalise stared at him. Like everyone in Haslewich, she knew that David Crighton had disappeared without leaving any explanation of where he was going or why.

'Yes, I saw him last night. He rang Uncle Jon and then came round and... Come on. I'm supposed to be giving you some tuition, not talking about my father.'

'No. I want to hear more,' Annalise argued. She had often wondered how she would react if her mother were to come back. Not that *she* had disappeared. Not in the way that Jack's father had done. No, she had simply abandoned them to go and live with someone else.

'No. I'm here to help you work, remember?' Jack chided her sternly.

An hour later, Annalise shook her head dispiritedly and said, 'It's no use. I'm getting worse, not better.'

'You're trying to push yourself too hard,' Jack comforted her. 'You'll get there. You just need more time and a few more lessons.' He started to frown. 'I've got to head off for university next week, but...' He paused. 'I'll be home again at Christmas. I'll have more time then.'

'You don't have to help me,' Annalise countered.

'No, I don't have to,' he agreed, 'but I do *want* to.'

'Why?' she challenged.

'Why do you think?' he answered huskily.

He was looking right at her mouth, Annalise realised as her heart started to beat frantically fast.

'I'm not going to go to bed with you,' she warned him hastily. 'And—'

'No, you're not,' Jack affirmed with surprising

sternness. 'For one thing, you're not yet ready and for another…'

Annalise stared at him. His stern response was the last thing she expected.

'You don't want to,' she gasped, too surprised to be cautious. 'But—'

'I didn't say I didn't *want* to,' Jack corrected her grimly. 'I just said we aren't going to…at least not yet.'

'Not yet…' Annalise hadn't thought it was possible for her heart to beat any faster, but apparently it could.

'No, not yet,' Jack repeated. 'Not until…' He paused. 'Will you write to me, Annalise?' he asked urgently.

Write to him… Bemusedly, she lifted her eyes to his, searching them to see if he was simply trying to make fun of her.

'It won't be too long before the Christmas break, and then—'

'Aren't you going to kiss me?' she asked in a shaky little voice.

'If I do, I don't think I'll be able to stop,' Jack replied, shaking his head, then, as tiny shivers of excitement quivered openly over her skin, he gave a small groan and pulled her into his arms.

Kissing someone and being kissed *by* them

when they made you feel as Jack was making her feel was a world away from your everyday experimental childish snogging, Annalise discovered dizzily.

'Oh, Jack,' she whispered in awed delight when he finally released her mouth.

'Oh, Jack what?' He gave her a tender smile.

'Do we really have to wait?'

'Yes, we *do*,' he told her firmly, quickly releasing her, then demanding thickly, 'Promise that you *will* write to me.'

'I promise,' Annalise declared fervently.

'LIVVY, HAVE YOU GOT a minute?'

'Only just, Uncle Jon,' Olivia responded tersely as her uncle stopped her on the way to her office. 'What is it?' she demanded as he put his hand on her arm and started to guide her towards his own office.

She had hardly slept the previous night. Caspar and the girls were leaving for America the day after tomorrow, but there was no way she was going to go with them, no way at all. He was wrong if he thought he could pressurise her, blackmail her, into changing her mind.

'Livvy, there's no easy way of telling you this,'

she heard Jon saying emotionally. 'Your father's back.'

'My *father*.' Olivia looked blankly at him. 'No, he *can't* be. He would *never* show his face in Haslewich again. He wouldn't *dare*. Not after what he's done. He'd be too afraid of ending up in prison where he deserves to be.'

'Olivia, please listen to me for a moment,' Jon begged her. 'I know how angry you were about what David did. I felt the same way, but—'

He stopped abruptly when he saw the look on his niece's face as she stared not so much *at* him but, much more frighteningly, right through him.

'Livvy, come and sit down.'

Jon took her gently by the arm. Beneath his touch her body felt rigid and cold and his heart sank even further. Allied to his anxiety was his understanding of why she was reacting the way she was and his love and compassion for her. Even as a child Olivia had been inclined to be sensitive, her pride easily bruised, retreating into herself as she fought desperately to try to conceal her hurt feelings from others. But she wasn't a child any more, and much as his instinct was to hold her tight and encourage her to cry out her shock and pain, he knew that any attempt to coax her to do so would result in her retreating into herself even more.

'I don't *want* to sit down,' she was telling him in a tight-lipped, strained voice now. 'I just want to know what the hell is going on. He can't come back just like that. He…'

She took a deep breath and Jon saw with concern that the effect of drawing it in ran like an electric shock right through her body. She had lost weight, he noticed.

'He came back because—'

'Because he needs money, is that what you're trying to say? What's gone wrong, Uncle Jon? Has he run out of frail old ladies to steal from?'

She was becoming agitated, dragging her arm from his grasp, pacing his office, her face as flushed as earlier it had been pale, her eyes full of passionate resentment.

'What is he expecting from us? To be paid to go away again? Is that what he's planning to do, to blackmail us? Has anyone told Ben he's back yet?'

Jon couldn't remember exactly when Olivia had stopped calling his father Gramps as the other grandchildren did. Jenny seemed to think it had been just after the birth of her and Caspar's second child, another daughter, when Ben had derisively pointed out that Max had been the first to present him with a great-grandson.

'No, I'm going to see Ben later,' Jon told her quietly. 'He'll be thrilled, of course, but too much excitement at his age…'

As he spoke, a warm, caring smile curved Jon's mouth, and looking at him Olivia burst out bitterly, 'How *can* you take it so calmly after what my father did? He nearly ruined your life, *all* our lives. He came close to destroying everything you've ever worked for. But for him, my mother—'

'No, Olivia,' Jon interrupted sternly. 'Your mother's…problems may have been exacerbated by the trouble within their marriage, but we know from what her parents and the doctors told us that Tania had already been suffering from her eating disorder as a teenager. In those days, such things weren't recognised for what they are—'

'Uncle Jon, I don't know how you can stand there so calmly and talk about what's happened like this,' Olivia exploded, her whole body trembling with angry emotion. 'My father has no right to just walk back into our lives and he certainly *isn't* walking back into mine. Did he tell you where he's been, what he's been doing, why he left?'

'Yes,' Jon began to reply. 'He—'

'No. Don't tell me. I don't want to know.' Olivia stared at him bleakly. 'Why should I? He didn't want to know about us...about me. I was just the daughter he never really wanted. The only people *he* ever cared about were himself, Ben and Max, with himself first and foremost.'

'Livvy, that just isn't true,' Jon protested. 'Your father has changed...suffered—'

'Suffered! How, by not having access to rich clients' bank accounts? What has he been doing for money? Did he tell you?'

The bitterness in her voice didn't surprise Jon, but it distressed him. He had been hoping to find some small chink in her protective armour that would allow him and, through him, David, to persuade her to at least listen to what her father wanted to say, but now...

'I don't want to see him, Uncle Jon,' she announced suddenly. 'I won't see him.' When Jon said nothing, she continued passionately, 'Have you *any* idea what it's like being his daughter? How it feels to know that I carry his genes in my blood, to know that no matter how hard I work, how much I prove myself, people will always wonder if, at some point, I'm going to show my true colours, if I'm going to turn out to be a thief?'

Jon was too shocked by her outburst to control his expression or his reaction. Immediately, he went over to her and tried to take hold of her, but she evaded him, turning to stand in front of the window with her back to him.

'Livvy, my dear,' he begged. 'I can understand how hurt you must have been...must *still* be by your father's behaviour, but to think...to believe... I can promise you that of the few people who *do* know the truth about events leading up to your father's disappearance, none of us believe for one minute that you would...' He found himself unable to finish. He was still battling against the shock her outburst had caused him and trying to find the right words to reassure her. It was like traversing a verbal minefield. This kind of situation needed Jenny's gentle, sure touch, not his clumsy, heavy-handed directness.

'*All* of us in the family share the same gene pool, Livvy,' he pointed out reasonably. 'If what you have just said is applicable to you, then it is equally applicable to any and all of us. What your father did was wrong—no one is trying to suggest otherwise—but to think you fear that you might somehow, as his daughter—'

'It's all very well for you to say that now,' Olivia charged wildly. 'But I've seen the way the others sometimes look at me. Luke...Saul...Max... they're just waiting for me to fall flat on my face.'

Jon was appalled. It had never occurred to him that Olivia felt this way and it was, he was sure, very significant that it was only her male family peers she referred to. Olivia was not the only woman in the family to have a career—far from it—and it disturbed Jon to have to acknowledge that her state of mind could be so dangerously off balance.

The words 'paranoia' and 'obsession' sprang uncomfortably into his mind, but he quickly dismissed them. Olivia was just suffering from shock and the pressure of the workload she had undertaken to carry.

'Livvy, all your father wants is a chance to talk to you...to apologise...to see his grandchildren,' Jon told her gently.

'*No!*' Olivia spun round to face him, her eyes black with bitterness. 'No way. My father is *never* going to be allowed anywhere near the girls. The rest of you can pretend that nothing ever happened if you want to,' she added scornfully, 'but there's no way *I'm* going to.'

'Olivia...' Jon protested unhappily.

She shook her head. 'I've got to go. I'm in court after lunch. A divorce case—' she gave him a bitter little smile '—and I intend to make sure my client gets what's due her. My father isn't the only man who's a liar and a cheat—unfortunately.'

'YOU'RE LATE,' Jenny commented when Jon walked into the kitchen later that evening.

'Yes, I'm sorry. I went straight to Queensmead from the office to see Dad.'

'Have you told him about David?'

'Yes,' Jon acknowledged.

'And how did he take it?'

'Very well. He behaved as though he'd known all along that David would come back. In fact, it was almost as though David had simply been away on holiday he took it so calmly.'

'And Olivia?' Jenny asked quietly. 'Did *she* take it calmly?'

Jon gave her a tired smile. 'I think you already know the answer to that one.' Without waiting for her response, he continued, 'She flatly refuses to see David and, in fact—' he took a deep breath '—she seems to have this…this blinkered belief…a fear that because she's David's daughter and because she's a woman, we're all waiting for her to...' He shook his head. 'She worried me, Jenny. I had no idea... Did you know?' he asked when she remained silent.

'Maddy *did* mention that Caspar had complained that Olivia was obsessed by the problems she'd had when she was growing up,' Jenny admitted. 'I'm afraid, though, that I put it down to a bit of marital discord rather than... She *was* very upset when what David had been doing came out, I know, but then we all were. Perhaps in the rush to sort out the practical problems he caused and to keep the truth from Ben, we none of us paid enough attention to what she was actually going through. Then she and Caspar got married and the children arrived.' She frowned. 'What do you plan to tell David?' she asked quietly.

'What *can* I tell him other than that she doesn't want to see him,' Jon responded unhappily.

What he hadn't yet told Jenny and what he didn't know how he was going to tell her was that just before she left for court, Olivia had come back into the office to tell him in a blank, over-controlled voice, 'And one more thing, Uncle Jon, whilst the rest of you are running about making plans to welcome the family's black sheep back into the fold, since I *don't* have any intention of seeing or speaking with my father and since you obviously do, I think it's best that I don't visit Queensmead…or you and Jenny.'

Her voice had faltered a little over her last few words, but her body had remained stubbornly taut.

'Livvy,' he had protested, but she had shaken her head.

'No…I'm not going to turn myself into a hypocrite and if he ever sets foot into these premises, then *I* shall walk out, and I mean that. The rest of you might be planning to let bygones be bygones and welcome him back with the traditional fatted calf, but I *never* will.'

Olivia's declaration had shocked Jon, leaving him feeling anxious and concerned for her but unable to find a way to reach across the barrier she had raised between them.

How could he turn his back on David and refuse to allow him a second chance? He couldn't. But to lose Olivia, who was so very dear to him…

'I doubt that David will want to come here' was all he had managed to say.

'He may not want to,' Olivia had retorted, 'but Ben will certainly expect him to.'

After she had gone, Jon realised that what she had said was probably true. However, David had made it clear he had no intention of returning to the practice, which would in any case have been impossible.

But he said nothing of this to Jenny who was bustling about the kitchen, looking tense and not at all like his normally relaxed, beloved wife.

'Jenny,' he commanded, reaching out to put his arm round her and draw her closer. 'Come and sit down. Relax.'

'I can't,' she returned shortly. 'Maddy was here this afternoon. She said that Max has been like a bear with a sore head. Oh, and Saul rang to ask if it was true that David was back. He said he'd heard the news from Katie and—'

'Jenny, Jenny...' Jon sighed. 'Something's wrong. What is it?'

'Do you really need to ask?' Jenny demanded crossly. 'David's back and suddenly everything's topsy-turvy. Everyone is on edge, and you, just like you always did, are taking his side, making everything easy and comfortable for him, putting him first.'

'Jenny, that isn't true,' Jon protested.

'Yes, it is,' she contradicted him flatly.

'Jenny,' Jon said gently, 'surely you of all people agree that David has a right to have a second chance. We're his *family*,' he persisted when she refused to respond or look at him. His expression changed to one of concern as she turned to face him and he saw that her eyes were full of tears. 'Jenny, my love, what is it?' he asked anxiously as he went to take her in his arms.

'I'm just so…so afraid that somehow things will change now that David's back,' Jenny confessed. 'We've been so happy these past few years, Jon, and I don't want—'

'David's coming back isn't going to change any of that,' Jon assured her. 'How can it?'

'I don't know,' Jenny admitted, but even though Jon was holding her and even though the warmth from the Aga was filling her kitchen, she still felt a sharp, prescient chill brushing warningly over her skin.

'You're still in shock,' Jon said soothingly. 'We all are. I had been going to suggest that we might ask David round for supper this weekend, have a bit of a family get-together sort of thing, to break the ice, but if you'd prefer not to…'

'No.' Jenny shook her head. 'Nothing can alter the fact that he *is* back and sooner or later everyone is going to know and want to see him. Oh, I do wish that Ruth wasn't in America. If she was here… What will we do about inviting Olivia and Caspar, though?' Jenny asked suddenly. 'I know you said Livvy wasn't prepared to talk to David.

I'll give her a ring,' she decided. 'Have a talk with her.'

AT QUEENSMEAD, Maddy and Max were also in their kitchen.

'I swear if Gramps mentions David's name one more time...' Max protested in exasperation.

Maddy gave him a sympathetic look. 'He is very cock-a-hoop about him coming back,' she agreed.

'Cock-a-hoop!' Max gave her a telling look. 'To listen to him, anyone would think we'd kept him incarcerated in a dungeon and that David had had to call out the troops to free him.'

Maddy couldn't help laughing. 'You've been watching too many cartoons with the children,' she teased him, then admitted, 'Ben *is* being a bit naughty.'

'A *bit*? I could have strangled him when he started telling me how Dad had never come up to matching David's intelligence or his sporting skills. Doesn't he realise...?' He shook his head. 'I've nothing against David *per se*, but if anyone thinks I'm going to stand back and let him walk all over Dad—'

'If you really want to do some hero stuff, then I think it's Jack and Olivia—especially Olivia—

who will be most in need of your support and protection,' Maddy told him seriously.

'Olivia! She and I have never really hit it off, and as for Jack—'

'This is bound to be a very difficult time for both of them, Max, and in very different ways. No matter how little David himself may want it and no matter how much we all know it isn't deserved, nothing's going to stop Gramps from lauding David to the sky.'

'OLIVIA, WHAT THE DEVIL is going on?' Caspar demanded in some alarm as he walked into the bedroom to discover the bed strewn with Olivia's clothes and a suitcase on the chest at the foot of the bed.

'What does it look like?' Olivia responded waspishly. 'I'm packing.'

'Packing?' Caspar's heart sank. They hadn't been getting on well recently. He realised that and knew both of them were inclined to be very stubborn, each refusing to compromise or give in, but the thought of Livvy's leaving him brought him out in a cold sweat of panic.

'Yes, packing. Isn't that what one normally does when one is going away?' Olivia asked acidly. 'How cold exactly is Philadelphia at this time of year, Caspar? I'm not sure which of these three outfits will be best for the wedding, and if we're touring afterwards—'

'You're packing for *Philadelphia*,' Caspar exclaimed in relief, his face breaking into a wide smile as he crossed the bedroom floor and, ignoring Olivia's objections, picked her up in his arms, swinging her round.

'No, not on the bed, Caspar,' Olivia protested as he lowered her towards it and tried to kiss her. 'I've just ironed these clothes.'

'You're coming with me!' Caspar exclaimed, ignoring her protests. 'Oh, God, Livvy…Livvy…' He tried to kiss her again, but she moved her head and pushed him away from her, then got up off the bed.

His reaction to her change of mind was making her feel both irritated and guilty. It infuriated her to think that he believed she had given way and that he had won, but these were not ordinary circumstances. Jenny had rung earlier to explain that she was giving a weekend supper party for David, and Olivia's fingers had curled around the receiver in protest as she listened to her.

'I won't be here, Jenny,' she had said with a cold voice. 'Caspar and I are flying out to the

States with the girls on Saturday afternoon to attend Caspar's half-brother's wedding.'

She had spent what was left of the afternoon
rearranging her work diary and cancelling appointments, all with a steely determination that
she didn't allow anything to shake. If her father
was going to be at Jon and Jenny's, then she
wasn't. It was as simple as that!

CHAPTER THIRTEEN

'MAX, WHAT ARE YOU DOING here?' Olivia demanded sharply as she answered the front door to find her cousin standing outside.

'Oh, I was just passing, so I thought I'd call in. Ma said you and Caspar are leaving for America this afternoon—a family wedding.'

'Yes,' Olivia acknowledged tersely as Max followed her into the hallway.

She had never felt completely at ease with her cousin. There was a history of enmity between them going back to when they were children, fostered by Ben Crighton's very different treatment of them. In recent years, that enmity might have softened down to a more adult tolerance, but its roots were still there—for Olivia at least.

'It will do you good to get away. Dad mentioned that he was concerned about how hard you've been working.'

As Olivia stiffened and turned towards him with a hostile look in her eyes, Max cursed himself under his breath. He just wasn't any good at this sort of thing and heaven alone knew why Maddy, a normally very perceptive woman, should have been so insistent that he be the one to try to talk to Olivia.

'Really. Well, he needn't be. I'm just as capable of doing my job properly as anyone else.'

Max stifled his irritation. It was so like Olivia to go on the defensive and to think she was being 'got at' when, in reality, all he had been doing was making polite conversation.

'I think we all know that, Livvy,' he tried to placate. 'Ma's a bit upset that you won't be there this evening,' he told her quietly.

Olivia tensed.

'I think that Caspar would be equally upset if I cancelled going to this wedding just so that I could pay court to the father we all know...' Her lips tightened. Then she informed him coldly, 'If Jenny has sent you here to try to make me change my mind, you're wasting your time, Max. I've already told Jon that I have no intention of seeing my father again—*ever*—and if that means I don't see any of *you* again, well, so be it.'

Max tried not to show his shock. He had been warned that Olivia was taking her father's return very badly but he had not realised just *how* badly.

'Look, Livvy, I can understand how you feel—' he began urgently, but it was as though he had put a lighted match under a keg of dynamite.

'No, you can't,' Olivia exploded without allowing him to finish. 'You *can't* understand at all. *Your* father didn't treat you as though you were an encumbrance, a nuisance, a useless piece of flesh he wished he had never given life to. He didn't laugh at *you* and put *you* down.'

'Livvy!' Max protested, dismayed not so much by her outburst but at the pain it revealed.

As he put his hand out towards her in an instinctive gesture of male comfort, she retreated from him, saying sharply, 'No, don't touch me.'

'Livvy…' Both of them turned towards the door as Caspar walked in. 'Oh, hello, Max.' He smiled, turned to Olivia and continued, 'I phoned for a taxi and asked them to pick us up a bit earlier—just in case the traffic is heavy. Everything's packed.'

'I won't delay you,' Max said formally. 'I have to get back for the kids anyway. Maddy is going round to give Ma a hand with this supper she's planned for Uncle David.'

'David?' Caspar looked from Max's face to

Olivia's in bewilderment. 'Does Max mean your father?' he demanded. 'But...'

Too late Max recognised that Olivia hadn't told Caspar about her father's return.

'My father has reappeared, yes,' Olivia agreed curtly. 'But as I've just told Max, I neither want to talk about him nor see him.'

'Olivia...!' Caspar began, but she only shook her head.

She turned to her cousin. 'I'll see you out, Max.'

As she ushered him towards the door, Caspar disappeared into the kitchen.

'Olivia, I'm sorry,' Max apologised. 'I didn't realise you hadn't told Caspar what's happened.'

'I didn't tell him because it simply isn't relevant to our lives,' Olivia retorted sharply as she opened the door.

'OLIVIA, WOULD YOU MIND explaining to me what's going on?' Caspar demanded as she walked back into the kitchen a few minutes later.

'The only thing that's going on so far as I know is that in—' she looked at the kitchen clock '—about five hours' time we shall be flying to New York.'

'Olivia,' Caspar warned grimly, 'don't play

games with me. You *know* what I'm talking
about. Why didn't you tell me that your father
was back?'

'Perhaps because it isn't something I want to
discuss with you,' Olivia said carefully.

'For God's sake, I'm your husband,' Caspar exploded. 'What the hell is going on? Your father
comes back after disappearing for years and years
and you act like…like it just isn't happening.' He
pushed his hand into his hair and looked at her in
exasperation. 'Sometimes, Livvy, you…

'Is this why you changed your mind about coming to the wedding?' he demanded sharply. 'Olivia! Answer me,' he said as she turned and started
to walk out of the kitchen.

'I've got to go and get the girls,' she told him.
'It's almost lunch-time.'

After she had gone, Caspar leaned his forehead
against the cool wood of the kitchen unit. There
was no point in provoking another argument. Not
now. Why on earth hadn't Livvy said something
to him instead of… God, but he just didn't have
time to think about the complexities of the situation now. He was on edge enough as it was because of the wedding, wondering what sort of re-
ception he was going to get from his now
complicated and disunified family without having

to cope with Olivia's almost neurotic resentment of her father.

Caspar knew that David hadn't exactly been a good father, but neither had his own, and he...

Impatiently, he pulled open the fridge door and took out a can of beer, flipping back the top and taking a deep gulp. Once he and Livvy got back from America, they needed to have a serious talk, a *very* serious talk.

Upstairs in the *en suite* bathroom of their bedroom, Olivia stared at her reflection in the mirror. Her face was white and drawn, her eyes dark and shuttered, but it wasn't her *own* face that she saw but her mother's. Tania with her pretty, delicately fey face and her too-thin, damaged body. Tania with her eating disorder and her loveless marriage. Then, next to her mother's face, Olivia could see her father's, his expression holding just the same irritation and impatience she had seen in Caspar's downstairs.

A tremor ran through her, quickly stilled, her muscles tensing tightly with the kind of pressure that might have been applied to an arterial wound, the kind of wound that if left would bleed away a life.

Distantly, Olivia was aware that behind her anger was fear—the kind of fear that choked out love and life. But just acknowledging that it might be there sent her into such a spiral of terror that she automatically drew back from it, ignoring it, denying it. She took a deep breath and opened the bathroom door.

'YOU DIDN'T CHANGE your mind about coming to the wedding with me at all, did you?' Caspar asked again after they had checked in for their flight. 'You're just coming so that you don't have to see your father.'

'Yes, that's right,' Olivia agreed tonelessly.

Caspar's mouth compressed and he turned his head away, too quickly to see the panic and fear that momentarily broke through the indifference clouding Olivia's eyes.

'DON'T WORRY, everything's going to be fine.'

In her car, David turned to smile at Honor. 'It's probably going to be harder for them than it is for me. I suspect that Jenny must be cursing me for putting her to such a lot of trouble. It was very good of Jon to offer to host a family get-together. At least it gets everything over and done with in one fell swoop and, much more importantly, it gives me an opportunity to show you off to my family,' he added tenderly.

He had heard the curiosity and the surprise in Jon's voice when he told him that he would like to bring Honor with him to the family supper. Typically though, Jon hadn't either pried or objected, simply saying warmly that they would look forward to seeing them both.

'Olivia won't be there, of course,' David remarked.

Honor said nothing. David had already told her of Jon's disclosure to him that Olivia felt unable as yet to see or talk with her father.

'As it happens, she wouldn't have been able to join us anyway,' Jon had told him, not quite truthfully. 'She and Caspar have a long-standing arrangement to fly out to attend a family wedding on his side in Philadelphia.'

They had almost reached the house now, and from the number of cars parked outside, David realised that he was about to face a pretty full family turnout.

'You don't *have* to go in,' Honor said, guessing what he was feeling.

'Yes, I do,' David corrected her with a small smile. 'I can't run away again, Honor.'

It was Jack who opened the door to them, a Jack who was a little stiff and unbending, nervous, as David was himself. He looked tenderly at his son but made no attempt to force any unwanted fatherly embrace or intimacy on him.

'Honor, this is Jack,' he said simply.

Jack's smile for Honor was, he noticed, much warmer than the one his son had given *him*. Then Jon was coming towards them, his eyes widening in recognition as he saw Honor, his touch on David's arm not just reassuring but somehow strengthening, as well, almost as though he was giving *him*, David, some of his own courage and life force. David suspected that it was no mistake that when he walked into Jon and Jenny's large drawing room, he was flanked on one side by Honor, who was gripping his hand protectively, and on the other by Jon, who was standing shoulder to shoulder with him, making a silent declaration to all those present that he accepted and supported him.

It was that far more than their father's emotional and in some ways almost distasteful glorifying of his return that made it possible for David to get through the evening. Every time he felt his spirits flagging, every time he saw doubts about him in someone's eyes, he found he was turning his head to search for Jon. He took strength from the quiet, calm reassurance he could see in Jon's eyes as he returned David's anxious look.

'I always knew he'd come back,' he could hear Ben boasting to Saul Crighton. 'And who could blame him for leaving that wife of his? All her doing that he damn near died.'

'My heart attack wasn't Tiggy's fault,' David denied immediately.

'Nonsense,' Ben declared. 'You should never have married her. She trapped him into the marriage,' he continued, addressing Maddy, who was standing next to Saul and his wife Tullah. 'Ruined his career, too. David would have been a QC if it hadn't been for that woman.'

'No, Dad,' David interrupted him firmly. 'I could never have been a QC, and the only person responsible for ruining my career was me.'

He saw that Jack was looking at him and went on to explain as though only the two of them were in the room.

'Your grandfather may have forgotten how idiotic I was, but I certainly haven't, Jack. I thought I knew it all…and that I could do it all. But as anyone with any sense will tell you, working for the bar and partying all night just don't mix!

'I behaved like a crass, arrogant fool and I deserved everything I got, including my dismissal from chambers.'

Into the small silence that followed his admission, David threw down the gauntlet as he knew he should have done to his father a long, long time ago.

'If it hadn't been for Jon, I dare say I would have got the punishment I richly deserved. Certainly there was no way I could ever have worked as a solicitor, never mind calling myself senior partner.'

'You had every right to be the senior partner,' Ben blustered. 'You were the first-born. Jon knows that it's your right to head the partnership, David.'

'No,' David corrected his father calmly. 'What Jon knows is that there is no way legally I should *ever* have been allowed to take that position. I don't have the qualifications, and besides...'

He paused, wondering how far he should go and how much he should say. Instinctively, his gaze was drawn to his twin, and from the other side of the room Jon gave a small shake of his head.

'Besides,' David continued, conceding authority to Jon, 'the law has never held any appeal for me. I'm far happier working with my hands than my brain.'

'*You've* done this,' he could hear Ben shouting to Jon, his face red with anger. '*You've* forced him to stand down in your favour. Well, I'm telling you…you'll *never* be the man that David is. You'll always stand in his shadow. You should be ashamed of yourself.'

'David,' Honor protested as David left her side and strode across to Ben, then leaned over him.

'That's *enough*,' he told him fiercely. Turning to face the room, he declared firmly, 'Whilst I'm well aware that no one apart from my father needs to hear me say just how wrong he is and whilst I know, too, that Jon himself has no need of my support…I have a need to say it.

'Dad, you're a fool,' he admonished Ben bluntly. 'Everyone else in this room knows perfectly well that, of the two of us, it is *Jon* who deserves the palm, Jon who should be fêted and praised. Nature might have decided that I should arrive in this world ten minutes ahead of him, but *she* wasn't responsible for the fact that instead of being protected and cherished by me, his twin brother, I allowed him to be cast in the role of second-best. The blame and the responsibility for that lies solely with me.

'We all know what you suffered as a child through losing your own twin, Dad,' David continued, 'and we sympathise with you because of it, but I'd like to put it on record that the reason

I came back, and the *only* reason, selfish though I know it is, is because *I* needed my brother.'

David could almost feel, as well as hear, the shocked reaction that rippled through his audience.

'That does not mean that I don't love my children—my daughter and my son—or my father. I do, but I can love them from any place in the world, wherever I happen to live. Probably the best gift I ever gave Jack was to absent myself from his life so that he was able to experience what true parenting is all about.

'Why I should feel so strongly that I needed Jon, I don't know. Perhaps it was to look for his forgiveness, to make reparation. I really don't know and maybe I never will know.

'As my family you have a right to reject or accept me as you choose.' He paused and looked at Honor and smiled.

'For those of you who choose to accept me, I shall be living permanently at Foxdean—when I am not acting as my wife-to-be's assistant and crawling through the Amazon rain forest picking flowers.'

David was all too aware of his family's astonishment and heard them offer their confused congratulations, but he wasn't really listening to them. Instead, he was watching Jon.

'I think you've given Dad a bit of a shock,' Jon remarked as he crossed the room to his side.

'Maybe, but it's no more than he deserves. He's much tougher than he likes to make out,' David assured him, 'or so Honor says, and she should know.'

'Mmm...*that* was rather a surprise,' Jon admitted.

'To us as well as you,' David agreed. 'If you don't want me to stay, Jon, you only have to say,' David told him seriously. 'Honor and I have agreed that we will move out of the area if necessary.'

'Haslewich is your home,' Jon reminded him.

In the background, David could hear corks popping as Ben insisted that the champagne he had asked Max to buy be opened.

'To my son...to David...' he started to toast when everyone's glass had been filled, but David immediately stopped him.

'No,' he said firmly, and raising his own glass, he announced clearly, 'To my brother. To Jon.'

'I think I'm going to like your father,' Joss admitted quietly to Jack as the two of them drank their champagne. Jack said nothing; he felt too

confused. He was proud of his father for what he
had said and done and yet, at the same time, he
felt that acknowledging that pride was somehow
being disloyal to Jon.

A little awkwardly at first, people began to
gather round David and Honor, offering them
their best wishes, several of them looking thoroughly bemused when they were told that the
wedding was not to take place in Haslewich but
in Jamaica.

'Jamaica! Goodness,' Jenny said a little uncertainly.

'It's what both of us want,' David told her
gently.

LATER THAT NIGHT when he and Honor were in
bed, David asked, 'Are you sure you know what
you're letting yourself in for?'

'I'm used to big families,' Honor answered, deliberately misunderstanding him.

'Ah, yes, but you are not the black sheep of
yours and your daughters have not refused to see
or speak to you.'

'Give Olivia time,' Honor counselled him. 'It
can't have been easy for her, growing up in the
shadows.'

COMING HOME

'It can't have been easy for Jon growing up in my shadow,' David reminded her.

'When she comes back from this wedding, you'll be able to talk with her,' Honor comforted him.

'Talking of weddings...' David murmured.

'Mmm...' Honor encouraged, snuggling closer to him.

'I know we agreed that it would just be us...us and the priest, but...'

'You want Jon to be there,' Honor guessed.

'Would you mind?' he asked.

Honor shook her head.

As he bent his head to kiss her, David wondered what on earth he had ever done to merit such happiness. He himself was convinced that it was totally undeserved.

LYING AT JON'S SIDE in their bed, Jenny murmured tiredly, 'Well, at least that's over with.'

David had surprised her with his firm championing of Jon, but she still couldn't feel totally relaxed about the situation. Because she was afraid that a new closeness between the two brothers might somehow push *her* into second place in Jon's life?

Now she was being foolish, but still she tensed as she heard Jon saying warmly, 'It really is good to have David back. It's odd but…I've missed him, Jenny, despite everything. Now that he's back…I feel…complete somehow.'

She was happy for Jon in his new-found closeness with his twin, of course she was…of course she was!

IN THEIR LARGE four-poster bed at Queensmead, Maddy sighed as Max turned over restlessly next to her.

'What's wrong?' she asked gently.

'Nothing. I was just thinking about Olivia,' Max said. 'I don't know if Uncle David or Dad really appreciate just how strongly she feels about David's coming back.' He paused and then said hesitantly, 'Do you know, it felt a little as though I was almost in the way this evening when Dad and Uncle David were talking to one another.'

Maddy sighed and leaned over, resting her chin on his bare chest. 'Try to be patient,' she urged him wisely. 'They've got a lot of catching up to do with one another. And Jon's not the only one to be drawn to David's side,' Maddy exclaimed as she told her husband she had suddenly realised just who Leo's 'Grampy Man' must have been. 'Leo recognised something of Jon in the man he saw in the garden. It has to have been David. No wonder Leo wasn't frightened.'

'Yes, you must be right,' Max agreed.

Maddy gave another small sigh.

Families! How very complicated and delicately balanced their relationships with one another could be. It would take time for the upheaval of emotion David's unexpected return had caused to settle down. Hopefully, the arrival of their new baby would take Max's mind off any sense of displacement he might feel over the new closeness between David and Jon. Certainly Ben was already reacting to David's stern refusal to allow him to denigrate Jon. He had been irritable all evening, refusing his medication once they got home, complaining that Jon had taken all David's time and attention, making it impossible for Ben or anyone else to have the chance to talk to him.

'He'll be coming round to see you tomorrow,' Maddy had reminded him soothingly.

'Yes, and you can make sure that Jon isn't with

him,' Ben had charged her crossly. 'I want to have David to myself.'

Families...

Maddy closed her eyes and snuggled closer to Max.

EPILOGUE

THE LAST OF THE morning mist was dispersing as they came down off the mountain, walking slowly in single file because that was all the path allowed.

The Jamaican official who had married them took his leave where the path broadened out and his car was waiting, whilst they took the fork that led to the mission.

The priest had insisted on preparing a breakfast for them. Jon and Jenny had looked a little uncertainly at one another when David had broken this news to them.

They had come out from their hotel in Kingston the previous day to see Father Ignatius. David had seen the shock in both their eyes as they witnessed for themselves the way that he had lived.

'It's not as bad as you think,' David had told them both as he saw Jenny looking round the bare rooms and the rolled-up, thin bedding that lay on the baked-mud floors. 'In this kind of climate one's needs are very simple.'

As David had predicted, Honor and the priest had greeted one another like twin souls, talking long into the night after their initial arrival. Jon and Jenny had been greeted warmly, as well. The one and only time Jon had been in Jamaica had been when he had flown out to Max's bedside, fearing to hear that his son was going to die. Those kinds of memories weren't easy to forget or suppress and he knew exactly why Jenny's hand tightened in his when they drove past the hospital on their way to their hotel.

The ceremony had been simple and short, a mutual exchange of vows as the sun rose over the mountain.

The married couple were to spend a few brief days in Jamaica and then return home. Honor had persuaded the priest to return to Haslewich with them.

'You're doing *what*?' Ellen and Abigail had demanded when she told them of their plans.

'I'm getting married—in Jamaica,' she had repeated calmly. They hadn't met David as yet. There hadn't been time. They had wanted to get married as quickly as they could.

'For mutual support when we face your disapproving daughters,' David had explained wryly.

Whilst Father Ignatius was now proudly showing Honor and Jenny round his 'pharmacy', David stood outside, looking out to sea. Without having to turn his head, he knew when Jon had joined him.

'I stood here the day I watched your plane leaving for England,' he told Jon emotionally. 'Father Ignatius prayed for Max's recovery. We both did.'

'It's hard to imagine your living here,' Jon admitted, shaking his head.

'Father Ignatius saved my life,' David replied quietly. 'Staying here to help and work alongside him was the only way I had of repaying him.'

'Breakfast,' the priest announced, coming out into the sunshine to beckon them into the shade where a feast of fruits and local delicacies had been prepared for them by the loving, grateful hands of the families of the patients they had nursed and cared for. On one side of the 'table', Honor and the priest were deep in discussion, no doubt exchanging herbal lore, David suspected. On the other, Jon and Jenny were holding hands like two slightly nervous children.

The next morning they were all returning to England. The priest, though he was loath to admit it, was becoming too frail to carry out his work alone any longer.

'I'm not really needed here any more,' he had informed Honor sadly. 'The government is opening its own hospice.'

'*I* need you,' Honor had said sincerely, and David had seen the way his eyes brightened and his back straightened. He wondered if she would ever realise just how much he loved her, how immensely and overwhelmingly. He was half-afraid to tell her in case she felt burdened by the intensity of his feelings, just as, in much the same way, he sometimes had to hold himself back from telling Jon how much he loved him.

'Love and harmony and all the blessings they bestow on us,' the priest toasted solemnly.

'Love and harmony.' David raised his glass.

* * * * *

There will be more to come from the Crighton family in future books from Penny Jordan.